HERE CASTS NO SHADOW

Bronwen Griffiths

HERE CASTS NO SHADOW

BRONWEN GRIFFITHS

Matador
9 Priory Business Park,
Wistow Road, Kibworth Beauchamp,
Leicestershire. LE8 0RX
Tel: 0116 279 2299
Email: books@troubador.co.uk
Web: www.troubador.co.uk/matador
Twitter: @matadorbooks

ISBN 978 1789013 382

British Library Cataloguing in Publication Data.
A catalogue record for this book is available from the British Library.

Printed on FSC accredited paper
Printed and bound in Great Britain by 4edge Limited
Typeset in 11pt Minion Pro by Troubador Publishing Ltd, Leicester, UK

Matador is an imprint of Troubador Publishing Ltd

Dedicated to my mother, Jean Griffiths, my grandmother Eva Pebody, my great-grandmother Burren, and all those strong women who came before you.

Acknowledgements

Thank you to everyone who supported me along the way – my friends and family, close and far, and those I know only from cyber-space. You have taught me well.

Thanks to Sarah Davis for the positive feedback on an early edit, to Cally Worden at Enigma Editorial for her meticulous copy-edit, to Claire Baldry for encouraging me to publish, and to Jennie Rawlings at Serifim, for the cover.

I started making notes for this novel in 2013 at the Stockholm Writer's House – a restful and quiet place in which to write before the long journey north to meet Hasan, a refugee from Damascus. His story, and the stories of refugees I encountered in Kramfors, Sweden, provided inspiration for the book.

Prologue

I'm in my apartment overlooking the square, watching the snow fall. The snow is like stars, you once said. Not stars, but birds, I argued; tiny flying birds.

You were so impatient that day. Do you remember? You kept asking me when the snow would come. 'Will it be like a fairy tale? How many days will it snow?' You wouldn't stop. You were like that. A chatterer. Always asking questions. I never imagined a time when you wouldn't talk at all.

A Saturday. Early January. Kaz in bed with a cold. Baby Moe yelling his head off downstairs in the kitchen. Ma banging pots. Pa out in the garden shed doing whatever he did out there. You were stood on tiptoes, at the window, your nose pressed against the glass. I was sprawled on the rug, pen in hand, planning a house –a house for Tam and me to live in overlooking the lake where Grandma lived. I so loved Tam. You just can't imagine it, Pearl, how he dizzied me, how my heart danced every time I set eyes on him. I still love him, though he is long gone now. He kissed me once, in the summer before everything turned. It was one of those hot summer days, the likes of which we never have here; the soles of my shoes stuck to the asphalt, the air shimmered like gossamer. Tam ran down the university steps, where I waited for Kaz. He ran down those steps, flung his arms around my shoulders and kissed me smack on the lips. The kiss didn't mean much, I knew that. I was only Kaz's sister, someone Tam liked to flirt with. But I kept hold of the hope his kiss brought me. Maybe one day, I thought, maybe one day life could bring another possibility like that.

You never knew how I felt about Tam. You were too young. You still don't know. There's so much you don't know. So much I should tell you.

1

The past: Zazour, Lyrian.

People suffering from post-traumatic stress syndrome
(PTSD) often re-live their experiences for many years
after the initial traumatic event. This can be distressing
for both the sufferer and their families.

Neeland Journal of Psychiatric Studies/Harrisson, J/Vol7/27

W e'd been out in the garden making snow angels and
throwing snowballs, and dancing about like dervishes.
Even Kaz had come out to join us, in spite of his cold. But Pearl
slipped and got wet; she cried and said she was turning into ice,
so Kaz took her back into the house. I was going to follow but
then I saw a tall figure at our back gate. My heart jumped – just
like the fish Kaz and I had seen leaping for insects by the old
stone bridge – because it was Tam.

'Hi, Mira.' Tam was breathing fast, as if he'd been running.
'Is Kaz home?'

'He's gone inside with Pearl.' *Don't you want to talk to me?*

Tam was dressed as always: in a long black coat and steel-tipped army boots without laces. He wore these clothes winter and summer. His one concession to the weather was a striped woollen hat: the dark, damp tendrils of his hair curled out from underneath it. Rey said Tam looked like a tramp and teased me about his long hair.

'Can you fetch him? It's important.' Tam smiled, and my insides turned to slush. 'There's something going on at the square.'

'What?' Rey knew about such things. I hadn't heard from her all day.

'We're organising against the regime. It's huge, Mira. Hasn't Kaz said anything?'

'No, he hasn't.'

'Perhaps he doesn't want to go.' Tam fixed me with his green eyes.

'He's been in bed all morning.'

'He can't miss this. We're on the edge of something beautiful. You'll see. Everything is about to change.'

Lyrian had been ruled with an iron rod for almost fifty years. Our president had been president half my life, and his father before him. Demonstrations weren't allowed. We had rallies to support the president where we waved flags and sang songs but protests were forbidden. That's how it was. We'd never have change, no matter what Tam thought.

'Won't you all be in trouble?' I said.

Another smile from Tam. 'Not if we're united, Mira.'

The snow was falling again but the wind had picked up and the flakes no longer resembled birds or stars. Now they appeared cold and hostile.

'Here he is. With your sister.'

Pearl was carrying our kitten, but when she saw Tam she dropped the kitten in the snow and flew into Tam's arms.

Tam hugged Pearl but his movements seemed mechanical,

as if his mind was elsewhere. 'I've been calling you all day,' he said to Kaz. 'The rally is now.'

'I thought it was next week.'

'We decided to bring it forward. I called but you didn't answer.'

'My phone was off. I was in bed all morning. A cold ...'

'Those boys who went missing ...' Tam stopped. He glanced at me and then at Pearl. I knew nothing about any missing boys. 'You have to be there, Kaz. It's extraordinary.' He lifted his arms to the sky. 'We'll fly. Like birds.'

My heart unsettled itself again. I didn't much like the president. He was known to be a cruel man. But I rarely thought about him. He was just there – like an endless bad period pain. Sometimes Pa would roll his eyes when the president appeared on the TV surrounded by cheering and adoring crowds, but if Kaz ever said anything critical, Pa told him to shut it.

'Our beloved president has the ability to turn people to stone with a single glance. I've heard he can even walk on water.' Kaz patted his backside. 'My arse he can.'

Tam laughed and Pearl giggled behind me.

'He killed a bear with his own hands. So they say.' Tam rolled his eyes. 'Do they really believe we buy that shit?'

I'd heard the story of the bear. We all had. It didn't matter if the stories were true or not. They were part of the president's mystique. Like his face on the banknotes. On posters in shop windows. On the walls of people's homes. No one could escape him. He was everywhere. Like a god.

'That's enough,' I said. 'Pearl is listening.'

'Why shouldn't she hear what we have to say?' Kaz cut the air with his hand. 'You'll see. Soon the president and his bootlickers will be finished.' Kaz slipped his hand into his pocket and drew out a banknote. He jabbed at it with his finger. 'What do you think?'

The words 'Damn your soul' were scrawled across the president's face, in thick felt-tip pen.

'You're crazy if you wrote that.'

Kaz flicked his fingers at me. 'I'm not the one who's crazy. We can't breathe in this fucking country. Isn't that right, Tam?'

Tam nodded.

'What about your studies?' I said.

'Fuck my studies.'

Tam waved his hand at us. 'This isn't the time for arguments. Are you coming or not?'

'I want to come.' Pearl pulled at my sleeve. 'Please, Mira.'

'Who said I was going? It's stupid and dangerous.'

'Kaz and I will look after you,' Tam said, smiling yet again. And that was it. I was decided.

'Keep to the edge of the crowd,' Kaz said, 'in case there's trouble.'

We were off, Kaz and Tam soon ahead, their scarves flying, but our feet were flying too and it was like a holiday. Zazour's central square was only a ten-minute walk from our house. It was called the Square of the Warriors after a battle in the twelfth century. Later, classical colonnades were built on the north and west sides. Behind the colonnades lay shops and cafes where Rey and I liked to spend our time after school, watching everyone go by.

Before we arrived I heard the crowd chanting, and I felt a tremor of anxiety but I kept on running because I was thinking only of Tam and the falling snow. At the end of the road that opened up onto the square, Pearl clutched at my coat. 'What's that big truck with smoke coming out?'

If my heart had leapt for Tam, now it shrunk in my chest. An army tank was creeping along the front of the colonnades. There were always soldiers stationed in Zazour – everywhere in Lyrian had soldiers – but I'd never seen a tank in our town. I grabbed

Pearl's hand and pulled her the few short steps to the sweet shop, but its green metal shutters were pulled down.

'A tank.' I tried to sound like it was nothing. 'An army truck.'

'I don't like it. Let's go home, Mira.'

Yet I was reluctant to leave. Something was drawing me in and it was even bigger than Tam. The square was packed; I'd never seen so many people. In spite of what Tam had said about looking after us, he and Kaz had begun to push their way into the crowd. I was afraid Pearl might get crushed in the melee and so we stayed where we were. People were singing and waving flags, though these weren't the flags people waved for the president with their red, white and green stripes: these were the old blue-and-white flags with the three stars. There were other flags too, home-made, and stitched with words like 'FREEDOM' and 'NO MORE' in large letters. It was incredible. Nothing like this had ever happened in Zazour.

A young guy climbed up onto the bronze statue of the leaping horse with the president astride its back. The statue had been placed in the square to commemorate the president's seventh year in office. When the guy blindfolded the president's head with a black scarf the crowd roared and cried out, '*Freedom, Freedom. Out with the president. Out, out, out!*' It was as if a weight had been lifted from us. As if, indeed, we could all grow wings and fly like Tam had said.

A sudden blast. The ground shaking under our feet. A woman screamed and the crowd surged forward. Instinctively I crouched, taking Pearl with me. It had been a mistake coming here. The president would never allow something like this. Now it was too late.

'Look at the monster, Mira, the fire coming out of it.'

The tank had gained on us. It was less than fifty metres away, cutting us off from the road that led back to our house. Staying where we were wasn't an option but I couldn't decide which way to go: towards the breaking crowd or to the right where a row of thin trees stood out against the white snow.

We had nothing to fear. We were just two girls.

The tank sped up. I never realised a tank could move so fast. Grey smoke poured from its exhaust and the mounted gun swung round in our direction. I yanked Pearl's arm and dragged her in the direction of the trees. Breath steamed out of our mouths. The snow was glassy underfoot where it had been trodden down and we ran and the trees were far away and how thin they were.

A loud crack. Not like thunder or the sound the whip used to make when Grandma couldn't get her mule to move, but a volcanic roar. Pearl's grip loosened on my hand. A second blast. Another loud crack. A terrible fiery heat.

Shouting, screaming, a roaring in my ears.

Silence.

2

Present day: Sundsholm, Neeland.

Years after the initial traumatic event PTSD sufferers may experience symptoms of hyperarousal (high alert). Even though no threat is present the person may believe the threat still exists. Other symptoms may include excessive startle responses, irritability, difficulty concentrating, and sleep problems, as well as emotional numbing, detachment and amnesia.

www.takecare.org.nee/post-traumatic-stress-disorder

Pearl and I are in the hospital in the southern suburb of Sundsholm. There's only one chair in the corridor, near the nurses' station. Pearl takes the chair. I don't mind. I'm quite all right with standing.

The overhead light flickers. On-off. On-off. It turns Pearl's face grey and creates a staccato beat to our movements. As we wait, an old woman shuffles along the corridor, shrouded in an over-large dressing gown, the hem trailing on the floor behind her.

Pearl stifles a giggle.

'Don't you remember the dressing gown I wore here last year? What a ridiculous thing it was. I can't think why I bought it.' There's an edge to my voice I can't keep out.

Her face falls. 'I remember.'

I smile at Pearl but she doesn't return the smile. It was Pearl who'd had me sectioned. Not that I blame her. I had needed help. I'd phoned her one morning after I'd seen patches of blood on the walls and heard that soldier whispering in my ear. Nothing he said had made sense. But he'd kept on, and on. The night before, I'd picked up another young man who reminded me of Tam and taken him back to my apartment. He'd already gone when Pearl arrived.

Pearl doesn't know about the soldier, or my sleeping around. She thinks my breakdown was a reaction to Ma's death. It wasn't. The psychiatrist had said I was suffering from PTSD. 'All these years later?' I'd asked.

'Perhaps there's something you haven't yet faced,' he had said. Because of his lovely grey eyes I had almost blurted out the truth. But in the end I'd shaken my head. I'd denied it.

'At least your gown was kind of glamorous.' Pearl points to the woman's receding back. 'Though you did look a clown, especially with your hair all messed up.'

My hand flies to my scalp. I had cut chunks out of my hair but it has grown back. I laugh, and this time Pearl laughs with me. It's a relief to laugh. We need it.

My attention moves back to the nurses' station. There's nothing much to look at here, only the patients who pass by and the porters hurrying, their shoes squeaking on the shiny floor.

'Do you wear the kimono I bought for you?'

'Of course. I gave the gown to one of my clients. It was still almost new.'

Pearl raises her eyebrows. The movement is almost imperceptible but I see it. 'I hope the gift was appreciated.'

'I'm sure it was.'

Pearl doesn't approve of my work at the refugee centre. That hasn't changed over the years either – the refugee crisis. In many ways it's worse. Pearl agrees refugees should be helped but she doesn't think I should be doing this work. When I left my translation job she said I was throwing away my chances in life.

'I'm going out for a vape,' I say.

'I thought you'd given up.'

'I have.'

Pearl clucks with disapproval. To be honest, I don't want a vape. I would like a cigarette, but it's almost impossible to get hold of them now. What I need is fresh air. I'm desperate to get away from this place of illness and death, away from the flickering light and brisk nurses, and to momentarily forget Pa lying in the specialist heart unit, hooked up to bleeping monitors and tubes, a mask on his face, his thin white hair plastered to his skull, his breath rasping. Hospitals bother me. They suck the air from my lungs.

After the warmth of the hospital the air outside is a slap to the face. I breathe in lungfuls, as if I were the one dying, not Pa. I stand on the hospital steps, rubbing my hands and stamping my feet to ward off the cold, and I look across to the small wooden church opposite. When we first arrived in Neeland, we were sent up to the far north, almost to the Arctic Circle. On the edge of the village there was a pretty church, painted red, with a bright blue door. I went inside one evening, in the middle of winter, and stared at the flickering candles. After all we'd been through, that was my first moment of calm.

The windows of this church are lit up now, and squares of yellow are falling onto the white snow. I consider crossing the street and stepping inside but, after five minutes, I go back to the stuffy, airless building.

Pearl looks up. 'Did you enjoy your vape?' Her nose is twitching.

'I didn't smoke. I needed air. Is there any news?'

She shakes her head and points in the direction of the nurses' station.

The nurse at the desk promises she'll check with the doctor. 'As soon as I have news of your father's condition, I'll let you know.' Her tone is kind but professional. Her eyes dart to Pearl in the chair, to her tapping foot and restless hands.

'My sister,' I say.

The nurse nods but I detect a shift in her expression. A slight frown. A small flicker of the eyes. She must guess where we're from; this is not something we can hide, even all these years later. Perhaps I'm being oversensitive. But prejudice still exists. Even Pearl can't deny it.

'He will be all right, won't he?' Pearl says on my return. Her voice trembles. Like it did when we were cramped in the dark cellar, the planes flying overhead, the bombs falling on Zazour. I want to hold her hand and sit her on my lap but she's not a child any more. I mumble a few words of reassurance. She bites her lip and turns away.

Pearl offers me the chair.

'You keep it. I'll sit here.' I slump against the scuffed, white wall and close my eyes. A faint humming fills my ears. I expect it's the heating system but the sound reminds me of the crowd on that snowy day in the main square of Zazour and I have to lean forward and hug my knees to calm myself.

A few moments later the nurse appears. 'You can see your father now.'

We follow the nurse down the corridor into the high-dependency ward. It's only a few days since I last visited but I'm shocked at what I see. The man in the bed is hardly recognisable as our father: he's a bag of bones, the flesh on him wasted away. How is it possible for him to have lost this much weight in such a short time?

'Pa,' Pearl whispers, bending close. When she looks up, her face is streaked with tears.

'He's on a drip,' the nurse says. 'He's not been eating. I'll get the consultant to come and talk to you both.'

When she has gone Pearl reaches out and takes my hand. 'Kaz must come this time.'

'Is that wise?'

'It's for Pa's sake, not ours.'

We've not set eyes on our older brother since we came to Neeland almost three decades ago. We keep in touch, intermittently. Pearl knows of Kaz's problems – his alcoholism, the break-up of his marriage – but she doesn't understand why he settled thousands of miles away and why he's stayed out of reach. I know. I understand. Thinking of Kaz makes me anxious. It's hard to breathe in here. The ward is so airless. I'd like to go outside again but we've only just arrived. I focus on Pa but seeing him in this condition only increases my disquiet.

I close my eyes. When I open them I see sandbags piled up against the windows and bloodstains on the floor, and I hear a young girl crying. She's hiding. Perhaps under the bed. Or in the cupboard. Yes, that must be it. She always fled to the cupboard when the bombs were falling. She thought it was safe. She's lost. Lost in the cold and the dark. *Where are you, Pearl? Where?*

'Mira!' Pearl's voice is strong; she calls me back. 'Here, take the chair. Sit down.'

I sit. I breathe. Now, when I look, I see the bed and the machines, and the windowless ward with its shiny, clean floor. There are no sandbags or bloodstains. No crying child, only a quiet bleeping. A nurse in the corner with her computerised clipboard, and Pa, thin and grey, his eyes closed but his chest still rising and falling.

'Do you want to leave? I can stay for a while. Stefan is at home with the boys. It's no problem.'

'I'm okay. I came over a little faint and sweaty. Maybe I should eat something.'

Pearl frowns. 'Are you sure it's only that? Did you take your pills today?'

'I didn't eat lunch.'

Pearl shakes her head. 'Have some chocolate.' And she digs out a few dusty squares from her smart red handbag.

I chew on the chocolate. It tastes good.

'I'll call Kaz,' I say. 'I'll get him here. I promise.'

'For God's sake.' Pearl is crying. In real time. 'Kaz never picks up the phone. He knows Pa is sick. Doesn't he care?' She brushes away her tears with the back of her hand, smudging her eyeliner. 'What if it's already too late?'

'Pa is tough. There's still life in him. He's pulled back before.'

'He's not been the same since Ma died. Look at him.'

Pa's face is peaceful, serene almost. 'Has Pa asked for Kaz?' Pa has said nothing to me.

Pearl dabs at her eyes with a tissue. 'He's always asking. Sometimes he forgets Kaz is so far away.' She lowers her voice. 'Oh, how he begged Kaz to come after Ma died. You heard. You were there, listening to the call. How could he have done that to Pa, to all of us?'

'He never has money.'

'That's no excuse. We offered to pay for his flight last time but he refused. If you remember.'

I was there. I remember. Part of me is always wanting to defend Kaz, but I'm angry with him too. 'The war broke him,' I say.

'We all went through the war. It's just another excuse. An excuse for his drinking, his lack of concern for us, his—'

Pa's machine makes a sudden loud noise. Some kind of alarm. The nurse comes running, her thick shoes slapping on the floor. Soon after, the door opens and the doctor arrives together with several other assistants, and we are ushered out.

Pearl is sobbing, gulping air. I take her in my arms and we lean against the wall in the corridor. 'I think it's me that needs to go home,' she says. 'I can't take this.'

'Shall I come with you?'

'No, I'll be fine. But will you be okay?'

'Mimi will keep me company.' I got a cat last year, after I came out of hospital. She's nothing like the coal-black kitten we once had – she's a tabby stray, with fur that falls out – but I wouldn't be without her. Not now.

We wait on the hospital steps for Pearl's taxi, our breath steaming out into the cold air. And across the road the lights from the church cast their yellow squares on the snow.

3

The past: Zazour, Lyrian.

Symptoms of PTSD often develop immediately after
the traumatic event but for some people the onset of
symptoms may be delayed by months and even years.

www.takecare.org.nee/post-traumatic-stress-disorder

A world that casts no shadow. White as a wordless page.
Later I felt someone moving me, hands lifting and
laying me down again. The starched crispness of a sheet under
my skin. A low murmuring of voices. The sharp bleep of
machines.

Later, later, I heard Baby Moe crying in the room next door,
Ma comforting him, and Pearl breathing softly in the bed next to
mine, her breath a small sound like a breeze soughing through
the trees.

Later still, I saw the blue winter light filtering in through the
window, and inhaled the warm smell of coffee.

Home. Everything safe and familiar. Yet something lingered
in the back of my mind, uncertain and dangerous.

Finally awake, I cast my eyes over the room. Two wooden chairs draped with clothes. A striped rug on the floor. A chest of drawers and an oval mirror. Pearl's doll next to our combs and brushes, its legs sticking out at an awkward angle. The doll dressed in a long red knitted coat and missing one of her white woollen shoes. The missing shoe bothered me, but soon there was a great deal more to worry about because when I tried to sit up my right hand hurt and my head swam as if I were under water.

'Pearl?'

'Yes?' Pearl rubbed her eyes. 'Is that you, Mira?'

'Of course it's me. I'm not a ghost.'

'Don't tease.' Pearl threw off her cover and jumped out of bed, her bare feet hitting the floorboards with a smack. 'I thought you were going to die.' Her voice sounded so fearful it made me afraid.

'Die? What are you talking about?' I drew out my hand from under the cover, only to find it swathed in a thick white bandage. 'What's this?'

'Can't you remember?' Pearl moved my pillows. Made me comfortable.

'Remember what?'

A shadow crossed her face. 'We went to the square with Kaz and Tam. There was a crowd of people in the square and everyone was shouting. Then fire came out of that big truck. The fire hit the tree and it exploded and a piece of the tree flew out and hit your hand and you fell down and you got taken to the hospital but you wouldn't wake up. Why did they shoot at us, Mira?'

My mind was like a television with a weak signal, all static and blurred lines. 'Who shot at us?'

'The soldiers. From the big truck.' Tears welled up in Pearl's eyes. She sat down cross-legged on my bed, her pink pyjamas bright in the winter gloom. 'It was horrible.'

*

They said I'd suffered a temporary amnesia caused by shock. For the next week everyone treated me like a precious ornament. Each morning Ma brought me breakfast in bed – eggs, flatbread, yoghurt, olives and her home-made apricot jam –more than I could ever possibly eat. She'd come in with her thick dark hair tied up, her face wrinkling with worry, and straighten the pillows and ask if I was okay; a hundred times she'd ask the same. Even Pa and Kaz stayed home and fussed. Pa brought me fruit and Kaz fetched glasses of water, while Pearl sat at my bedside for hours and told me stories of princesses and enchanted forests, as if I were the one nine years old, and she almost sixteen.

A nurse came every second day to change the dressing. She said the burns were healing; there was some nerve damage but my hand would be okay. Perhaps some scarring, some loss of movement. I wanted to ask more questions but she seemed nervous, always looking over her shoulder, in a hurry to be gone.

Though I couldn't remember the details I hadn't forgotten the reason we'd gone to the square, and I noticed how jittery Kaz was. He never seemed to sit still. He'd come into my room and start pacing about and then he'd leave again. I asked him about the nurse. 'Everyone is nervous now. After the demonstration the regime rounded up a lot of people.'

'What about Tam? Is he okay?'

Kaz shook his head at me. 'You're sweet on Tam, am I right?'

I felt myself blush but I said nothing.

'Don't worry. He's quite safe.'

I checked my mobile. There were no messages from Rey. Which was odd. I asked Kaz what he thought.

'Maybe she's left Zazour,' he said.

A tear spilled down my cheek. 'She'd tell me. And why would she leave, anyway?'

16

Kaz perched on the edge of my bed. 'People are, Mira,' he said in a low voice. 'The army is crawling all over the place.'

I examined my brother's face. His eyes were dark hollows and there was a pimple on his nose. He never got pimples. 'We've always had soldiers in Zazour.'

'Up north in Naran the authorities rounded up a group of teenagers – hardly more than kids – just because they painted slogans on the walls criticising the president. The kids were tortured in prison. When the parents asked for their sons back they were sent dead bodies. I've seen the pictures.'

'Oh my God.'

'There's no way we're staying quiet now.' Kaz reached for my uninjured hand.

I didn't know what to say, or even what I felt. I was afraid, yes, but a part of me was excited that we could be part of some big change. Yet I was cautious. I understood the possible consequences. 'What are you going to do?'

'We're organising. More rallies are planned. You'll see. We can beat them. There have been hundreds of demonstrations already, all across Lyrian, though it hasn't all been peaceful. After people heard about those kids, there were riots and some police and soldiers were injured. One policeman was killed. That's wrong, I know, but the regime retaliated by shooting at the protestors.'

'Did people die?'

'News is hard to come by.' Kaz waved his arms in the air. 'Everything that comes from the regime is lies and propaganda. It's a hall of mirrors. Now they're saying that our movement is part of a foreign plot. Can you believe it? Of course it isn't. The regime knows it isn't. They just want to cause trouble for us.' He started pacing the room. He picked up Pearl's doll and put her down again. He went to the window and came back. Then he stopped moving and turned back to me. There was no light in his eyes.

'Sit down, Kaz. You're making me dizzy.'

He sat. He swallowed and his Adam's apple bobbed in his throat. 'We were so worried about you, Mira.'

I felt like crying but my tears were stopped up in my throat. 'It will work out.' Kaz kissed my forehead. He hadn't done that since I was a baby.

After he went downstairs, I shook off the bedclothes and got out of bed. The floor seemed strangely uneven and I had to place my good hand on the wall to steady myself. But I made it to the window. The snow was still there in the garden but it looked cold and impassive, something to avoid.

*

One morning, Kaz declared he was going into town to buy fresh bread. And it was an announcement. As if buying bread had suddenly become something to shout about.

'Let me come.' My hand was still painful, but my head had cleared and I needed to stretch my legs and breathe the air.

'No,' Ma and Pa said together.

'You can't keep her here like a prisoner,' Kaz said. I was surprised; he didn't often stand up for me.

Ma's face turned quite pink. 'Don't talk like that, Kaz. She's not a prisoner. But we're worried for her. For you too.' She was talking as if I wasn't in the room.

'Ma, please,' I said. 'I can't stay inside forever.'

'They're only after the demonstrators.' Kaz twisted a strand of hair between his fingers. I could hear Pearl running the tap upstairs.

Ma banged her hand on the table. She'd never done that before – not even Pa did that. 'Exactly! You were all on the demonstration and look what happened to Mira ... to her hand. It's not safe out there.'

18

'People still have to shop.' Kaz walked over to the door and removed Ma's shopping basket from the hook. 'We'll be careful.'

Ma turned to Pa. 'Shouldn't you go instead? Are you going to let your son and daughter run out into danger?'

Pa put his head in his hands and we stayed silent awhile, waiting for him to speak. Ma was a strong woman but she always conceded to Pa. When Pa looked up again, he said wearily, 'Let them go. We must get bread. Who knows how long it will be available. Better that Mira goes with Kaz. Together they will be safer.'

'Safer?' Ma said. 'But not safe.'

Pa sighed. 'Nothing is safe anymore. It's time we accepted that as fact.'

*

The day was bitter; snow piled up on the pavements, the side roads thick with it. I pulled my scarf tight round my neck, linked my arm through Kaz's and placed my burned hand inside my coat. I could smell a faint aroma of cigarette smoke on Kaz's jacket.

'If we get stopped by soldiers, just keep quiet. I'll tell them I'm accompanying you because of your age.'

'It's come to that, has it?'

'For now we need to think of our safety. They've already arrested a number of students and activists.'

'Are you sure Tam is okay?'

'Not worried for me?' Kaz grinned. 'You're in love with him, aren't you?'

'He already has a girlfriend.' I didn't want Kaz to know that every time I saw Tam my heart skittered in my chest, that sometimes I couldn't eat for thinking about him, that I'd written his name a hundred times in my school exercise book. When Rey saw his name she'd laughed. Not in a nasty way. Though she thought I was crazy.

Rey still hadn't messaged or answered my calls. It wasn't right, but I was trying not to think about it. 'Why isn't Pa at work?'

'He took a few days off. Because of the snow.'

I wasn't sure I believed Kaz's explanation but I decided not to question him. It was eerily quiet in the neighbourhood. The snow had a muffling effect but the town, usually bustling, had never seemed so empty or silent. I almost said we should turn back but Kaz spoke again. 'People aren't just being arrested, they're disappearing too. We don't know where they're being taken.' He guided me across the road and we turned to the left.

'What about Rey?' I said, and my heart banged even louder in my chest. 'You don't think ...'

'I'm sure she'll turn up. Her parents aren't activists ... are they?'

'I don't think so.' Suddenly I realised how little I knew about her family. I'd always turned away from knowing because to know too much was dangerous. This behaviour was a reflex action, something we did automatically. Like breathing and eating.

There were few car tracks in the snow and despite the gloomy, wintry day, the windows in the houses were dark. 'Where is everyone?'

'Keeping out of the weather.'

'Why are there no lights?'

'Maybe there's been another power cut. We had several while you were sick.' Kaz set his mouth in a tight line and on we went.

We took another left. Now we were on Ezfa Street, the road that led to our school, a wide residential road lined with tall trees and large houses, and a much grander street than the one we lived in. We were following a line of footprints, but we'd still not seen anyone.

Our school consisted of two buildings: an older block close to the road which hosted the infants and juniors; and, up on higher ground, a modern glass and steel edifice which was the secondary school. The infant and junior block had been built in the 1950s. Kaz and I had both spent our early years there, and Pearl still attended. It was an ugly concrete construction, familiar as my well-worn boots. Except now it wasn't. The secondary school stood unchanged, apart from a thick layer of snow on its roof, but the roof of the infant and junior school had collapsed, leaving hanging wires and slabs of concrete, exposing the classrooms to the elements.

I gripped Kaz's arm and closed my eyes but when I opened them the mounds of rubble were still there, the desks covered in dust and debris, the blue painted walls of the classrooms stained with the damp of the snow. Tattered drawings of trees, butterflies and flowers flapped in the chill wind. 'Who did this?'

'The regime, on the orders of the president.' Kaz's face was drained of colour and he was hunched up like an old man, though his eyes were blazing. 'They will blame it on the extremists. How convenient.'

I let go of Kaz's arm. 'Why a school? What have we ever done to them?' The foundations of my world were cracking and pulling apart. As if the bomb had fallen on my own head.

'It's a punishment for the demonstrations; a warning. They don't want us to have freedom. They want our silence.'

'Surely they made a mistake? Perhaps they intended another target.' I knew the regime was rotten but I could hardly believe what I was seeing. It made no sense. Nothing was making sense.

'It's not a mistake, Mira.'

'Do Ma and Pa know about this?'

'Pa knows, but we haven't talked about it.'

'Is Pa …' I hesitated, unsure of what to say.

'Pa hates the president. He always has done but you know how it is, Mira. No one can say what they think in this country.'

'Was anyone killed here? What about Ahbet, our caretaker?'

'Ahbet is okay. No one was harmed. The school was empty when the rocket was fired. It was just a warning, but next time … who knows.' Kaz pulled down his hat and we continued walking to the square and did not speak again.

The square, too, was changed but not in a good way. Nothing had changed in a good way. The base of the fountain had been damaged and several of the paving stones uprooted. Someone had daubed white paint on the bronze statue of the president astride his horse and covered the walls behind the stone colonnades with graffiti:

DEATH TO THE PRESIDENT!
MAY HE ROT IN HELL
FREE
DOM
FREE
DOOM

'What a mess,' I said.

'Where else can we write?' Kaz said, and I wondered if he too had written on the walls.

The snow had melted in places but dirty mounds of it lay at the edges, criss-crossed with the footprints of those who had passed through. A group of soldiers stood shivering under the colonnades, though there was no sign of any tanks or heavy artillery. But all the shops were closed, the shutters pulled down. I looked across to the charred trees on the right, one of which had fallen, its trunk split in two. When I hesitated, Kaz pulled at my arm and told me to hurry.

We turned down a side street into the old part of Zazour with its narrow, winding streets and high stone walls, its arches and balconies. You couldn't see far in the old town because of the tightly-packed buildings, but every time you turned a corner you'd glimpse something: the tall column of the minaret; the stone church tower peering up above the buildings; a courtyard behind an open door filled with geraniums; a stone archway leading to a dark alley; a thin cat scurrying along the cobbles; sheets hanging out to dry. That morning a few distant figures hurried along, but otherwise the area was empty.

Next we entered Stone Street with its small stores – the florist's, the second-hand bookshop where Pearl and I liked to browse sometimes, the barber's with its red and white pole, the bric-a-brac shop Ma loved dearly, and the ironmongers which had always fascinated me as a child – but these were also all shuttered.

We turned right into Olive Walk, an old cobbled street where Babbs' bakery lay, along with a number of other small shops and three gnarled olive trees that were said to be a thousand years old. There were other bakeries in town but Babbs' was our favourite. We bought all our bread there, and their cinnamon rolls, which were famous across all of Lyrian. Unlike the other shops, Babbs' was open but a long queue snaked along the pavement. Yet no one was talking. It made the silence big and ominous.

'Why are there so many people?' I asked Kaz.

'The army takes most of the bread.'

It came back to me then, clear as light: the tank creeping along the colonnades, me taking Pearl's hand. The explosion. Falling into the snow. I had buried the memory because I didn't want to remember but now that memory had returned. I took a few deep breaths of cold air to try and settle my fear. If only I could smell the warm yeastiness of newly-baked bread, perhaps that would calm me. But all that reached my nose was the rankness of the drains and the cold damp air.

Kaz placed his hand on my arm. 'Are you okay? You look pale.'

'I'll be all right.'

'You wait here. Keep an eye out for anything untoward.' Kaz pointed to the doorway of a flower shop and ran across the road leaving me no time to protest or ask more questions.

The snow was no longer falling but mounds of it were piled up at the edges of the pavement. While I waited I peered at the queue shuffling forward. Everyone was wrapped up in thick coats, hats and scarves on heads, boots on feet, gloves on hands – layers and layers of clothes. The woman in the dark green coat might have been Mrs Haseen, our neighbour opposite, but I couldn't be certain as she never looked my way. I kept my eyes on Kaz but he didn't look up as he inched along opposite. And still no one spoke.

Kaz had asked me to be vigilant. Now I was alerted to a movement in the street, though it wasn't a soldier but a young guy. In defiance of the cold, he was dressed in a short-sleeved T-shirt and he wore leather sandals on his feet; he was waving a home-made flag, fashioned from a small square of white cotton. On the flag, stitched in green, was the word, 'FREEDOM'.

Oh God – Tam. It was Tam. I hadn't recognised him in those clothes.

What are you doing, have you lost your mind? But my mouth wouldn't make the words and anyhow, Tam wasn't looking at me, his eyes were focused on some distant point and he was marching forward, marching on and my heart was pounding in my chest but my legs were stone.

No one spoke but a ripple passed through the queue like a carp moving upriver.

He was close now, almost close enough to touch. 'Tam, Tam!' I called, my mouth at last doing my bidding.

He turned. His curly hair was damp and beads of sweat clung to his forehead, and there was a small spot of blood on his bottom lip where he must have been biting it. Our eyes met; he smiled and I smiled back and I thought, everything will be okay. Perhaps he'll come back home with us and Ma will lend him a coat; we have a spare coat that Pa never wears.

'What are you doing?' I looked across to the bread queue but Kaz had gone inside. 'It's not safe with that flag out here. There are soldiers about.'

He slowed his pace. 'Mira,' he said, his voice soft and gentle. 'It's good to see you. How is your hand? I've been meaning to visit but it's been difficult.'

'Put the flag away, Tam. Please.'

He lifted his hands. 'We'll fly – like birds. Remember that, Mira. Remember.' He turned. He took two paces forward. The flag fluttered in the icy wind and a sharp crack echoed down the silent street.

I froze. We all froze.

A second crack, a sound that would echo in my ears down the long years.

Tam's arms flailed. He toppled forward and crashed onto the snow-covered cobbles and a red stain bloomed across the white of his shirt like a rose and the flag fell too and there were more shots, the bullets catching the edges of the buildings and sending small pieces of stone leaping into the air and I screamed and there were more screams and people ran in all directions.

'Mira!' Kaz catapulted across the road, a loaf of bread clutched under his arm. He grabbed me and we were running, running, not stopping.

'What happened out there?' Kaz pulled me into the shelter of another doorway. 'I heard shots.'

'Tam. It was Tam.' I had to bend over to catch my breath, to catch at the sense of it. But there was no sense to it. 'They shot Tam. Didn't you see?'

'Tam? Where?'

'In the street.'

Kaz's mouth was moving but he wasn't saying anything and he was far away and I was shaking and my burned hand throbbed and I looked at Kaz again, at his moving mouth. Then, as if a switch had been turned on, I heard him saying, 'Go home. I must go back.'

'I'm coming with you. I have to help Tam.'

'Go home, Mira!'

Before I turned the corner I glanced over my shoulder. Kaz was kneeling on the snowy ground but he no longer looked like my older brother; he looked like a child.

I felt nothing. Only a great emptiness. Like a sky without stars.

4

Present day: Sundsholm, Neeland.

Our Missing is a small charity, funded entirely by
donations. Our aim is to locate persons in Lyrian who
went missing during the long war. We employ a small
team but we are also reliant on the services of experts:
forensic scientists, forensic archaeologists, geophysicists,
soil scientists and others.

www.OurMissing.com/AboutUs

The entry phone buzzes. I jump up to let Pearl in and wait
at the top of the stairs, listening to her heels clicking on the
concrete steps. But just as Pearl reaches my door, Mimi streaks off.
I clatter down the stairs after her but before I can reach the entry
door someone else comes in and she slips out. I don't worry too
much. She can look after herself. But it's annoying, all the same.

'Sorry … about that,' I say, out of breath from running back
up.

Pearl takes off her cashmere coat and embraces me, and I
smell the heavy perfume she always wears.

'How is Pa?' I ask. She's been to see him again.

Pearl hangs her coat on the hook in the hallway and follows me into the kitchen. 'One minute it seems like he's on death's door, the next he's chatty as ever.' She blows air through her lipstick mouth. 'I'm finding it hard, Mira. And so soon after Ma ...'

'It is hard,' I say, putting the kettle on. 'Do you want a mint tea?'

'Yes, if you have it.' Pearl doesn't drink coffee. It affects her nerves, she claims.

'I'm considering going back. After Pa dies.' Why have I said this? I haven't given it much thought, but now the words have spilled from my mouth I'm thinking, yes, I need to return. But could I take seeing how much Lyrian has changed, all that was lost and broken turned into something I no longer recognise?

Pearl's eyes flash. She doesn't want me to talk about Pa dying. 'It's not the same country we grew up in.' Her tone is brisk and businesslike. She never used to speak like that. She teaches economics and business studies at a local college and she's cultivated that voice to match her profession – at least that's my impression. I ought not to be so critical. We've all had to adapt to survive.

'I feel it's time.'

'You don't intend to move back there for good, do you?' She regards me with suspicion.

'It's possible.' Do I mean this? 'But I should visit. Why don't we go together? To be honest, I can't understand why we haven't already. It's relatively safe there now.'

Pearl gestures theatrically with her hands. 'We have nothing in Lyrian. What is there to go back to?'

Our country fell off the map and broke into a thousand pieces and those of us who are left from that time are ghosts, scattered across the globe. Pearl has a husband and children to anchor her but, even all these years later, I'm without a mooring. Yes, I have chosen to be alone, so people are always telling me, Pearl included, but sometimes I'm not certain I did choose this life. Maybe this life chose me. Yet to go back … what would it be for?

'It's different for you,' I say. 'You have family here.'

'You never wanted kids and a husband.' Pearl frowns and bites at her thumb, flaking her crimson nail polish.

'It's too late for me now.' I laugh, but my laugh sounds like a chicken being strangled.

'Too late for kids maybe, but not too late to meet someone.'

I shake my head. It's a sore subject, this. 'I'm too used to my own company. I don't think I could make the necessary compromises.'

'All relationships require compromises.' Pearl sounds a little sad.

The kettle is boiling, filling the area with steam.

'What happened to Johann?' Pearl takes another bite out of her thumbnail and turns to look out of the window. 'Do you ever hear from him?'

I shake my head. I liked Johann, even if I was never in love with him, but after I ended up in the psychiatric unit he stopped answering my texts. 'He couldn't cope with a woman who'd lost her marbles.' I'm smiling at Pearl as if I've told some big joke but I'm not smiling inside. And I'm not being honest with Pearl. Johann discovered I'd been picking up men in bars and bringing them back to my apartment. That's what drove him away. I can't say I blame him. I just wish I'd been able to explain.

Pearl crosses her legs and sits back in the chair. 'What a bastard.' She flicks at something in her eyelashes. Mascara probably. I wish she didn't wear quite so much make-up. It makes her face look harsh. It's weird. I'm not a judgemental person but when it comes to Pearl I can't seem to help myself.

I place the mint tea bag into a cup and pour on the boiling water. I spoon coffee into the Turkish copper pot and place it on the hob.

'Can I say something?' Pearl asks.

'Even if I say no, you'll say it anyway.'

I expect her to frown but she grins instead. 'Johann had the most ridiculous ears. The boys used to laugh about them. I didn't want to say, of course, in case it upset you. Oscar said they looked like two flying saucers stuck on the side of his head.' She giggles.

I shake my head but I'm grinning too. 'Oscar should have told me.' I hand Pearl her tea.

'You will meet someone one day,' Pearl says, serious now. 'Don't give up.'

'Do you never consider going back?'

Pearl sighs and runs her hands through her perfectly styled hair. She used to wear it long but now she wears it in a chic bob. My hair is a tangled mess, as usual. 'No, I don't.' She sighs again. 'You live too much in the past, Mira. You should let go. Move on.'

'I can't forget what we lost.'

'Nothing will be as you remember it. Going back to Lyrian will only make things worse for you.' She picks up her cup and stares into its steamy depths, then looks back at me. 'I suppose because you were older when we left, you remember more. I was only nine. Everything is a little hazy from that time.' Now her voice is softer, more forgiving.

I take the coffee off the heat. 'I understand. It's different for you.' The truth is, neither of us quite understands the other.

'Do you still think about Tam?'

We haven't spoken of Tam in a long time. I feel like denying it but I say, 'Yes, I do. I often think of him.'

I'm looking for Tam but this I don't tell Pearl. I keep my silence – it's safer. No one in my family knows I'm doing this work. The only people who know are the people I contact through the website, the ones who are also searching. For answers. For loved ones long gone; the missing and the disappeared. The tortured, the murdered, the lost. Sometimes people get lucky – if you can call it luck. It's a lottery yet I still hold on to my hopes. Tam's body must be somewhere. Though after all this time only bones will remain, white and pure like bleached shells. But if his bones are under the soil, perhaps they'll be stained, or broken down to dust. I know how the body decays. I have spent hours researching the conditions which affect decomposition. Pearl is right. I should forget and move on. And it's quite possible Tam's remains will never be found. Yet I feel I owe him. I owe them all – the vanished. Because I survived and they did not.

I pour my coffee and sit down. Pearl leans across the table and rests her hand on mine.

'Do you remember that long black coat Tam used to wear?' I ask.

Pearl nods. 'Of course I remember. Tam was Kaz's best friend. I liked him too, you know.'

'Do you still have nightmares?'

'Sometimes. You?'

'Yes, sometimes.'

Pearl removes her hand and sips at the tea. I look out of the window but I don't see the lime, its leafless branches golden in the winter sunlight, or the pale blue sky behind and the elegant buildings in the square. What I see is a small bloodied shoe, a broken doll and a girl staring into space, her face a terrible blank. I see a grey and dusty hand reaching out from the rubble. A man cradling a dead child. A boy kneeling on the ground beside a collapsed house. Burned flakes of books falling on soldiers' uniforms. An orchard ablaze. Dead tree stumps. Our river running red.

This is what I see.

'What time are you visiting Pa?' Pearl asks.

I shake off the images that have crowded into my head. 'At seven.'

'Do you have a biscuit? It's an age since lunch.'

I hand Pearl the tin. She's put on a little weight recently but I won't say anything because I know how sensitive she is about it. She's still stunningly beautiful. She has a perfect oval face and high cheekbones – looks she inherited from Ma. Even now men turn and stare at her on the street. I don't think men ever looked at me in quite the same way. Our baby brother, Moe, has the same good looks but Kaz and I inherited our features from Pa. We both have lopsided mouths and oversized hands, and our skin is darker. Kaz's hands always seemed too large for his body. Pa used to tease him, saying, 'You'll never be an architect, Kaz. You have builder's hands.' I count myself lucky I don't have Kaz's woolly, unruly hair. Whenever he let it grow, it resembled a sheep's fleece caught in barbed wire and Ma would try and get him to cut it. But he had perfect teeth – just as Pearl does. Mine have always been crooked, like a falling-down building.

'We need to talk about Kaz,' Pearl says.

'What about him?' A sudden chill runs up my spine.

'I still don't get it, why he avoids us so.'

'Like I said … the war …'

Pearl slams the tin down on the table. Crumbs scatter from shattered biscuits and coffee slops out of my cup. 'Don't give me that about his drinking and the war again. He's selfish, that's what he is.'

I stare out of the window willing clouds to gather, flakes of snow to fall. This city is happier in the snow. The hard edges of the buildings soften and children in bright jackets rush out with their sledges.

'Do you remember the day it snowed, the day we went to the square? The sky was silver and grey, the edges yellow like old paper. You were so excited when the first flakes came down.' I pause. 'Oh, I'm talking about the past again. Like an old woman.'

Pearl smiles, her anger at Kaz already gone. 'There's a lot I don't remember. Maybe I avoid it. But I do remember that day. How could I forget? The flakes looked like tiny white stars.' She takes a bite of the biscuit. More crumbs fall onto the table. She wipes them up and drops them onto the tin.

'We should never have gone to the square,' I say. 'I shouldn't have allowed you to come. It was reckless.'

'No one blames you, least of all me. I don't know why you should think that. You were the one who suffered most that day. Kaz and Tam were just as much to blame …'

'Kaz blames himself.'

'We all make mistakes.' Pearl's voice falters, then she frowns and runs her hands through her hair again.

The church clock in the square chimes the half hour. 'I don't think you really understand quite how much the war broke him.'

'There's no need to labour the point, Mira. It's the same for every man who goes to war. War is what it is, and men are always at war somewhere.' Now Pearl sounds tired. 'Kaz didn't have to go back and fight. He should have stayed with us. We needed him.'

'He didn't want to be thought a coward.'

Pearl's lipstick is smeared. She will check her face in the hall mirror before she leaves, like she always does. 'He ran away in the end. If that isn't cowardice, I don't know what is.'

I don't argue. There isn't any point.

*

After Pearl has left I sit back down at the small table by the window. I sit there a long time, watching the grey clouds slipping by, the people crossing and re-crossing the square. There's no sign of the old man who's often outside his apartment, or Mimi. Later, I slip on my coat and boots and go out. Sometimes Mimi hangs out by the bins at the back of the mini-market on the far side of the square. I wander over there and call her name but she doesn't appear.

I walk back out of the alley and head into the mini-market to purchase a bag of coffee. 'Have you seen Mimi?' I ask Mr Engman, who runs the shop.

He shakes his bald head. 'Why, is she missing?'

'She ran out of my apartment earlier this afternoon.'

When he lost his wife three years ago, Mr Engman and I became good friends. It wasn't something planned, it just happened over a few months. Sometimes, when the shop is closed, we take coffee together and discuss the state of the world. We like the big topics. We're not good on small talk. Except for cats. Mr Engman's own cat died a week after his wife passed away, though he didn't get another. 'I'll keep an eye out for her, my dear Mira. But surely there's no need to worry yourself just yet. How is your father, by the way? Are they looking after him properly?'

'He's well cared for but he's so very frail.'

Mr Engman shakes his head, slowly. 'I'm sorry to hear that.'

I pay for the coffee and return to the apartment. It seems so empty with Mimi absent. Perhaps, after dark when the temperature drops, she'll come back into the warmth. Someone will let her into the block, they usually do. I can't afford for Mimi to go missing too. My heart is broken enough.

5

The past: Zazour, Lyrian.

Traumatic events are extremely stressful. The stress that results from such traumatic events often results in a range of emotional and physiological problems.

Neeland Journal of Psychiatric Studies/Harrisson, J/Vol7/27

Ma was bent over the table, chopping onions. I ran in gasping for breath. Ma startled and spun round, the knife still in her hand. She had onion tears in her eyes.

'Where's Kaz?' She dropped the knife on the wooden kitchen table and wiped her hands on a cloth. I stood in the kitchen doorway, silent. Ma was wearing an apron, the one printed with pink roses and I was thinking how the roses looked so terribly out of place, how they mocked me with their reminder of happy summer days.

She snapped her fingers. 'Mira, what is it? You look awful. Has something happened?'

'It's Tam.' My words fell out like broken stones. 'He's been shot.'

'Shot? Oh my God.' Ma held out her arms and I buried myself in her embrace. She pulled back. 'Why isn't Kaz with you?'

'He went back there.'

'Where was this? You need to tell me, Mira.' I could hear panic in Ma's voice and it scared me. She wasn't a person who easily panicked. When Kaz had cut his head open last summer after falling on a rock in the river, she had hardly batted an eyelid.

'I was waiting for Kaz outside the bakery when I saw Tam walking down the road ... oh, Ma ... I heard the shot and Tam fell. There was blood on his white T-shirt. He's dead ... I know for sure he is.'

'I don't understand. Who shot him?' Ma took a step back and gripped the table edge.

'The soldiers. Tam was carrying a flag. They shot him because of the flag and he fell and I should have gone to him but I was scared ...'

'Shh,' Ma said, holding me tight again. She stroked my hair and I breathed in her scent, a mix of onions, spices and soap.

Footsteps. Not Pearl's – Pa's. Heavy, slow footsteps.

Ma said something to Pa in a low tone and Pa placed his big arms around me. He smelled of engine oil but he wasn't a mechanic, he wasn't even interested in cars, he worked as an accountant at the university. 'It's okay,' he said. 'It will be okay,' and he sat me down in a chair and Ma made me sweet tea and I couldn't stop shaking. It won't be okay, I was thinking. It will never be okay.

Ma and Pa asked so many questions. The soldiers shot Tam, I said. That's all I know. Ma wanted to call Kaz but I said no, that might put him in danger. Better to be patient and wait.

Now our comfortable living room with its soft armchairs, striped cushions and thick velvet drapes, felt more like the doctor's waiting room. We hardly spoke. Ma kept getting up and looking out of the window which overlooked the street and

Pa wouldn't stop jiggling his leg, and all the while I replayed that scene over and over in my head; Tam falling and the blood blooming on the back of his T-shirt like a large red rose.

Pearl was upstairs. Perhaps she was playing a game on her phone. It was odd that she didn't come down or that none of us went to fetch her, though I didn't think about it at the time. As for Baby Moe, blissfully unaware, he sat on his floor mat and chewed on a soft plastic car.

Ma and Pa seemed lost, like planets spun out of orbit. The minutes passed slow and heavy like boots on a staircase. Maybe the soldiers had picked up Kaz. Or worse. How could we just sit and wait? I had to do something. I went to the front door and out into the street. Already the day had faded but the lights from the Haseen house opposite cast a friendly glow on the snow and then a car passed by, its tyres spinning a little on the ice, and I thought how ordinary the scene looked and yet there was nothing ordinary in Zazour anymore. Everything had turned upside down. Tam was gone, my heart was torn to shreds and now I was afraid for my brother. Then I saw Kaz, his head bent low like an old man. When he looked up and saw me he broke into a run, and I ran to him and we embraced and he cried a little.

Ma and Pa rushed to meet us, but Pearl stayed upstairs though surely she must have heard the commotion. Then Ma was asking questions and Kaz was answering. The soldiers had gone. Tam was gone. The people were gone. He knocked on doors, he said, but everyone hid, then Mr Barak opened his.

'Mr Barak the ironmonger?' Ma asked. As if that were important.

'Yes,' Kaz said, impatient. 'He didn't see Tam shot but he witnessed the aftermath. Everyone in the queue ran. Soon after, a group of soldiers drove up in a pickup truck. Two of them got out and threw Tam's body into the back and the truck drove off.'

'His body?' Ma echoed. She clamped her hand over her mouth.

I felt sick.

'Do his parents know? Have you called them?' Dear Pa. Practical Pa. Always thinking of others.

Pearl had come down the stairs. I don't know how long she had been there in the doorway. Her footsteps were quiet that day: everything silenced except for the sound of those gunshots still ringing in my ears.

'What are you talking about?' Pearl stood rigid against the door jamb, her hands two small fists.

'Tam's had an accident,' Ma said.

Pearl's face paled and she clenched her fists tighter.

'He fell and hit his head on the pavement,' Pa said.

I looked at Pearl and then at Kaz. *Why are you lying?*

'Is he going to be all right?' Pearl asked.

'No, he's not.' Kaz was still wearing his coat. He went to take it off and I saw tears in his eyes.

'I'm afraid we have bad news, Pearl,' Pa said. 'Tam is dead. The doctors couldn't save him.'

Pearl ran to Ma and buried her head in Ma's lap, while I sat staring at the painting of Grandma's lake that hung on our wall and wished I could dive into its blue water and never surface.

*

After Ma had settled Moe and Pearl had gone to bed, I sat with Kaz and Pa. 'Why did you lie to Pearl?'

Ma was in the kitchen clearing up supper, the supper each of us had picked at because we had no appetite for food.

'She's too young to understand.' The lines on Pa's forehead turned deep like the fissures in the northern mountains. 'It's better this way.'

'She saw my hand burned, the soldiers shooting at us. Why shouldn't she know this time?'

Pa was scratching his head as though he had fleas. 'Your mother and I feel we have a duty to protect Pearl from the worst ... at least for now. I fear the situation is only going to deteriorate, Mira.'

'Deteriorate? How?'

'Let's go outside,' Kaz said, nodding in the direction of the kitchen. 'I need a cigarette.'

'Me too,' Pa added.

'But you don't smoke any more,' I said. In response to Ma's constant nagging, Pa had given up two years previously.

'I do now.' Pa gave me a long look. I'd never seen his face so sad.

We stood outside the back door, and Pa and Kaz lit their cigarettes. The stars glittered cold in the sky and the snow was white like a shroud. For a while none of us spoke. Ma must have known we were out there but she continued her clattering in the kitchen and did not call us in. I watched the curls of smoke dissipate into the freezing air. Still we did not speak. Then Pa ground his cigarette out on the step and said, 'This has got out of control. There was no need for it.'

'Why are you so surprised?' A tiredness to Kaz's voice.

'I thought this president would be different. He promised us reform.'

Kaz threw the stub of his cigarette into the rose bed. Not that there were any roses, just bare dark sticks poking up through the snow. 'Reform? You're an idiot if you believe anything that comes out of his mouth.'

I'd never heard Kaz speak to Pa like that. I expected Pa to remonstrate with him, but Pa only said, 'If you have any leaflets or books in the house that could incriminate us, get rid of them. You hear me?'

'What leaflets?' I blurted out.

'I have nothing here,' Kaz said.

Pa turned to me, but I could not see his expression in the darkness. 'Why would I have anything like that?' I said, sharply. Pa sighed. 'All right. Best to be sure.'

'Where will they have taken Tam's body?' I feared the worst.

'I'll make enquiries, but I'll need to be very careful. Things are getting dangerous out there. We must stay vigilant.' Pa dropped his voice. 'I don't want to worry your mother but there have been problems at the university. People have been disappearing – students and staff.'

'Why didn't you say anything?'

'You were ill, Mira, if you remember. And I'm saying it now.'

'Who's disappeared?'

'The Dean of Studies, and Dr Hodesh from the economics department. Among others. We'll talk another time. We should go inside.'

Ma brought us tea. We sat at the kitchen table. Ma was still wearing her printed apron and she kept wiping her hands on it, over and over.

'Our school got bombed.' I said to Ma.

'What?' Ma's hands flew to her face. 'I heard an explosion. Your father said it was gas canisters exploding.'

'Pa said that?'

Ma looked at Pa but he turned away and Ma rubbed her forehead as if she had a headache.

'I meant to tell you.' Pa reached for Ma and took her hand. He raised his eyebrows at me but I didn't care, I was sick of all the pretence.

Kaz was turning his teacup round and round in his large hands. If anyone had looked in through the window, we'd have seemed like any other family in Zazour, chatting together. It felt so unreal, as if I were watching a film. I tried to focus on the things that might tether me to the material world: the olive jars on the shelf, the white lace underneath, the plates drying on the rack, the butterfly stickers on the fridge door. But I couldn't stop myself from seeing Tam lying on that frozen street, motionless, bloodstained.

'Where have they taken Tam?' Tears spilled down Ma's cheeks. Pa squeezed her hand and Kaz looked down at the table and continued to fiddle with his cup and we were silent again, lost in our own thoughts. Then the lights flickered and went out for the second time that week and Ma got up and lit the candles and our shadows danced on the wall like grotesque cartoons.

'I'm going to make enquiries in the morning,' Pa said.

'What about Tam's parents, do they know?' The fridge gurgled as Ma's words settled in the darkness.

'I called. Three times, maybe four. No one answered. I didn't – I couldn't – leave a message.' Kaz sounded so broken. I had loved Tam, but Tam was Kaz's best friend. I needed to remember that.

A deep sigh from Pa. 'Would you like me to make the call?'

'It's okay. I should do it.' As Kaz picked up his mobile and the glow from the screen lit up his tired face, Moe began to cry upstairs.

'I'll go and check on Moe,' I said.

Moe needed his nappy changed. He wriggled and whined as I lay him on the mat, but afterwards I rocked him in my arms and his breathing softened and he drifted back to sleep. I had felt death would be preferable to losing Tam, but when I kissed Moe and placed him back in his cot, I knew I would go on.

*

After Tam was shot, more people came out on the streets, in Zazour and across Lyrian. There wasn't much on the news but Kaz got information through social media and his student friends. I wouldn't go to any of the rallies; I couldn't, not with Tam gone. Part of me wanted to believe that violence could be avoided, that we could fight with words as Tam had promised, but in my heart I knew it wasn't true.

But Kaz went and it worried Ma, especially after some of his friends were arrested. She tried to persuade him against going, and then he and Pa had a blazing row about it, but Kaz ignored Ma's pleas and Pa's anger.

I still hadn't heard anything from Rey. After one of the rallies, Kaz visited her house at my request. The shutters were closed, he said. No one had answered when he knocked on the door.

I don't know if it was that day or the next when I found Pearl drawing a butterfly, but when I told her how pretty it was she shouted and said it was horrible and stupid, and she scoured thick black lines across the page.

'Why did you do that?'

'Because Tam is dead. Nothing is pretty any more.' And she burst into tears.

I held Pearl until she calmed. Then I sat on my bed and looked out at the snow and dreary winter sky and wondered if spring would ever return.

Two days later six soldiers were murdered in Zazour. None of us knew who the perpetrators were. I can't say we were surprised by the murders: people had been disappearing in town and there were rumours of torture and summary executions. Now the regime really came for us.

*

When the first bomb fell Pearl wet her pants and ran to the cupboard under the stairs. I found her there, shaking and weeping, sitting tight against the vacuum cleaner, her knees drawn up to her chest, the kitten in her arms.

'Come in and close the door ... please, Mira.'

It was cramped with the door closed and the darkness was suffocating. I thought how terrible it would be to die like this, entombed in the house, that to be shot in the street might be preferable.

'What if we all die?'

'We'll be okay,' I said. 'The bombs sound loud but they're on the far side of town.'

'What if they send more bombs?'

'We'll go and live in the cellar. It'll be safe there.'

'I won't go! The cellar is horrible and creepy. It's full of spiders. Can't we go to Grandma's instead?'

'Maybe.' But Grandma lived so far away.

The bombing went on and on, while we cowered in the dark with the kitten and the vacuum cleaner, the smell of polish and wax, and the sour stink of urine from Pearl's wet pants. Finally, the sounds died away and silence fell.

'Are the bombs gone?'

'I think so, yes.'

'Will they come back?'

'I don't know, Pearl. I hope not.'

'Why are they shooting at us?'

I wasn't sure how to explain. How can you explain something that makes no sense? I was saved by Kaz, banging on the cupboard door. 'You can come out, Pearl. It's safe. I have sweets for you.'

We went out into the light and Pearl ate the sweets. We called Grandma but we got no reply. Pearl worried again and asked if they were sending bombs to Grandma's but I said no, the planes would never go there. Then Kaz came and sat on the edge of Pearl's bed. I thought he was going to read her a story but instead he said, 'Why don't I teach you how to use a gun?'

'A gun?' I said. 'Are you crazy? We don't even have a gun in the house.'

'What's wrong with her knowing how to defend herself?' Kaz glared at me. His eyes were sunken, as if he hadn't slept in weeks.

'I don't want to use a gun,' Pearl said, in a small voice. 'Do you have a gun?'

'There are soldiers in town, shooting at people,' Kaz said.

Pearl picked up her doll and held it against her thin chest. 'Are they shooting at the terrorists?'

'Where did you hear that?' I was shocked by Pearl's words.

'On TV.'

'It's a lie, Pearl. You mustn't believe what they say on TV. The soldiers aren't shooting at terrorists, they're shooting at us.' I walked over to the window. The snow had turned dirty at the edges, its perfection spoiled. The kitten was outside, stalking a bird, his small pawprints scattered across the snowy lawn like the shadows of flowers.

'Will you kill someone?' I heard Pearl say to Kaz.

'If I have to, yes.'

My heart flew about in my chest like a bird trying to escape the kitten's claws. I swirled round, almost hitting my burned hand on the windowpane in the process. 'You're scaring her.'

He shrugged. 'We can't protect Pearl from what's going on. It's too late for that.'

I knew he was right. We couldn't hold back the truth, even though we'd agreed to say nothing. Pearl needed to know. And so I blurted out the words I'd promised never to say. 'Tam was shot. He didn't slip in the snow. The soldiers shot him dead.'

Pearl gasped as if she were drowning. 'They can't have, they can't. You're lying, Mira.'

'I saw it with my own eyes.'

Pearl threw her doll on the floor. 'The soldiers wouldn't shoot unless Tam had done something really bad. Did he do something bad?' Tears were streaming down her face.

'He didn't do anything bad. He was doing something good. He was carrying a flag that said, 'Freedom'. They think if you do that, you're against the president and the soldiers are told to shoot anyone who doesn't like the president. But he's a bad man, a terrible man. If I had a gun I'd shoot him straight through the heart.'

'You mustn't say that, Mira.' Pearl's face had turned as white as the snow outside.

'The president is responsible for Tam's death. He ordered the soldiers to shoot. He deserves to die.'

'Stop!' Pearl cried. 'Stop or they'll kill you too.'

'Now you're the one upsetting Pearl,' Kaz said. 'For goodness sake, Mira.'

'You started it with your talk of guns. They already shot at me and Pearl knows it. She was there. She saw what happened.'

'They made a mistake,' Pearl said. 'They were aiming at the bad people.'

'You're stupid if you think that. You've been watching their propaganda, their lies, because that's what it is. Everything you see on that television is a lie.' I should have said sorry to Pearl – I'd gone too far and I knew it – but I didn't. I ran out into the garden and knelt in the snow. Everything was muddy and hopeless and the faded snow smelled strangely of disinfectant. I don't know how long I stayed there. It probably wasn't long. Pa came out of the shed and knelt down with me and held me tight and I wanted to cry and let everything go, but I couldn't.

*

After the first bombing it snowed non-stop for three days and three nights. Pa said he'd never witnessed a snowfall like it. The electricity went off and it was freezing cold in the house but at least the snow and low cloud kept the planes away. In that brief, quiet time I thought a lot about Tam. Sometimes I even wondered if he was not dead and that I might find him somewhere. In a hospital. In prison. Anywhere. But I couldn't even leave the house. Pa would scarcely let me out of his sight and Ma was the same. Pa hadn't gone back to work; he said he was taking time off because of the weather, but I knew that wasn't so.

Tam's parents called to say they had left town. Later we heard his father had a heart attack. Then we lost touch. Everyone lost touch. That's how it was.

On the fourth morning – a Thursday – we woke up to sunshine. Pearl was so excited. At breakfast she chattered on about how we'd spend the day making snow angels and building a big snowman. She had it all planned out. Two apples for the snowman's eyes, a carrot for his nose, Pa's old garden hat for his head. But we hadn't finished our coffee when the first bomb fell. All morning they struck, one after the other.

'We'll have to take shelter in the cellar,' Pa said, after Pearl had hidden in the cupboard again. 'I'm sure it won't be for long. The regime is just trying to scare us. They'll see sense soon enough.'

None of us believed him but we didn't argue. Except for Pearl who stamped her foot and screamed. But she went down. We all did, though none of us wanted to. It was simply necessary, as many things became. We packed up what we needed – clothes, bedding, crockery, tins and packets, the old camping stove, a hundred and one things – and carried them downstairs. My hand hurt and my heart hurt and everything hurt so bad it was like carrying an extra weight. But we all carried it, I know we did.

It was late when we finally trudged down the worn stone steps into the darkness. Pa bolted the door and Ma lit the gas lamp, and our shadows grew large on the lime-washed walls. The cellar smelled of must, old apples, damp and earth. It wasn't an unpleasant smell but, though we'd made it as comfortable as we could, the place felt like a prison.

We'd only be there five minutes when Pearl started to cry. 'I left baby doll upstairs. What if she gets killed by a bomb? I have to go and get her.'

'Not now,' Pa said. 'We'll find her tomorrow.'

He'd hardly completed his sentence when a terrible sound split our ears. The whole cellar shook, the lamp fell and died, and the cellar turned darker than a moonless night. Moe and Pearl wailed, and I thought, *The house has been hit and we're done for.* Because of Tam, I'd considered death but now I discovered I wanted to hold onto life. I didn't want it to end, shuttered up in the dark. I didn't want it to end at all.

The silence after the explosion was like the end of everything. Pa got up and re-lit the lamp. 'Is everyone okay?'

'What about the house? Is it hit?' In the flickering shadows cast by the lamp Ma's face looked old and misshapen.

'I don't think so,' Pa said, cautiously. He unbolted the door. Pearl buried her head in my lap.

'Be careful,' Ma said. 'What if the whole house has fallen?'

'The house is fine,' Pa called from the steps. 'Come on, Kaz. We must check on our neighbours.'

I followed. Ma held up her hands as if to try and stop me, but she put them down when she realised I would go anyway. Pearl ran to Ma and clung to her, and Moe cried in fright.

The house opposite had been hit. Half the front had been blasted off, the roof collapsed. Pa had brought a torch but some of our other neighbours were already outside, the light from their own torches making small circles of yellow in the darkness. A choking, burning smell lingered in the air. The smell made me retch. I decided to return to the cellar. What use could I be here? Then a beam from one of the torches lit up an object in the rubble. I stared. It looked like a white glove. A woman screamed – it might have been Mrs Dalimi from the house next door – and a man shouted, 'God have mercy, God have mercy.'

What I was seeing wasn't a glove. It was severed hand.

As I stumbled down the steps, bile rose into my throat and I retched again. 'The house opposite has been hit,' I said to Ma. 'The Haseens are all gone.'

Pearl cried out and Ma rocked Moe in her arms, back and forth, back and forth, rocking, rocking, rocking and I felt as if even the earth under our feet could no longer be trusted.

6

Present day: Sundsholm, Neeland.

Teeth and bones are valuable sources of DNA evidence.
Dental enamel, the hardest substance in the human
body, protects the DNA-rich pulp.

www.OurMissing.com/howwework/evidence

'Pa? Are you awake?'

He's trying to say something. I lean close. His breath smells stale.

'What is it?'

'Will Kaz come?' His words fall out slow and ragged.

My throat tightens. 'I hope so.' I pull a tissue out of my pocket and pretend to cough.

I look at Pa again. He's scrutinising my face in a way that he hasn't done for a long time. It occurs to me that perhaps he knows, but I throw the thought away. Of course he doesn't. I'm being paranoid. 'Kaz is a devil to get hold of,' I add, grinning and speaking almost carelessly to throw him off the scent.

'I see.' Pa's voice is hoarse, barely more than a whisper

now. 'Kaz is his own man. Always was.'

'Do you want him to come, Pa?'

He doesn't answer my question. 'Your mother. She was such a good person.' He looks at me with his rheumy eyes. 'How I miss her, Mira.'

'We all do.'

Tomorrow, or later today, he will forget she is dead. I almost envy him that. The ability to forget, to be present in the moment. Pa reaches out, takes my disfigured hand and weighs it in his. Instead of the cold I felt earlier, I feel warmth in his skin and for a few moments I consider the possibility of him getting better, getting out of here.

Getting out. The story of our lives.

'Kaz will visit this time,' Pa says suddenly. 'I feel it in my bones.'

I've told Pearl I've been calling Kaz. I haven't. I can't. But now I must. For Pa. The thought makes my stomach tighten.

I let go of Pa's hand and pick up the clock he keeps on his bedside table. It's eight fifteen and the lights are low in the ward. The bed opposite Pa's is empty. The friendly nurse told me the old man died this morning. The men in the other two beds lie under the covers, their backs to me. Neither moved when I walked in. I suppose they must be asleep or perhaps they simply don't wish to talk. There are no visitors with them tonight. I turn back to Pa. His eyes are closed, his breathing quiet.

The friendly nurse comes by again. She's a slim woman with fair hair scraped up away from her face, a web of tiny wrinkles above her pale mouth. I squint at her badge; Kerstin, that's her name. 'Your father had a bad night yesterday. He was shouting,' she says. 'It's good to see him peaceful now.'

'What was he shouting?'

'I'm not sure. I can't speak your language. But I know he misses your mother.' She looks at me with tired, grey eyes. 'My father is the same. My own mother passed away last year and he's not coping so well.'

'I'm sorry.' I sit back in the chair. I, too, am tired. I didn't sleep well but that's not unusual for me. When I was a child, my mother said I slept like the dead but ever since that week I spent in a state of shock and amnesia after my hand was burned, I've been a restless and erratic sleeper. And last night I was worrying about Mimi. She still hasn't returned.

'He's a good man, your father. Never gives us any bother. Not like some.' The nurse nods in the direction of the bed next to Pa's, then she picks up the computerised chart at the end of Pa's bed and examines it.

I think about her words. 'Yes. He is a good man.' But what does it mean to be good? We've had no reason to complain. Pa never beat us or prevented us from following the paths we wished to take in life. But there's a distance between us and I know Pearl feels it too. He wasn't like that before the war. Before the war he was warm and sociable. Like Kaz, he liked to tell silly jokes. He knew hundreds of them: *A man and his wife are traveling in the desert, far from home. A local approaches the husband, saying, 'I'll give you one hundred camels for your woman.' The husband thinks, and after a very long silence he says, 'She's not for sale.' The indignant wife says, 'What took you so long to answer?' The husband replies, 'I was trying to figure out how to get one hundred camels back home.'* How Pearl and I used to groan. Yet we missed his jokes when they ceased. Pa withdrew into himself. Sometimes he'd get angry over a trifle. A broken glass. Ma forgetting to put cardamom seeds in his coffee. A remark one of us made. He was always quick to apologise but we began to tread more carefully around him. Then there were the times I'd catch him staring into space, but if I ever asked him what was wrong he'd say, 'Nothing, dear. Nothing. Just your old Pa thinking,' and he'd slap his hand on his thigh and laugh it off.

The nurse, Kerstin, replaces the chart. 'I ought to check his temperature. It's been rather low, but perhaps I'll wait until he wakes up. It seems a pity to disturb him.'

'It's been two years since my mother died. It was sudden.'

'It's not easy losing a parent.' She sighs. A moment ago she appeared efficient, in charge, but now she looks small and vulnerable. 'There is always so much unresolved. Things that one feels one ought to have said and didn't.' She looks at me and I feel afraid. But she can't see anything.

'My mother was the one who held the family together,' she continues. 'I'm sure it's like that for most families.'

I think about Ma. She dedicated her life to us. After Kaz was born, she gave up her job at the pharmacy. She said it didn't bother her, that we were enough, but I'm not certain it was the whole truth. When I got my job as a translator she was so happy it made me feel guilty. Later, she kept asking when I'd get married and have children. When Pearl gave her two-longed for grandsons she was delighted, but I always had the feeling she was secretly pleased I'd carved out a different path.

'My mother was the same.'

'I'd love to stay and chat but I must be getting on with my rounds. I'll be back later to take your father's temperature. In the meantime, if there's anything urgent just ring the bell.' And she is gone.

Pa opens one eye and then the other. 'How are you feeling?' I ask.

He gives me a weak smile and holds out his hand. His fingers are so thin and gnarled it is as if I were holding his bones, not flesh; and how sunken his face is, the skin grey as the sky outside, his silver hair almost all gone. Each time I visit I am shocked again at how aged he seems and yet he is not so old.

'The clock is loud,' I say.

'What clock? Why isn't your mother with you? She can't be busy at this time of night.' He sounds irritated.

'She's not busy, Pa. She's not with us any more.'

He peers at me and frowns. 'Tell her to come as soon as possible and to bring Kaz with her.'

'Are you comfortable? Shall I sit you up?'

He nods, and I plump up the pillows for him and hand him his water. He has to drink from a child's beaker now. Watching Pa clutch the beaker with his trembling hand is painful to watch. I remember holding a similar beaker to Moe's lips. Once, he snatched it from my grasp and threw it into the mud and I scolded him and slapped his leg. That memory is painful to think of.

Pa puts the beaker on the table and his eyes close. I sit and listen to the clock tick and Pa's shallow breathing. Sometimes voices drift in from the corridor outside, or one of the men moves on a nearby bed. No one else comes in. At nine o'clock, I get up to leave but as I'm zipping up my parka, Pa wakes. 'Where are you going?'

'Home. The bus leaves in ten minutes.'

'Home?' Tears well up in his old eyes. 'I wish we could go home, Mira. I'd like to see our country one last time ... the house ... if it still stands.' He tries to smile but he doesn't quite manage it. Dribble falls from the side of his mouth.

'Perhaps you and Ma should have gone back a few years ago.' I hesitate. 'Why didn't you?'

He waves his hand at me. 'Your mother didn't want to.' This is the first time I've heard him say this. I always assumed he and Ma had been in agreement. He always said he wouldn't return. 'The past is a different country.' Those were his words. 'Never look back.'

Out of the blue, Pa says, 'What happened after they killed Tam?'

My heart jumps. 'What do you mean?'

He waves his trembling hand at me again. 'I know I'm old and finished, Mira, but I'm not stupid.' He taps his forehead.

I perch on the edge of the chair. 'You know what happened, Pa. We wouldn't be silent, and the regime came for us with bullets and bombs.'

'Was it worth it?'

I breathe a sigh of relief. So this is what he wants to talk about. I think on his question. Was it worth it, the years of grief and terror, the countless lives shattered, the thousands of dead and maimed, the long years of exile, the broken hearts, the trauma? I'm not sure this question can ever be answered. 'I don't know, Pa. At least there's hope now for a better future. The country is healing.' Yet my words sound hollow and bland.

'Do you think really think that, or are you just giving your old Pa the answers you want him to hear?' He smiles at me, such a gentle smile, and my heart contracts. The thought of him going from my life, from all our lives, is suddenly unbearable.

'I do think that.' Now I feel more definite. I put the other thing to the back of my mind.

'Will you go back to Lyrian sometime? It's too late for me now. Don't tell me otherwise.' He closes his eyes and I think he's falling asleep but the moment I get to my feet he says, 'You're a good girl.' The words echo the nurse's words. Perhaps he heard us talking earlier.

I laugh. 'I'm hardly a girl, Pa. I'm forty-three.'

'Do you ever wish you'd married, like Pearl, and had children?'

'No, I don't. That life wouldn't have suited me, Pa.'

'Maybe not. You've always been one to go your own way. Like Kaz. Two peas in a pod.'

I lean over and kiss his forehead. 'I should go. It's late.'

'We lost so much.' A tear drips down his wrinkled cheek.

'Don't cry.' I locate another tissue and hand it to him. 'I'll be back tomorrow. Pearl will come too.' I kiss his damp cheek and walk towards the door but he calls me back.

'What is it?' I move to the bed and stand there, my hands in my pockets.

'Make sure you bring Kaz here before I leave this world. Promise me, Mira.'

'I promise.'

He fixes his gaze on me and I see something of the old Pa – his fierceness and bravery. 'Kaz told me. Years ago.'

A chill runs through my body. 'Told you what?'

His face softens. 'I forgave you both years ago.' He puts his hand to his chest and wheezes. 'Don't worry, Mira. No one else needs to know. I will take it to my grave.'

I turn and scramble for the exit and on the way out I almost run into one of the nurses.

*

I've missed the bus but I decide not to wait for the next one. Instead I walk home through the falling snow and sometimes I stop to watch the flakes in the light of the street lamps. Tonight, they look like hundreds and thousands of tiny whirling dervishes, and I think of the day Pearl and I stood together at the window when she said the flakes were stars, and I think of Tam, his hat and long coat pocked with snow. Tears flood down my cheeks, cold tears, frozen tears, and on I go through the snow, through the town with its lights and people, and each step I take is weighted with grief. Yet that fear is back again too. The fear and the guilt and the terrible shame.

*

I'm kicking off my boots in the hall when my phone rings. It's Moe. 'It's not too late is it?' He always speaks to me in English but even now the language and his American accent sometimes catch me off guard.

'I've just got back from visiting Pa.'

'You sound like you have a cold.'

'I walked home. My nose is running. It's freezing out there.'

'It's cold here, too. How is Pa?'

'He was quite chatty tonight.' I pause. I don't want to think of what Pa said. I fish the used tissue out of my pocket and blow my nose. 'I won't bullshit you, Moe. He's very weak. But sometimes he rallies. You know how it is.'

'I've arranged a locum to cover my work. She can fill in at short notice. Perhaps I should fly over this week?'

'Why don't you speak to his consultant? Then you can make the right call.'

'Yes, I'll do that.'

We mull over possible travel plans. I ask him about work. He works in a children's hospital in Boston. He's a paediatrician – a surgeon. It hardly seems possible that it is nearly three decades since he was a baby. I remember holding him in my arms, how he smelled of milk, how good it felt to cradle him. Now, like Kaz, he's thousands of miles away and has children of his own.

'I still plan to come over in the summer.' Moe always brings his children with him – Todd and Daisy. They're good kids, although they know almost nothing of Lyrian. Sometimes his wife Moira comes with him, sometimes not. 'We'll go to the lake and hire canoes.'

'I'd like that.' We don't mention the fact that Pa will probably no longer be with us.

'How are Pearl's boys? Every time I call her we end up talking about Pa. I haven't had much news about them lately.'

'They're fine. Lucas is rather quiet.'

'Quiet? God, when Todd capsized last year Lucas was screaming at him.'

I think of Grandma's lake. Moe never visited. He only met Grandma once; he doesn't remember her at all. I wish I could go back there. I need to remember how it felt in the heat of summer, the cool water like silk on my skin, the sun burning the top of my head, my moving limbs shattering the reflection of the pine trees and turning the water into a mosaic of green and blue. I miss Grandma: I miss that we never said goodbye properly, that she died alone after we were gone. We should have taken her with us. But how could we have done? We had no way to reach her.

The guilt of the survivor is something we do not discuss. Any of us.

'I never swim in the lake here,' I say to Moe. 'Why don't I? I used to love swimming. Kaz, Pearl and I would swim every summer, either in the river at home or in the lake when we visited Grandma.' My voice breaking.

'Mira,' Moe says gently.

'I'm sorry. I was thinking aloud.'

I'm afraid of the lake here, afraid of the memories it evokes. Each time I sit at the water's edge I think of how Grandma is gone, and I think of the river and the dead body floating under the bridge. And soon other pictures fill my head, like the group of young men laid out along the riverbank, close to where we used to swim, their bodies bloated and decaying.

Some of those men were students, people Kaz knew.

'Mira?' Moe's voice cuts through my gloomy thoughts. 'You've gone quiet. Are you sure you're okay?'

'Sorry. My mind wandered ... like my cat.'

Now he laughs. 'Don't let it wander too far. Give it some reins. But what's this about your cat?'

'Mimi ... I expect she'll be back. She's been missing two days.' I pause. Then I say, 'Pa has asked for Kaz.'

'Have you spoken to Kaz recently?' Moe's voice is tight.

'No.'

'I wouldn't bother. What makes you think he'll care this time?' There's anger in Moe's voice now.

Silence on the line. My neighbour calling down the stairs. 'Moe? Are you still there?'

'Is Pa that definite?'

'Yes,' I say. 'He is.'

Moe sighs down the miles that separate us. 'Well … if that's what he wants.'

After we say goodbye I stare out of the window. I hate to pull down the blind: it makes me feel locked in. The snow is still falling, softly now, the flakes sleepwalking on their journey to the ground. I watch for a while, hoping I might see Mimi, but there's no sign of her or any other cat. Then I go to the fridge and take out a carton of yoghurt. I spoon some into a bowl, together with a dollop of apricot jam. After we came to Neeland Ma continued to make apricot jam, but it was never the same. These days I buy it from the supermarket.

When I've finished, I make myself a cup of jasmine tea. I sit at the table and worry about Kaz. After all this time, what we did has turned into a grey concrete barrier that separates us from each other, from everyone, and I don't know if we can ever knock it down.

7

The past: Zazour, Lyrian.

The emotions that fuel revenge differ across cultures. Researchers have discovered that anger drives revenge in more individualistic cultures, while shame tends to drive revenge in more collectivist cultures.

Neeland Journal of Cultural Studies/Klasson,J/Vol 48/19

The family killed in the house opposite were given a funeral. None of them survived. Six of them exterminated in just a moment: mother, father, grandmother and three little girls, Amra, Asiya and Allia. The oldest, Amra, had been Pearl's friend. The Haseens' deaths were terrible but at least their relatives had bodies – or parts of bodies – to bury, while I had none. With Tam there never would be a funeral. No one to weep over his grave, to bring him flowers, to whisper to him.

We didn't attend the funeral. Pa forbade it. He said it was not safe for us to go.

'Why did they have to die?' Pearl had cried until her eyes were so swollen she could scarcely see out of them.

'Only God can answer that question.' Ma's words surprised me because she'd never been particularly religious.

'There is no God,' Kaz said. 'Everything is random chance.'

'That's not true,' Pearl said, bursting into tears again. Pa had retrieved her doll from upstairs but now she threw it onto the damp, earth floor. 'It's the bad people. The bad people are coming and they're going to kill us.'

I tried to put my arms around Pearl to comfort her but she wriggled away and then she sat twisting her fingers in her lap as if a rope lay there that she needed to knot. And all the while her doll lay on the floor like a dead body.

'We're safe here,' I said but the words were not long out of my mouth when we heard the sound of a plane flying low overhead. Pearl screamed and we all ducked but the plane flew on and we heard nothing more.

'You're a liar,' Pearl said. 'The bad men can get in anywhere.' Now she picked up her doll and smoothed its hair.

'I didn't say the planes wouldn't come. Only that we'd be safe down in the cellar.' There was too much truth in Pearl's words. The soldiers could easily find us here and in reality we weren't much safer in the cellar than up in the house above; we might end up buried under rubble with no way out. Chance was our only ally, and if Ma wanted to call that God, so be it.

'Let's play snap,' Pa said, getting up from the camping chair where he had been sitting.

'I don't like snap,' Pearl said. 'Snap is for babies. I want to go upstairs.'

'You know you can't go upstairs,' Pa said, his voice firm but patient. 'How about a game of snakes and ladders instead?'

'I want to go upstairs,' Pearl said again. In the end Kaz persuaded her to play. What else was there to do? We had to have something to take our minds off our situation. I just hoped there would be enough ladders and not too many snakes.

*

After the Haseens' house had been hit, the neighbourhood stayed relatively quiet for several days although we could still hear rocket fire and explosions in the distance. Soon we all started to demand to move back upstairs, but Pa insisted we stay in the cellar. By then cracks were beginning to appear – not in the walls of the cellar but inside us – hidden cracks none of us wanted to talk of.

'How long must we endure this?' Ma asked. All we'd had for breakfast that morning was thin coffee and the last of the stale bread, with Ma's plum jam.

'We must be patient,' Pa said.

'There's not enough food left and we have nothing fresh. All we have is tins and rice,' Ma said, pointing to the dwindling supplies on the old wooden shelves.

'We have jam,' I said. I was trying to make light of things, but I wasn't doing a very good job of it. 'There's plum, cherry, peach, apricot, fig ...'

'That's all very well,' Ma said, irritably, 'but no one can live on jam alone.' She picked up the feather duster and started dusting.

'I don't like jam,' Pearl said, in a whiny voice. 'I want a biscuit.'

'There are no biscuits.' Ma flicked the duster into a corner. 'Why are there so many cobwebs in this damned place?'

'This won't continue forever.' Pa's voice was small and tentative, not like Pa at all.

'How do you know?' Ma snapped. 'This isn't living, it's mere existence. We'll have to go to mother's house. We can't stay locked up in this dreadful place. We'll go crazy, I'll go crazy ...' She whacked the duster on the ceiling. Dust flew down. 'Pearl's right. We should have biscuits and bread and a proper life.'

'We can't go to your mother's, you know that. The roads are far too dangerous.' Pa put his hand to his head as if he could somehow think us out of the situation. 'Kaz and I will go out and see if we can find food.'

'What if the nasty men drop a bomb on your head or shoot you?' Pearl's voice was now so quiet we had to strain our ears to hear the words.

Pa walked over and took Pearl in his arms. 'We'll be careful,' he whispered. 'Don't you worry, honey.'

While Pa and Kaz were gone, Ma kept pacing up and down, and Moe whimpered and fretted, though usually he was no trouble. Pearl stayed quiet. Too quiet. As if she'd locked up her voice and thrown away the key.

*

Pa and Kaz returned with two tins of tomatoes, a small can of tuna and a kilo of rice.

'Is that all?' Ma frowned and shook her head. 'I can't see that lasting us very long.'

'We couldn't get bread or any fresh stuff,' Kaz said. 'The bakery and the indoor market are shuttered, and most of the shops are either closed or empty. We're lucky to get this.'

'I see.' Ma set her mouth in tight line. 'So now they wish to starve us.'

'The weather is bad,' Pa said. 'Maybe that's why food is short. At least it's quiet in town. The soldiers have been moved to the other side of the river, so I hear.'

'They'll be back,' Ma said, opening the rice.

'What is it they want with us here?' I said to Pa. 'Zazour is only a small town.'

'It may be small, but its location is strategic.' Pa smiled at me, but his smile was like one of Pearl's drawings – half-rubbed out. 'I'm sure our troubles will be over soon enough. The regime is bound to come to its senses. Everything will calm down.'

Behind Pa's back, Kaz rolled his eyes and although I didn't argue with Pa, I wondered who he was speaking for.

*

I dreamed of Tam that night. We met on the college steps and then, all of a sudden, as dreams are, we were sitting by Grandma's lake. Its water was as blue and clear as a late September sky. We sat on the shore and Tam held my hand and I said we should go swimming but Tam said he couldn't swim. 'Don't be stupid,' I said. 'Of course you can. I saw you in the river, remember?' He shook his head in a sad kind of way and walked with me to the water's edge. I didn't wait for him; I dived right in. There were weeds at the bottom of the lake the colour of jewels. When I surfaced the day had grown dark and Tam was nowhere to be seen. I called and called but he didn't appear.

I woke up shouting. Ma asked if I was okay. I said I'd had a bad dream. I didn't tell her what it was about.

The quiet continued for several more days. In spite of our food shortage Kaz and Pa didn't go into town again, although they went into the garden to make calls. I don't know who they were calling and they didn't say. I could have asked but I didn't want to know but I had my suspicions. I never saw Kaz or Pa with a gun but I was sure they had one, or perhaps even more than one, hidden in the shed. One morning a big, burly guy I'd never seen before turned up at the door. He didn't come down into the cellar, but I crept up into our room upstairs and saw him talking to Kaz and Pa in the garden.

Ma and I had been going upstairs to the house to fetch clean water each day, but the day after the burly man turned up, we found the taps dry. Pa said it must be because of the cold but Ma argued with him and said the regime had turned the water off deliberately. It turned into quite a heated row, which upset me, because Ma and Pa rarely argued. Afterwards, when they'd both calmed down, Pa and Kaz went to the allotments to fill up from the tap there.

The days passed, heavy like boulders. We weren't chatting much – there didn't seem anything to talk about any more – but Pearl stopped speaking altogether. She'd always been such a fidget and a chatterbox, driving us crazy with endless questions, but now she was silent. And nothing we did, not Pa's jokes or Ma's cajoling, or even Moe's chuckling, changed that. Every time there was a boom, however distant, Pearl sat on the mattress, her hands over her ears, trembling from head to toe. Whenever I tried to comfort her, she turned away.

Eventually Pa said, 'That's it. We can't continue living like rats.' In the flickering, dim light the strain was obvious on his face and he'd developed the habit of scratching at his head, as if ants were living in his hair. He looked terrible. I suppose we all did. Like Kaz, he hadn't shaved and his chin was covered in white stubble.

'Are we moving back into the house?' Ma asked. 'Do you think it's safe?'

'Not yet,' Pa said. 'Kaz and I need to go out. We're running low on food.'

Ma laughed. Not a laugh of amusement. She sounded almost hysterical. 'Why now? We've been running short for days.'

'I'll go with you,' I said. The thought of staying in the cellar for another minute felt like torture.

'I'm sorry,' Pa said. 'But I just can't allow it.'

'What about Pearl? She needs fresh air. Even if we just go to the end of the street ...'

'No,' Pa said again. Ma was nursing Moe, but he snuffled and pulled away from her breast as if he had understood the gravity of our situation. As for Pearl, she just stood there, clutching her doll, saying nothing.

'What about my hand? I need fresh bandages.'

'Kaz and I will get you some clean bandages. What else do you need?'

I swallowed. Looked at Ma.

'Tampax,' Ma said. 'We need Tampax, bandages and antiseptic cream.'

'I'll see what I can do.' Pa had turned a little pink. This was not something we normally spoke of in front of him.

'Please let me come. I'd rather die out there than put up with this,' I said.

'Don't be an idiot,' Kaz said. He was stood at the foot of the steps that led up to the outside. His hair had grown and with the stubble on his chin he looked not just unkempt but somehow harder.

'It's because I'm a girl.' My cheeks burned with the injustice of my brother's words.

'That's not true.' Kaz grabbed his coat from the hook. 'Come on, Pa, we should go.'

'Why don't you want me with you then? What is it you and Pa are doing out there?'

Pa raised his hand. 'Enough. Stop this arguing. I said no, Mira, and I mean no. You can go out into the garden with Pearl and no further. The weather is poor again today and the planes are unlikely to fly but that could change in the flicker of an eye. Keep your eyes and ears peeled. If you hear anything unusual – and I mean anything – you are to go right back inside again. You hear me?'

'I hear you.'

I'd heard but it didn't mean I was going to obey. Soon after Kaz and Pa had left, Ma went up into the house to search for something she'd forgotten and I took my chance. 'Look after Moe for me,' I said to Pearl, putting on my parka. 'Ma will be back in a minute. We'll go out in the garden later, okay?'

Pearl opened her mouth and closed it again.

'I'm just going to the end of the street to look for the kitten.'
We hadn't seen the kitten for twenty-four hours. We'd let him
out and he hadn't come back, and Pearl had been very upset.

I zipped up the parka, pulled on my woollen hat and walked
up the stairs. I almost expected Pearl to call after me. She didn't.

*

Small flakes of snow fluttered down from the white sky. The
wind bit at my face like a hungry dog. I picked my way down the
icy steps and out into the road. The ruined house opposite was
dark, like an old bloodied wound, and the lines of bare aspens
trembled in that bitter, angry wind.

My boots crunched on the packed snow. Pa was right about
the planes. The low cloud was keeping them away. I was taking
a risk being out but I didn't care. It was wonderful to breathe
again, to stretch my legs and be alone. For a while I forgot Tam,
I forgot the soldiers and the bombs. I was almost happy.

Pa had said the soldiers were being deployed to the industrial
area of Zazour, north of the river. Either that had been a lie to
placate us or the situation had changed, for the square fairly
bristled with soldiers. Groups of them stood around shuffling
in agitation at the cold, guns slung across their shoulders. It was
early afternoon. Usually at this time of day the square would
have been crowded with people out shopping, drinking coffee in
one of the numerous cafes, gossiping in the square and feeding
the pigeons, but few townspeople were about and the ones I did
see were hurrying along, heads bent towards the ground.

I thought of Tam and how brave he'd been to walk down the
street with his freedom flag. My heart was beating uncomfortably
fast but I wasn't going to allow the presence of the soldiers to
intimidate me. Already they'd injured my hand, killed the one
person I loved more than anyone in the world, and they'd forced

66

me to live in a cellar like an unwanted dog. Now I'd show them that a girl could walk through town alone with her head held high.

As I passed the first group, one called, 'Come 'ere, sweetheart!' My mouth turned dry because I'd heard stories about soldiers and what some did to girls, but I carried on walking. Another soldier whistled. I turned and stared, willing knives to shoot from my eyes and grenades to fly from my hands. Something in my expression spooked him because, instead of whistling again or shouting abuse, he averted his gaze. I started thinking about what the soldiers had done to Tam and a cold anger built up inside me and it grew larger than my fear.

At the far side of the square close to Café Yasmina – where Rey and I used to spend a lot of our time (the cafe was closed like all the others) – I spotted a young soldier sitting on the kerb, eating a sandwich. He seemed quite relaxed, as if he were just taking a picnic. I don't know what made me do it but walked across the square, leant against the cafe wall and watched him. He didn't look up.

He appeared to be around the same age as Kaz and Tam and yet he was fighting against people like them. I wondered what he thought, but probably he didn't. He had no need to; he simply carried out orders. As I was thinking about this and hating him for his blind obedience, he looked up and smiled. It was such a friendly, surprising smile that I found myself smiling back.

'Hi,' he said, as if he knew me.

'Why are there so many of you?'

'So many of us?' The soldier's face flushed. 'Don't you know?'

'No.' I folded my arms and scrutinised his face.

He flushed again. He had pale blue eyes and fair hair, cropped short like the others.

'There are terrorists in town. We came across a group of them only yesterday.' He gestured with his hands. 'Out there.

Past the orchards. We hit an ambush and one of our guys was killed. I reckon we got some of them.'

'You killed a man?'

'Not yet.' He flushed a deeper shade of pink. 'We're here for everyone's security.'

'I never heard about any terrorists, not here.'

He shrugged. 'Only what we've been told. What's your name?'

'Dania,' I lied. I didn't ask his.

'That's a pretty name.' He bent forward, so that he was closer to me. 'A pretty face too.' He was still swallowing, even though he'd stopped eating. 'It's not safe for a girl to be out on her own.'

'I need bread. For my family. My little sister. She's hungry.'

'I can get you bread.' He screwed up the greaseproof paper his sandwich had been wrapped in and dropped it on the ground. As he stood up, several shots rang out in the distance. 'What did I tell you?' His expression hardened. 'Go home.'

'We must eat.'

His friendly smile disappeared and something sly and devious settled in its place. 'I can get you bread.' His tone too had changed. He stood up and took a step towards me. 'You really want bread?'

I held my ground. 'We must eat.'

'There's a price.' He took another step forward. Now he was inches from me. The smell of onion on his breath was overpowering. 'You understand?'

I wasn't so young and naïve to think he'd do me a favour with nothing in return. I didn't have much experience of boys but I knew enough. I held his eyes. He no longer looked young and sweet. How I hated him then. We weren't friends. We were enemies. 'Oh,' I said. 'I see.'

'I don't think you do.' He pulled me towards him. He had a powerful grip. We were about the same size but he was stronger than I was. He pulled at the zipper on my parka, reached in through the opening and squeezed my left breast. I felt disgusted and cheap; I wanted to smash my fist into his face and break his nose. Yet another part of me was thinking differently. Clear thoughts. Like the water in Grandma's lake.

'All right. What about tomorrow? If I stay out too long now my mother will get suspicious.' I smiled. A false smile.

He let me go. 'I can get you cheese and oranges too.' He narrowed his eyes. 'But nothing without the payment.'

'Of course,' I said, zipping up my parka. 'We can't meet here. I know somewhere nice and quiet. Where we won't get disturbed.'

I told him when and where. It was that easy. There was a burst of gunfire and the soldier's companions shouted at him to move. And he was gone.

*

I wondered if Pearl would say anything about the kitten, or if perhaps the kitten would return by itself and then Ma would know for sure I'd lied. But first there was somewhere I had to go. I might never get the chance again.

A river ran through the middle of Zazour. It was known as the singing river because it always had a song. The song varied according to the seasons and the rainfall. Sometimes fast and unsettling, sometimes melodic, sometimes just a ripple and a gurgle. Even now, when I'm half asleep and I hear the wind sighing through the tree outside my window in Sundsholm I often think it's the river singing and then, when I remember where I am, the tears fall.

Another group of soldiers was gathered near to the bridge but I passed by almost unnoticed. Later, no one would get by. Halfway across I stopped for a moment and looked down into the churning water. It seemed to me that the river's melody had been lost, that it only shouted war and death.

I hurried on.

The cemetery lay on higher ground, surrounded by pines, cypress and cedar trees; the neat rows of grave markers rose like knives out of the icy, white earth. The place was empty, as I'd expected it to be. I walked along the familiar paths – past the snow-covered rose garden and the small chapel, the long rows of stones, past the children's section and the cypresses – until I reached Grandpa's resting place. Pearl had been a baby when he'd died and she hardly remembers him, but he and I were always close. Soon after he passed away, Grandma left town and moved back to the village in Kalatia where she'd grown up.

'Grandpa,' I whispered, sitting down at the edge of the grave. 'It's Mira.'

When Ma was not around, if perhaps she'd gone to change the flowers, I liked to chat to Grandpa. Pearl used to think it was funny. Once she asked Grandpa for a new dress for her doll. I told her she could ask Grandpa's advice but she couldn't ask for presents.

The wind whistled through the trees, bringing with it a flurry of sleety snow. I shivered and shrank into my parka. 'They killed Tam,' I said to Grandpa. 'Did they bring him here?' But I knew the regime would never give Tam the honour of a decent burial. Something had turned rotten there years ago but even after I'd started to grow up and understand more about my world, I hadn't wanted to see it.

'What should I do?' I told him everything. About how I loved Tam and why I'd gone to the square and what had happened there. How Tam had waved his flag but how none of us had expected the regime to shoot an unarmed civilian. How the soldiers had dumped Tam's body in the back of a truck. I told him about the bombs and the family and Pearl's silence.

I told him about the soldier I'd just met who'd offered me sex in exchange for food. Then I waited. It sounds stupid now, but I really was waiting for some kind of sign. Nothing happened. It grew colder. I leant over and kissed his stone, and I started crying uncontrollably – the first time I'd cried since I'd seen Tam shot. I thought again of my own death, of how much easier it would be if I took off my parka and lay down in the cold snow; but then I thought of my family and Grandma in her house far away. I couldn't do it. I loved life too much. Even in that time of despair, I loved it.

It had started to snow again and the flakes were settling on my eyelashes like pale cold butterflies. 'Goodbye, Grandpa,' I said.

A round of machine-gun fire blasted out from the direction of town, shattering the silence. I jumped to my feet and retraced my footsteps in the snow, back through the rows of stones. Just before the entrance to the cemetery, a deer bounded out of a copse of trees. I'd never seen a deer in Zazour before. There were deer up in the pine forests above town, beyond the orchards, but they rarely came into town. On catching sight of me, the animal came to a halt. Its nose and flanks quivered and its warm breath sent small sprites into the cold air. We examined each other a moment and continued our separate ways.

The soldiers close to the bridge had gone. The machine-gun fire had also stopped although several rifle shots rang out. Then everything fell silent. I could hear the roar of the river but beyond that, nothing.

I stopped and leant on the stone parapet. We'd spent so many happy hours on that bridge, Kaz, Pearl and I. Dropping in sticks. Throwing in stones. So many hours.

I knew I was a sitting duck there, an easy target for any trigger-happy soldier but I didn't care. If God, fate or random chance wanted me dead, so be it. That wasn't the same as lying in the snow and waiting for death. The truth was: I never could have done that.

The next round of gunfire was too loud to ignore. But as I turned to leave something caught my eye floating downstream towards the bridge. At first I thought it might be a tree trunk, or even a large dog.

I clamped my mouth shut with my hand. Else I would have screamed. For this was no dog but the body of a man, face down in the water. He was wearing a torn red T-shirt and his hands were tied behind his back.

I fled. Across the bridge, past the square. There was smoke on the horizon and a smell of burning. As I ran, I saw Tam falling, the blood on his shirt. I saw the man in the river, and the young soldier smiling at me. And now it came to me – what I would do. What we would do, Kaz and I.

*

When I reached our street, the light had faded from the sky. I waited on the steps of our house. To catch my breath. To catch at my thoughts.

An arm gripped my shoulder and I shouted out. 'Who's there?'

It was only Kaz. I'd been breathing so hard I hadn't heard his footsteps. 'Where the hell have you been? Pa and I have been looking for you. Ma's been out of her mind with worry.' He shook me. 'What's the matter with you? Don't you know there's a war going on?'

'I saw a dead body,' I blurted out. 'Floating down the river.'

'You've been to the river? For fuck's sake, Mira.'

'I went to Grandpa's grave. Please don't be angry.'

'We were worried. There's been a lot of shooting today. You must have heard it.'

'They're killing people. For no reason.'

Kaz put his hand to his head. 'The regime has been killing people for years, Mira.' He spoke so quietly it was almost as if he didn't want me to hear.

The burning anger I'd experienced when the soldier groped me returned. 'We have to stop them.'

'What can we do against an army? Against guns and bombs?'

I started to cry and Kaz put his arm around me. 'You're upset. We should go in. It's freezing out here and Ma and Pa are waiting.'

It had to be now or never. 'Kaz?'

'What?'

I told Kaz my plan. Then I asked if he was in or out. Without Kaz it would not be possible.

We stood in the dark and the silence. A few snowflakes fluttered down from the sky. 'In,' he said. 'As long as you understand the consequences. Do you?'

'I do.'

'You're certain. One hundred per cent?'

'Yes,' I said.

Before we went down into the cellar I looked across the road. The bombed house stared back at me like a toothless beggar-woman. There would be women like that soon enough. Children too. But we would be gone by then, dragging our guilt and sadness with us like heavy suitcases.

8

Present day: Sundsholm, Neeland.

Some sufferers with PTSD recover with no or limited interventions. However, without effective treatment, sufferers often go on to develop chronic problems which can last years, or even a lifetime.

www.takecare.org.nee/post-traumatic-stress-disorder

It's a ten-minute walk to the refugee centre where I work two days a week. I love my work here. I don't miss my old job. Not at all.

The square is busy at this time of the morning. People walking and cycling to work. Mothers – and some fathers – taking their children to school. The birch trees stand out like strips of lace against the clear sky; a child is running across the square with his mother and both are laughing. I'm happy today, in spite of everything. Today I feel like everything's going to work out. Even though I haven't yet called Kaz. Even though Pa is in hospital. Even though Mimi hasn't turned up. A few minutes ago I called in at the mini-market. Mr Engman has promised to put up some posters of Mimi. He's always so kind. He's lonely with his wife gone.

I walk briskly, pulling my scarf close round my neck against the chill wind. Across the square. Down Langagarten with its strange lopped trees, whose branches resemble knobbly fingers. The centre is halfway along the street and is a plain building, painted a dirty yellow. It's situated between a bank and a kitchenware shop. Most people probably pass it by without noticing.

The foyer is busy, as always. There are people milling about, waiting to be seen. Women in bright scarves, kids playing, babies crying, young men gazing at the girls, the girls giving the boys long sideways glances.

I greet Sofia at the reception desk and walk into the room I use for my clients. I counsel people, help them negotiate their way through the maze of bureaucracy, fill in forms, make calls, visit government departments, and a host of other stuff. I don't choose the people I advise: they're chosen for me. There are always more people who need help than there are helpers.

I sit down at the desk and check through the paperwork relating to my first client, Tomas. We've already met several times. Soon he's knocking on the door. 'Come in,' I shout, and he enters. 'How are you today?'

'Fine,' he mumbles. I gesture, and he sits down.

Tomas claims to be seventeen though he looks younger. He's a small, slight young man with a crop of raven-black hair and dark, intense eyes. Tomas had to leave his country because he's gay. You'd think by now, after all these years of conflict and hatred, humanity would learn forgiveness and tolerance but his country still punishes homosexuality by torture and death. He told me he couldn't let his family know because they too would have been punished, so he left one day without telling them and by various means he arrived here in Neeland. I'm not quite

75

certain how he managed the journey. He said it was hard, it took him months, he lost weight and more than once, he said, he thought he was going to die. For a while he was at sea, stuck in the hold of a cargo ship crammed in with many others, and was very sick. I told him that my family and I had also travelled by sea from our country and he looked at me for a long while and said, 'It is bad, is it not?' I nodded and we moved on.

Tomas and I don't speak each other's languages, so we use our common language, English. His English is good and I never have a problem understanding what he's saying. With other clients it can be problematic and we never have enough translators.

'We need to discuss your accommodation.'

Tomas won't look me in the eye. He's jumpy today.

'You seem a little uneasy.'

'I'm good. You have no need to worry.' He turns to look at the picture on the office wall, painted, as I was told, by the previous director. It's pleasant enough although not quite to my taste. A landscape, in oils. A blue lake, surrounded by birch trees, the background painted in the yellows, reds and russets of autumn. Tomas has seen the painting before, but he continues to fix on it.

'Do you like this picture?' He doesn't respond. Usually he's quite chatty. 'I find it a little conventional,' I continue. 'Though I like the colours.'

Tomas gives me a half-smile. I'm encouraged by this. I lean forward and place my hands on the desk. 'How is the new accommodation? Is it working out for you?' Recently Tomas moved from the far north of the country where he was living in an old army camp into an apartment in town which he shares with three other refugees.

He shrugs.

'How are you getting along with the others?'

'Okay.' He focuses on me a moment. He continually jigs his right leg. Then his eyes return to the painting.

I get up and stretch my arms. Something's definitely up with Tomas: I can almost smell it. I examine the familiar surroundings. Besides the painting on the wall, which gives the room a splash of colour, the place is dull and spartan. There are two chairs and a desk, and a single lamp in the corner. The carpet is grey, the walls white. I turn back to Tomas. 'There's a nice cafe just around the corner. We could get a coffee and chat there.'

He stares down at the carpet and says nothing. Now I think of all the times Ma and I tried to get Pearl to talk. It never worked.

I pull out a pad of paper and a pen and place them on the desk close to Tomas. He pushes the paper back in my direction. I can't see the expression in his eyes, but I can see his jaw moving.

'Has someone upset you? Someone here? Or one of your flatmates perhaps?'

He shakes his head. I'm frustrated. We were managing so well before. 'Would you prefer to talk to someone else today?' Again he shakes his head. I push the paper back towards him. We're not supposed to discuss our own circumstances but the boundaries aren't concrete or laced with barbed wire. 'My sister stopped talking after bombs fell on our town. She started drawing pictures instead.'

His eyes turn to me and I see a glimmer of something on his face. I walk to the window. There's a small garden at the back of the centre but the plants are buried under snow and only a few stalks of tall grass are poking up. The snow is patterned with footprints – birds' feet and larger prints which might be the tracks of deer. They wander into this part of the city sometimes. I think of the deer I saw in the cemetery; how close I was to it. But I had moved and it had bounded off.

A rustling of paper. I turn my head, slow. I stay by the window. Tomas is hunched up, leant over my desk, his hand moving across the page.

'Here,' he says. 'This for you.'

The drawing is beautifully done. A group of four men is standing on top of a tower. One of the men has his arm outstretched. There is a fifth man, but this man is falling and his legs are upside down, pointing to the sky, which is scattered with stars. The man's head is level with a small window.

'What is this?' I say, pointing to the falling man.

'My friend.' With those two words, he gets up and walks out of the door, and when I look at the drawing again I notice a face at the window of the tower. It is Tomas.

*

After Tomas, I meet with Solomon. There are more young men than women because it is easier for the men to travel. Solomon's story is the story of our times, of all times.'How are you today?'

Solomon smiles and his whole face lights up. 'I good,' he says. 'Always good.'

Solomon is at college. He intends to study to become a plumber. He's had some problems but he appears to be coping well now. Soon we won't be seeing each other any more. That's sad in its way but it is also a relief to see clients go. To know they are beginning a new life.

'No more problems at the house?'

Last week he got into an argument with one of his housemates, and someone called the police.

'All fine. We friends now.'

I laugh, and he laughs with me.

We discuss some practical issues and he leaves. After Solomon I have two further cases and then I leave the office to talk to Anna, the senior caseworker. I show her Tomas' drawing and we mull over possible strategies.

'People only talk when they're ready,' she says. 'You can't force things.'

'Sometimes people bury things so deep down they never surface.'

A slight frown passes across Anna's face and her calm grey eyes darken. She knows some of my history but there's much she doesn't know.

My hand is already on the door handle when my words come tumbling out. 'Maybe Tomas senses there's something on my mind. Perhaps that's why he's clammed up.'

Anna doesn't press me. She stands by her desk, looking at me without judgement. Her clothes, like Pearl's, are subdued and classy, and her greying hair is highlighted with blonde streaks. She always looks elegant and in control. But whereas a single look from Pearl can often cause me to flounder, I always feel at ease with Anna.

'It concerns Kaz, my brother.' Anna knows I have a brother in Australia but she has no idea why we are estranged. 'My sister wants Kaz to come and see Pa ... you know ... before he goes. We haven't seen Kaz since we left. His visit is going to be difficult for all of us. I'm particularly worried about my nephew, Lucas. He's been so withdrawn lately. You see, my sister stopped speaking for a while ... during the war.' In all the time Anna and I have been working together, I've never mentioned this.

'You think your brother is going to reopen old wounds, is that it?'

I feel suddenly close to tears. 'Kaz has had a lot of problems. Alcoholism, a marriage break-up. I know his problems are related to the war but my sister seems to think he's playing on it.'

Anna glances at her watch. 'We could take lunch together if you'd like. I have no more clients until two.'

'Yes,' I say. 'Thanks.' I realise I'm hungry. I didn't eat breakfast this morning. I'm prone to missing meals. Anxiety makes me nauseous but not eating only feeds my anxiety. How careless I am sometimes. Careless and stupid. That's what Pearl would say.

Anna and I walk up to Norrviken Park. There's a cafe here, close to the lake; a friendly, busy place, filled mostly with students and arty types. Some brave souls are sitting outside in the cold but we decide to stay inside in the warm and we manage to locate a table in one corner. Over lunch, I open up to Anna. I tell her how Tam was gunned down in the street right in front of my eyes. How we fled Zazour because of the bombing. How Kaz went back to fight and refused to come with us to Neeland. How I'm still searching online for news of Tam's final resting place. I even tell her about Mimi. She listens without interrupting. But there's one thing I don't say. I cannot speak of that.

*

Before I go up to my apartment I stop by the mini-market to buy fresh coriander and ginger.

'The posters are up,' Mr Engman says. 'I got my grandson to put them up.'

'Thanks,' I say. I don't admit I haven't seen the posters: I was lost in my own thoughts walking home from work. 'How much do I owe you? For the printing.'

'Nothing. I just hope you find her. How's your father doing?'

'He's still very frail. I'll be seeing him later.' I pay for the coriander and ginger, thank him again for the posters and go out to look for Mimi. Mr Engman's grandson has done a good job. The posters are everywhere. As soon as I see one, I notice others – on lampposts and buildings – some already curling in the damp air. But there's still no sign of Mimi herself. First, I check the bins behind the Turkish restaurant. The owner of the restaurant discovered Mimi there as a kitten; he told me about her and I took her in. I don't go inside the restaurant as the owner retired last year. Now it's been taken over by another family.

Next, I check the small park at the southern end of the square but I can't see anything in the darkness. I call her name and a teenage boy on a bicycle asks me if I'm looking for a cat. 'Yes,' I say. 'The one on the poster. Have you seen the poster?'

He has, he says, but he hasn't seen Mimi, though he promises to let me know if he does.

'My number's on the poster,' I say.

'I have it already,' he says. 'Our cat went missing last year but he came back. I'm sure yours will too. You could try the missing animals' website. Do you know it?'

'No,' I say. 'I don't.'

'Just type in Sundsholm missing animals site. You'll find it easily. I hope you find Mimi soon.'

*

I must call Kaz. Time is ticking by. I pick up my mobile: the conversation with Anna has encouraged me. I hold it in my hands and stare at Kaz's number. I can't do it. Not now. I put the mobile down on the table and make myself a stir-fry. I season it with the fresh ginger and coriander, and a little chilli paste. Wandering around in the cold has given me an appetite.

As soon as I've finished eating I check the missing animals' site. I log in Mimi's details and scroll through the pictures of cats in this area, but she's not featured. At this time of night she's usually curled up next to me, purring. It feels lonely without her.

Next, I log onto Missing.com. I've been using the site since it was set up twenty-five years ago by a guy called Eka. We've never met although we've shared a lot over the years. He's a couple of years older than Kaz and he lives in the capital, Lyri.

He studied law at Lyri University but during the war he fought for the opposition, and afterwards he decided to set up the site. Eka and his team have uncovered many mass grave sites across Lyrian, including one in Zazour, close to the cemetery. But there's never been any news of Tam – or of Rey. I don't know if Rey made it to Europe. I'm convinced she's alive though she may have married and changed her name. As for Tam – I've tried to be positive but, as time goes by, I have grown increasingly pessimistic. When I was ill last year, I started thinking that God was punishing me because of what I did but now I have to remember what came first and what came later. I don't know. Even now it can be difficult to entangle right from wrong. But that's war for you. The longer it continues, the more uncertain one becomes.

Eka isn't online today and there's nothing new on the site. I check the live-chat. A message pops up from someone who calls himself Adam1. 'Hi,' he says. 'What are u here for?'

'Looking for an old flame and a school friend. You?' I may sound blasé but it's for my own protection because anyone can access this site. Eka tries to screen people but there have been instances of bullying and worse. Not all wounds can be healed in a generation. It's still too soon.

'My father. I was four when he disappeared. Police came. Took him in the middle of the night. Ma was screaming. Even now I have nightmares about it.'

'I'm so sorry,' I write back. Adam seems genuine. But I won't reveal any details about myself or Tam. Not yet. 'Do you have photos?'

'Everything was lost when we left. Any info on your friends yet?'

'I'm still waiting.'

We talk awhile. No one else comes on. There are so many horror stories from our war. It's a wonder any of us survived.

After we've said our goodbyes, I turn out the kitchen light and stare out of the window. A black cat is skulking in the doorway of Tata's Takeaway but there's no sign of Mimi, no sign at all.

It's almost eight o'clock. I must get to the hospital.

9

The past: Zazour, Lyrian.

'The old law of "an eye for an eye" leaves everybody blind.'
Martin Luther King.

A wind blew the snow into my face; the flakes were hard, stinging arrows against my cheeks. The blizzard was keeping the planes locked in their hangars but we knew they'd return with their cargoes of death, and I kept wondering what the pilots thought when they looked down on the roofs of our town and unleashed those bombs. Did they think of their children, their mothers, sisters and brothers? Did they imagine we'd shoot back at them when all we had were a few rusted old muskets that had belonged to our grandfathers? Did any of them even care?

I stood on our steps, looking at the house opposite. One side of the roof was collapsed. Part of the front wall was also gone, exposing the living room. An armchair with a brocade seat and gilded arms stood in the middle of that space, untouched by the destruction, though it was surrounded on all sides by debris: chunks of ceiling plaster, hanging wires and exploded brickwork. The chair looked so surreal and absurd in the chaos, I actually laughed. But no one heard me because the street was empty. Even the cats seemed to have vanished. Nor could I hear the cockerel that used to crow morning, noon and night, and annoy us. Perhaps it had been eaten. Many of our neighbours had already left. We, too, had been talking about leaving.

I crossed the road, pushed open the front gate, stepped into the ruined house and sat on the chair. At any moment a beam could have fallen on my head, but life had turned into a lottery and I almost didn't care anymore. It was either your turn or it was not. The seat was cold and wet from the snow leaking in through the broken roof and the damp seeped into the pants of my trousers, but I stayed there a while and thought about how fast life could turn into a nightmare.

When I got up to go, I spotted a doll lying in the rubble. Her head had broken away from her body and lay to one side. She was wearing a white blouse with lace frills and a short blue skater's skirt but the blue had faded and her clothes were covered in a fine, grey dust. I fixed her head back onto her body as best as I could, placed her on the brocade chair and walked back across the street.

The doll's empty eyes stared at me, unblinking. Then Kaz came out from the cellar, wearing his green woollen hat and a chequered scarf and we set off into the snow as we had agreed.

*

The weather was our friend that day. It had sent everyone scurrying inside, even the soldiers, and the falling snow covered up our tracks. We walked fast and did not talk. There were no soldiers at the bridge and Kaz and I crossed unchallenged before taking different paths.

It was icy cold but I was sweating and my hands were shaking. I waited at the wooden shed as I'd agreed. The shed belonged to the town council who ran the cemetery but I knew there'd be no one there that day. My mouth got so dry while I was waiting, I melted some snow on my tongue. The soldier had said he'd be there at two and I was fifteen minutes early. I kept checking my watch. When it got to two I was so nervous I started to feel sick. Part of me was afraid he wouldn't turn up, and part of me was really hoping he wouldn't.

The soldier was ten minutes late. But suddenly he was there with his sly smile.

I try never to think of what came after: I blanked it out. But I remember us running, Kaz and I. Past the grave markers and the copse of trees. Over the bridge and the black river. Through the empty streets, our feet pounding the snow, our breath ragged, our hearts beating, beating, beating. Over the crossroads. Along our street, past the unlit lamps.

'Where have you been?' Ma asked, as we tumbled down the steps to the cellar, kicking the snow off our boots and pretending, yes pretending, we were the same people who'd left the house two hours earlier. 'Your father's not back. Did you get any bread? Anything?'

'We have a loaf and four oranges,' Kaz said, and he handed them to Ma.

'Why are you so out of breath? Did someone chase you?' Ma gave us a searching look and I thought, *She's going to ask more questions and we're not prepared,* but all she said was, 'Moe's not well.'

'What's wrong with him?' I asked. How could we have been gone while Moe was sick?

'He has a fever. He hardly stopped crying while you were out. Now he's gone quiet. You take him for a while, Mira.'

Moe's cheeks were red and his breathing was uneven and shallow. I tried to stroke his hair but it was plastered to his scalp. 'We ought to get him cooled down,' I said to Ma.

'I'll get you a wet cloth. Where's your father? Maybe you should call him, Kaz.'

While I bathed Moe's head. Pearl sat on her mattress, watching, saying not a word while Kaz stood by the door, looking at us, his mobile in his hand.

'You're shivering,' Ma said to me.

'Am I? I must have got chilled out there. Moe will warm me up.' I smiled at Ma but it was a clown's smile.

'Pa will be here in minute,' Kaz said. He sounded as if nothing had happened. But I could not look at him.

Pearl was at the back of the cellar, where she always sat. Her face was shadowy and ghost-like in the glow of the gas lamp. I turned to look at her and she stared into my eyes. I did not hold her gaze. It frightened me. I felt she could see right into the darkness I was hiding inside.

*

In the night I heard Moe coughing and Ma singing to him in a low voice. I heard Pa snoring and, just once, Kaz sighing. There was nothing from Pearl but her steady breathing. Everything stayed quiet outside. The cellar muffled noise from the road but I would have heard the sound of a car engine if there'd been one. I was almost expecting someone to turn up, but no one did. Once, I thought I heard a fox barking in the garden but I wasn't sure.

I lay on my mattress, tossing and turning. I wasn't afraid. I'm not sure what my other feelings were. They were confused and dark. I lay awake for a long while and when I finally did sleep, I dreamed I was lost in a maze. The hedges were tall and dense, and each turn I took led me to a dead end but I kept on, moving ever deeper into its dark centre. The paths were covered in small stones which crunched under the thin shoes I was wearing. When I arrived at the heart of the maze, I discovered a stone plinth. On top of this plinth stood a white marble statue of a horse. There was a young man astride the horse's back, also made of marble; his white hands were clutching its mane. Before, the place had been dark, but now a full moon appeared in the sky. It shone on the statue and the surrounding hedges, bathing everything in an eerie light. As I looked at the statue, drops of blood trickled down from the rider's eyes and dripped onto my feet.

I woke up sweating, my heart exploding in my chest.

*

Moe was still sick in the morning. He lay at Ma's side quiet and pale and Pearl was quiet with him.

Breakfast was a sombre affair. When I dared glance at Kaz he was staring at his cup, turning it round and round until even Ma said, 'Kaz, please will you stop that? It's getting on my nerves.'

Once our meagre breakfast was over, Pa and Kaz left to search for medicine for Moe. Ma had wanted to go, but Pa said no and Ma didn't argue. But barely five minutes after they'd left, she fetched her beautiful blue wool coat and said, 'I need to go out, Mira. I must get something for Moe. I don't trust your father and brother.'

Ma looked so elegant in that coat. But her hair needed washing and there were dark circles under her eyes.

'Where are you going?'

'To Mrs Consuala, the herbalist. If she's still there.' She smiled and gave me a brief hug. There were faint traces of perfume on her coat. 'Stay strong, Mira. You too, Pearl.' She kissed Pearl on the forehead and was gone.

Moe was asleep again. I looked at Pearl and then at the oranges on the sideboard. We'd shared one for breakfast. Now there were three left. What had it cost us, Kaz and me, to get those oranges?

'Would you like a story?' I asked Pearl.

No reaction. Not a word.

'Why won't you talk, Pearl?'

She shrugged and turned away.

Ma was gone perhaps half an hour. I was so relieved when I heard the door opening and I saw her walking down those steps.

'How is he?'

'Still asleep,' I said, 'But sometimes he's coughing in his sleep. Did you get anything?'

'I did. Mrs Consuala was at home, luckily, but she's thinking of leaving. She says it's too dangerous to stay. So, I have the herbs. They should help.' Ma slipped off her coat and hung it on the back of the door where Pa had put up a row of hooks. Then she poured the herbs into a pan of water and set it on the stove. And began to cry softly.

I walked over and placed my hand on her back. 'Everything will turn out all right, Ma.'

'I'm scared,' she said.

'Did something happen out there?'

'No. It's quiet at the moment. But what about tomorrow and the next day?'

'I don't know, Ma.'

We sat and waited for the water to boil and Ma strained the herbs through a sieve. All the while, Pearl sat in her place, saying nothing, playing with her hands. When the mixture had cooled sufficiently, Ma woke up Moe and he started to cry and cough. I helped Ma hold Moe while she spooned the concoction into his mouth. He protested and spat it out, but between us we somehow managed to get enough of it down him. Then Pa and Kaz arrived back, stinking of cigarette smoke.

'Did you find anything for Moe?' Ma said nothing about her trip to the herbalist. Or the cigarette smoke.

'No. The pharmacy is closed.' Pa closed his eyes and rubbed his forehead as if he had a headache.

'What about the one close to the market?'

'That's closed too.' Pa sat down, his shoulders slumped. He was a strong, upright man but he looked as if the air had been pumped right out of him. 'The centre of town is swarming with soldiers.'

'What about the doctor's? Did you go there?'

'The doctor has left,' Kaz said. 'We bumped into Hadi. He told us.'

'Rats escaping the sinking ship,' Pa said angrily. 'Everyone is leaving.'

'Are we to leave soon?' Ma looked at Pa and then at Kaz. 'Where will we go – to my mother's?'

Pa shook his head. 'We've already discussed that, Sara. It's too dangerous.' He leant forward on the chair, his right hand under his chin, the finger of his left pulling at his eyebrow.

'Then where?'

'Over the border.'

'The border? Are you serious?' Ma put Moe down and went over to the stove. She picked up an empty pan and banged it down. The noise made us jump. And she started to cry again. Now Pearl ran over and tried to comfort her but Pa just sat there, scratching his eyebrow and staring at the dirt floor. Normally he would have been the one to go over to Ma. He was tired, I understood, but it made me sad to see him like that, Ma too. As for Kaz, he remained by the door, tapping his foot, one hand in the pocket of his jacket.

No one spoke. There was nothing left to say.

10

Present day: Sundsholm, Neeland.

Soils are the physical context within which forensic evidence is found. It is important to understand some of the potential implications of different physical and chemical soil properties. Soil properties such as the depth of soil, rock fragment content, soil reaction, soil temperature, soil texture, and soil moisture play a significant role in bone decomposition and in locating a clandestine grave.

www.OurMissing.com/Soil analysis and human remains

I pick up the phone three times before I call Kaz. We do keep in touch – from time to time – but the truth is, I haven't called him in over six months. I wonder if he's moved and not told me, or if perhaps Moe is right and Kaz is drinking again. Even though he promised me last time he'd never touch another drop. I've heard that one before, we all have. Even so, I had real hopes for him this time.

There's no answer. I leave a message. 'It's Mira. Call me. It's urgent.' I ought to say why I'm calling. I don't.

It's my day off. In the morning I go looking for Mimi again but I don't find her. Mr Engman tells me not to give up but I'm beginning to think something bad has happened. Perhaps I should check the local vets' surgeries in case she's been run over. I can't bear to think of it. To take my mind off Mimi I visit the art gallery later. I haven't been in a long while. The place reminds me of my lost ambition to become an architect. I never draw now, nor does Pearl. It's something that got lost along with all the other losses, something I've had to grow used to.

I walk up the steps past the stone lions and in through the revolving doors, where I have my ID and bag checked. Even here there is security. The bags used to be checked by a bot but the guards complained they had nothing to do. Now the bag goes through a machine – it does the checking – while a security guard scans faces. I suppose he relies on his intuition. He smiles. The bots can't quite smile, but they're working on that.

The place is quiet, although that's not surprising. It's winter and midweek.

First, I go to the sculpture gallery. I prefer sculptures to paintings. I even like the ones that look like someone's rummaged in a junkyard and thrown the bits together, although that style has gone out of fashion now. I stop in front of a piece called *We are Living Now*, put together from old guns and bullet casings. Pearl thinks it's trash but I like it: it's a hopeful piece of art – death and destruction turned into creation. Today we have drones and 'smart' bombs. We're not smarter than we were before. Sometimes I feel we're hurtling backwards to the future.

I move on to one of my favourites, a large figure cast from bronze. I peer through the spaces and it's as if I were a child again playing in our garden. How I miss our garden: those gnarled old fruit trees, Ma's roses wilting in the summer sun, Pa's shed creaking in the wind, the kitten padding about. I don't have a garden here – few people can afford a garden in the city – but I can sit in Pearl's garden in the summer and listen to the birds. The city is generous with its parks and if I need wilder space, I can pedal out to the lake though I rarely visit in winter; the place is too bleak and cold and I don't have a car.

No one is in the sculpture gallery. I sit on the wooden bench and drop my head to my knees so that I can view the sculpture upside down. I often look at trees that way. A different perspective. That's what I need on Kaz. On the past, too.

'It's all about reframing,' the psychiatrist said. 'Or, to put it another way, we create paths in our brains and after a while these paths get deep and rutted, perhaps full of mud and even rubbish. Then we need to seek an alternative path.'

I liked the way he talked, the psychiatrist. He made sense.

I walk on. In the temporary space there's a photographic exhibition, *The Memory of Conflict*. I'm expecting to see iconic pictures of soldiers and battles but it's not like that. A series of large-scale landscapes hangs on one wall. Weeds growing through ruined buildings. A lovely white church, its dome cracked open like a broken egg. A minaret smashed to the ground, the tiled space around it pockmarked with bomb craters. A Roman amphitheatre, its columns upended as if there had been an earthquake – but this earthquake was man-made.

Here it is: our war.

It may be *our* war, *my* war, but I feel like a voyeur. The first image that catches my eye is a photograph of an abandoned house – not the whole house but the kitchen. It could even be our house. Certainly it feels familiar. The glass in the window is smashed, and someone has drawn an erect penis on the wall. Besides the graffiti and the broken window, things are as the family left them. Cups in the sink. Plates on the drying rack. A clock stopped on the wall at a quarter to twelve. A table pushed against the wall, covered in a chequered cloth. A striped jug on a shelf.

Next to the photograph of the ruined kitchen there's a black and white photograph of a doll sitting on a chair in a bombed-out building. The doll herself isn't monochrome – her clothes are a brilliant, startling red. Of course it's not *that* house, the one opposite ours, and it isn't the gilt chair I sat on in the snow, but nevertheless I turn and flee.

Back in the sculpture gallery I sit down on the wooden bench and wait for my heart to settle. There's nothing here to alarm me, only a wire pterodactyl hanging from the ceiling – the kind of thing Oscar loved when he was a child. We used to come here, Pearl and I, with Lucas and Oscar but we haven't been in years.

*

The guard is looking at his watch, jangling his keys. I check my own watch. It's only ten minutes to the museum's closing time. When he walks away, I lean forward and stroke the bronze leg of a reclining woman. It's against the rules but I can't resist. The metal is silky and cold under my fingers and it has a calming effect. I still feel agitated after viewing that picture.

Next to reclining woman, on a stone plinth, is a wooden sculpture shaped into a perfect oval. Its dark brown colour and smooth, burnished surface reminds me of the chestnuts that used to fall from the tree in Grandma's garden. She was lucky to survive the war but we never saw her again. She died a year after the final peace agreements were signed. Not that there was real peace. That took another fifteen long years.

The guard returns. 'We're closing in five minutes.' The sound of his keys jangling from his belt makes me tense up again. While he's closing the heavy doors at the far end of the gallery a young man walks in through the other door. The young man looks so like Tam – he could almost be Tam as he was – he takes my breath away. He has the same curly hair, the same slight build and there's something else, something I can't quite define, that confuses my brain. For a moment I really believe I'm seeing Tam again. And it happens. Everything spins and dissolves and now I'm in the street, opposite the bakery, sheltering in a shop doorway. The queue is moving slowly and no one is talking and I can feel fear in the pit of my belly. I look up. Here he is, walking towards me. How brave he is, his head held high, waving his flag. He's going to be our saviour. We will be free. He is our freedom.

A shot rings out. Or is it a door closing? There's blood staining Tam's white T-shirt. I can't breathe. I clutch my chest.

'Are you okay?' The person speaking is dressed in uniform. He's not that soldier. He might be a prison guard. There are keys hanging from his belt. Perhaps they've taken Tam to prison.

'Excuse me, are you all right?'

I blink. Look up. I see the sculptures in the room, the white walls and the door behind. 'I think so.'

'You're very pale.'

'I felt a little faint. I'm sure I'll be fine in a moment.'

The guard waits by my side. There is no sign of the young man.

I take a few deep breaths. I'm a little spaced out but the worst is over.

'Would you like me to help you to your feet?'

'That's most kind of you.'

He takes my arm and walks me to the entrance hall. I feel like an old woman. 'You can sit here for a few minutes.' He gestures to a stone bench. 'Would you like a drink of water?'

I spot the young man again. So, he was real. He's striding down the upper steps towards the doorway where another guard is standing, keys in hand, ready to close the grille. He's not Tam, I know that, but he looks so much like the Tam I remember from thirty years ago. It breaks my heart. As if my heart isn't broken already.

'Thank you,' I say to the guard who is still hovering close by. 'I'll get some fresh air. That will help. In any case, you're closing up.'

I stand on the museum steps but the young man is already out of sight. Last summer I followed a young man like this and we ended up having sex in a doorway. I wouldn't do that now. That's just how I was – reckless, crazy.

The short winter day is fading and the lights of the city blink like so many eyes. An icy wind thrusts its way around the corner of the building and a terrible homesickness bears down on me. I want to feel the heat on the stones and smell the jasmine, the herbs and spices in Zazour's market. I want to hear my mother tongue on the streets and wander along the riverbank, past the old houses, and stand on the bridge staring at the water below, listening to the river's song. I want to forget we ever had a war and lost each other. But so much I want is impossible.

*

I switch on my mobile as soon as I've taken off my coat. It rings almost immediately.

It's Pearl. 'Where were you? They said you weren't at work and I couldn't reach you on your mobile. Pa is really sick again. I'm at the hospital.'

'I was at the museum. I'll come right away.'

I order one of the fast, driverless taxis; the bus will take too long.

By the time I arrive at the hospital, Pa has stabilised but Pearl seems lost. 'It was touch and go earlier,' she says. 'Did you manage to reach Kaz?'

'Not yet. I've left a message.'

'He'll live to regret this.' Pearl's eyes fill with tears. She wipes them away with the back of her hand.

Pa is hooked up to a machine in the high dependency ward. How grey and worn he looks. Like an old coat discarded at the side of the road.

'You see?' Pearl says. 'Look at him. He can't have much time left. This time they saved him but next ...' Her eyes fill with tears again.

'I'll call him again.'

Pearl lowers her voice. 'I don't want to see Kaz but Pa wants it, he wants it so much.'

The idea of Kaz coming here fills me with dread. But when I look at Pa lying there in his bed, small and fragile, and Pearl, her hair in disarray, her mouth quivering like it did when we were stuck in that cellar, I know I must persuade him to come, however it turns out.

'Let's get a coffee,' I say. 'They can always come and get us if we're needed.'

Pearl nods. I hold out my hand and she takes it.

Once upon a time we were just two girls walking towards the trees in the snow with hope in our hearts.

11

The past: Zazour, Lyrian.

What do we think? Is revenge an irrational act that has
no place in civilised society? Or is it both rational and
morally justifiable in the face of injustice?

www.issues_talk.com/revenge

Moe's health improved and the kitten came back but
everything else was as bad as before. The snowstorms
blew themselves out and the jets came back and so we stayed
in that cold, damp cellar listening to the thud of artillery and
the sound of the death planes flying overhead. Every time
Pearl heard their engines whining, she slapped her hands over
her ears. We found it impossible to get close to her. Only the
kitten was allowed in. He'd sit on her lap for hours and when
we had to let him out into the garden, Pearl would suddenly
find her voice and scream and one of us had to try and calm
her down. Most of the time she sat on the mattress, picking at
the threads on her blanket or sucking her thumb like a toddler.
She rarely spoke but once she tapped me on the shoulder and

whispered, 'Where have Tam and my friends from the house gone?'

'To heaven,' I said, even though I no longer believed in heaven. 'The angels will care for them now.'

'How can you be sure, Mira?'

'Good people always go to heaven.'

Pearl opened her empty sketchbook and drew a house with bars at the windows. Above the house she sketched a plane dropping bombs, and a child by the front door, lying down with its eyes closed. Then she picked up a red felt-tip pen and coloured in a lake of blood.

'What's that?' Ma asked.

Pearl dropped the red pen and scribbled thick black lines across the drawing and tore the paper into small pieces. She was very methodical.

'Don't you want to draw something nice?' Ma said.

'There's nothing nice,' Pearl said, turning away.

*

I was sleeping badly. We all were. I'd wake up in the middle of the night after a bad dream, sweating, my heart thudding; my mouth dry. One time I woke up yelling and Ma came over to comfort me.

'What is it?' Ma stroked my hair like she used to do when I was small.

'Just a bad dream.' I never dreamed of Tam. I dreamed of the soldier.

'I have them too.'

'When will we be out of here?'

'Your father and Kaz are working on it. Now go back to sleep.'

*

The morning after that dream I woke up groggy and irritable to find Kaz and Pa gone. When I asked Ma where they'd disappeared to, she said she thought they'd gone looking for food but she didn't seem certain. The snow had returned, and the town stayed quiet although we were always on the alert. I tried to read but I couldn't concentrate and Moe kept whining and needing attention. Ma scuttled about the place, tidying and dusting, though there was almost nothing for her to tidy. As for Pearl, she just sat on her mattress, silent as ever. Sometimes she picked up her doll, sometimes she stared into space and played with her fingers. Ma and I spoke to each other from time to time, but we said nothing to Pearl. We didn't know what to do any more.

Pa and Kaz didn't come back until the early afternoon. I could see that Ma was getting nervous. She kept pacing up and down but when I said I'd call Pa, she told me not to. I was considering going out into the street to look for them when Pa came running down the steps, Kaz close behind. 'We must pack,' Pa said, breathlessly. 'We're leaving tonight. It's all arranged. Anything you need from upstairs, go and get it now.'

'Tonight?' Ma said.

'Yes, tonight,' Pa said.

'Where are we going?' I asked.

'Over the border, into northern Sufra. We can't stay here any more. It's too dangerous to stay in Zazour. There's going to be a new offensive. Kaz and I learnt of it today.'

The border had been mentioned before but I'd never believed we would leave Zazour. Pa had been born here and his father before that. Zazour was our life. We loved it here. And none of us had travelled outside Lyrian before.

'Where in Sufra – and for how long?'

'I don't know, Mira.' Pa looked as worn as the trousers he was wearing. 'We must get packed. We don't have much time.'

He tried to smile, but his smile looked like that of a man at the gallows. 'Just one bag each. Warm clothes.'

Ma was stood by the stove, her head in her hands. Kaz went over and wrapped his arms around her. I hadn't see him do that in a long while. 'It will work out. Better than staying here. You'll see,' I heard him say.

Ma nodded. I couldn't see her expression.

I pulled Pearl's arm. 'Come on Pearl. We should go upstairs and see if there's anything we need.'

She shook me off.

'Don't you want to come?'

'No.' The first word she'd spoken all day.

Ma stepped away from Kaz and shook her head at me. 'Don't force her, Mira. Just get her some more socks and pants and that pink sweatshirt she likes.'

'Aren't you coming up?' I said.

'No. I have everything I need. Don't be long.'

The electricity in the house was off – it had been off for days – and the place felt chill and unfamiliar. I remembered family parties we'd had, filled with light and laughter. I remembered bouncing on the bed with Pearl, giggling over something, and Rey dancing crazily to music. I remembered the few times Tam had come to the house and how stupidly shy I'd been. Now the house was dark and silent, the light of the winter afternoon already faded into twilight. I went into our bedroom but I wasn't sure what else to pack. The things Pearl and I really cared for had already been brought down to the cellar and there was no possibility of me taking heavy books, or even extra clothes. I opened our wardrobe and pulled out Pearl's socks and pants, her pink sweatshirt and a thick sweater for myself. I took nothing else. Then I sat on Pearl's bed. The springs creaked under my weight; a lonely sound. How I wished Pearl was there with me, warm and chatty like she used to be. I would even have welcomed her annoying and endless questions. I wanted to hear Ma clattering plates in the kitchen. I wanted to smell spices and coffee wafting through the house. I wanted to hear Moe gurgling in his cot. I wanted to see Pa and Kaz in the garden, digging the earth, arguing a little as they went.

We'd be leaving soon. Perhaps we'd never be back.

Next, I went over to the window and looked out. In the twilight, the snow glowed, phosphorescent and surreal; it all felt unfamiliar and strange, as if the garden were already just a dream.

Before leaving, I picked up my notebook. It contained my drawings and plans for buildings. There was also a photo of Grandma tucked inside one of the pages. Then I walked out of the door. I didn't look back. It's not good to look back. Now I do it all the time.

*

We didn't talk, stepping into the car. It wasn't our car. I don't know whose car it was or how Pa had acquired it, or why we didn't take our car, or if I even asked. There was too much else to think of. The car was bigger and older than ours, with torn leather seats and it smelled of engine oil and air freshener. Kaz sat in the front with Pa, Pearl and I in the back with Ma and Moe. My seat belt was broken. Pearl put her hand in mine – my good hand – and I asked if she was all right and she nodded. Pa turned on the engine and we trundled slowly down the unlit, empty street, the headlights off, and I craned my neck to catch one last glimpse of our house, the place I'd been born.

At the junction, there was another car waiting, its headlights also dark. Pearl squeezed my hand and I heard Ma gasp but Pa said, 'It's okay. Just keep your heads down and stay quiet. These are friends.'

We followed the car. I couldn't see who was inside. We drove past the allotments and took the road that led east towards the orchards, then we swerved back towards town again. I kept thinking we'd hit a roadblock and soldiers, that we'd all be arrested and disappear, but we didn't see a soul. It was a miracle. I'm still not sure how we managed it.

Moe lay slumped on Ma's lap. Sometimes he spluttered, but the worst of the fever and cough were gone.

After leaving the straggle of buildings at the edge of town, we turned down a long dirt road. A layer of snow covered the surface but it was muddy underneath and sometimes the tyres skidded and spun, and once the car in front got stuck and Ma had to help push and mud spattered all over her skirt. I wanted to help, but Pa said, 'No. You stay inside with Pearl and Moe.' He was trying to be kind because of my injured hand, but his words hurt and I felt heavy with grief and uselessness.

Still following the other car, we passed through farmland and up into the thick, pine forest. The sky cleared a little, revealing an emaciated moon and a sprinkling of stars. It still wasn't safe to use the headlights, Pa said, and we moved with care. None of us spoke. The only sounds were the car creaking over the ruts, the clank of the engine, and soft swish of the tyres. Pearl fell asleep, her head on my lap. But I couldn't rest and kept my eyes on the unravelling road.

An hour went by, perhaps longer although I couldn't be sure as it wasn't possible to see the hands on my watch. Although I felt I must stay awake, I drifted off. A jolt woke me. Pa slamming on the brakes. The car skidding to a halt.

'What the …?' Kaz hissed.

The car in front had stopped without warning. We'd almost driven into the back of it.

'What's going on?' Ma's voice was high with panic.

'Shh! Lie down,' Pa ordered.

He and Kaz leapt out and crouched behind the other car. The half-moon shining gave out enough light for me to make out the driver of the other car – he too had got out – a burly man, with a scarf wound about his head and throat. He was carrying something in his hand.

Moe whimpered. Ma shushed him.

The man was soon swallowed up in the gloom, but he'd switched on a torch and I could see the dancing circles of its light.

A crack. I knew that sound. Pearl cried out and curled herself up tight.

'Oh, God,' Ma said. 'Can you see anything, Mira?'

Pa and Kaz bolted out from behind the car and then they too were swallowed up by the forest.

'I can't see a thing.'

'If it was an ambush we'd hear voices … wouldn't we?' Ma said.

I could just make out the other people huddled in the car in front. They were moving their heads, trying to make out what was happening, I supposed. It was difficult to see how many they were, perhaps six, although there might have been others lying down in the back. I wondered who they were. Pa had muttered something about a colleague at work, but they were not friends we knew.

We waited. How much more waiting could we endure? My heart felt like a football being kicked against a wall. But no more shots were fired and finally Pa and Kaz came back into view, along with the other driver. Ma sighed and Pearl sat up and the tension in the car lessened.

Now Pearl cried out again, Ma with her.

I pushed myself up so that my head was above the seat and peered through the windscreen. Pa, Kaz and the man were dragging a heavy object through the snow.

'Have they killed someone?' Ma said, her voice sharp and tight.

I too had feared the worst but then I noticed the antlers and I realised what it was they were dragging. 'It's a deer. A stag.'

'Are you sure that's what it is?'

'It's okay, Ma, I'm sure.'

Ma and Pearl sat up and we watched as Pa and Kaz helped the man lift the lifeless stag into the boot of his car, but the animal wouldn't quite fit and Pa had to fetch a length of rope from our vehicle to tie it down. By the time Pa and Kaz returned, Pearl was sobbing.

'Don't cry, my little Pearl,' Pa said. 'Unfortunately, the stag ran straight out in front of the other car. We were lucky it didn't do more damage. It was injured. That's why the man had to shoot it. Better that than allowing it to suffer.'

'I don't want anything to die,' Pearl said.

'Of course not,' Pa answered. 'No one wants that. Here, let me find you a tissue. Sara, do you have one?'

Ma rummaged in the pocket of her coat and handed Pearl a crumpled sheet of kitchen roll. Pearl sniffed and wiped her eyes. Then she wriggled in the seat and poked me twice with her elbow. 'What is it?'

Pearl pointed between her legs.

'We need to get out for a moment,' I said to Pa.

'You'll need to be quick.' Pa wound down the window and signalled to the car in front.

It was so dark and silent out there, crouched behind the car. Only the sound of our breathing and the trickle of our urine hitting the snow. Not the hooting of an owl nor the crack of a twig, not even the smallest wind sighing. Maybe, I thought, we could live in the forest. We'd be safe here, wouldn't we? But what would we live on – berries and leaves? And how would we keep warm? My idea was pure fantasy. Yet the wild, stark beauty of that place struck a chord in my heart.

Pearl pulled up her pants and got into the car and I heard Pa saying, 'Hurry up, Mira.'

I stood and looked across to the forest's edge. There, close to the road, a doe stood, motionless, its black silhouette edged with silver light, like an image from the film *Bambi* that Pearl and I had watched together. Perhaps she was the mate of the stag who'd been shot. I was surprised she hadn't bounded off when the gun fired. Or maybe she'd slipped into the trees and had now returned.

I wanted her to know it had all been a terrible mistake.

The car in front began to move. 'GET IN NOW!' Pa bellowed.

I jumped in. As we drove away I turned to look through the back window but the doe was no longer in sight. Silent tears tracked down my face. But why was I crying for a doe, when I couldn't cry for Tam?

Pearl cuddled me and lay her head on my shoulder, and on we went. Through the forest and out into farmland, the wheels turning, our hearts turning, but on to what we did not know.

*

A rumble as we drove off the narrow roadway and along a bumpy track, the wheels spinning.

Five minutes later we stopped at the edge of a field.

'We've arrived,' Pa said.

We piled out, and our feet sank into the deep snow. I heard the distant bleat of a sheep. The occupants of the other car got out too. There were six of them: a mother, a father, an older woman (perhaps the grandmother), and three children. We nodded and greeted each other but we didn't chat.

'Now what?' Ma whispered to Pa.

'We take our bags. We must go on foot from here.'

The father of the other family said, 'Good luck,' and his wife turned and said the same and we smiled and shook their hands.

'Where are we?' I asked.

'Close to the border,' Pa said.

A truck was parked nearby, two men standing at its side. The men beckoned everyone forward and we followed on foot, carrying our bags. I'm not sure what happened to the dead stag. I was too preoccupied to look. Perhaps someone went back later to collect it.

Pearl kept looking over her shoulder. 'What is it?' I asked.

'We forgot the kitten, Mira. I hope he will be all right.'

How could we have done such a thing? He must have been outside in the garden when we fled and, in all the packing and anxiety, he'd been left behind. 'It's better he stays at home,' I said. 'He'll hunt mice and he'll be perfectly fine. Anyway, we won't be away long. I'm sure of it.'

I was lying to Pearl. I knew we might never return; I could feel it in my bones.

'When will we go home? Will it be soon?'

'Perhaps a week or two. Come on, we must walk faster. We mustn't fall behind.' I was glad Pearl was talking again and asking questions, even if it was of things that made us sad.

We walked. It was cold and mist lay in the hollows like bandaged fingers. We walked. Only the quiet sound of our shoes on the grass. We walked until we came to a ditch and saw the lights of many torches.

Finally, we crossed. To another country. Another life.

12

Present day: Sundsholm, Neeland.

> Revenge is both an act and a desire.
>
> *www.issues_talk.com/revenge*

Pearl calls. Pa's condition has improved overnight and Moe will hold off coming for now. I dial Kaz again but there's still no answer. This time I explain why I'm calling. 'It's Mira. Pa is gravely ill. Call as soon as you can.' I keep my voice businesslike and say nothing else.

I have work this morning; it's a relief to have something to take my mind off Pa's condition. My first meeting is with a new arrival, an older woman called Sabina. Her husband, a political dissident, was gunned down in the street in Azerbaijan. After he was killed she fled here to Neeland, like so many others, and now she's waiting to hear if she can stay. Her faltering words unsettle me. I'm still grieving for Tam and yet all we had was a brief kiss all those years ago – this woman has lost her husband.

'I don't want much,' Sabina says, giving me a half-smile. 'Just a little peace in my life, somewhere safe I can call home.'

She taps me on the arm. 'You're not wearing a wedding ring. How is this?'

'I never met the right man.'

I'm surprised when she throws back her head and laughs. I don't know how to react.

'Sorry,' she says, when she's composed herself. 'This is me at your age. I never want to marry. I only want to work.' She leans forward again and puts her hand on mine. Her skin is wrinkled and covered in age spots. 'Then I fall head over in love. I am like young girl again. And to think I am fifty years.' She moves her hand away and laughs again.

'You didn't meet your husband until you were fifty?'

'Yes, yes. This is true.' She sighs. 'We were happy, happy. You see there is time for you, young lady.' Her eyes moisten. She blinks and a tear trickles down her cheek. 'Now I am sad. But this is life we lead. This is the life.'

'I'm sorry.' I always say I'm sorry – and I am – but my words are like cheap trinkets. 'We have some formalities to complete. Paperwork, you understand?'

She nods. 'I have papers. Passport.' She's not smiling now. 'I think you have broken heart. Not mended yet. This is a problem for you.'

I feel myself colour. 'Maybe,' I say, a little more curtly than I mean to.

'I think so, yes.'

We fill in the paperwork together and she does not raise the matter again. It's strange she should see something no one else sees. When we've finished, Sabina hugs me tight and thanks me for the help, and I walk with her to the foyer. Before she takes her leave, she clasps my hand in hers. 'You have change soon. Big change,' she says.

I watch her walk down the street in her bright, flowery clothes, her head bent against the cold wind, and I persuade myself she's nothing more than a fortune teller. There are dozens of them in the city, selling their posies of flowers, saying exactly the same things, and yet I cannot quite let go of her words.

Then a new client comes in – a young pregnant woman from Gabon. Her situation is complex. Anna joins me for a while and between us we agree to find accommodation more suitable for her condition and mental health. After, I see another three clients, but they're all doing well and need only some help with form-filling.

I'm about to go for lunch when there's a knocking on my door. It's Tomas. I wasn't due to see him today. He's agitated but at least now he's talking. 'I have nowhere to stay. Last night I sleep in doorway. It so cold, so very cold. I almost freeze to the death.'

'Why are you sleeping outside?'

'I cannot stay in that other place. They call me names. They …' A tear trickles down his cheek.

'What kind of names?'

'Lady-man. Nancy. They force me to wear a dress. Make-up.' He points to his lips. 'And they say they want sex with me.'

'Were you attacked?'

'No, but I fear it so I take my clothes and leave. I cannot stay in this place with these people. I cannot, Mira.'

'No, you can't. I'll see what I can do.' While I make calls, I send Tomas out with cash to buy a hot drink and something to eat and I go and talk to Anna. But we can't manage to find him anywhere at such short notice. Upon his return, I beckon Tomas over. 'Here,' I whisper, handing him my address and personal number. 'I'm not supposed to give this out. Please only call if there's a real emergency. The shelter should be able to give you a bed tonight.'

However, I know that the shelter is often full in the winter months. Sometimes Anna and I, and other colleagues, have had to make frantic calls to other organisations in the city trying to locate a place for a client. And Tomas is not exaggerating about the cold: last year a young man did freeze to death. He was just seventeen years old.

*

I take the afternoon off to visit Pearl. My work hours are flexible: I like this about the job. As I travel out to the suburbs on the bus, I wonder why Pearl and I so rarely talk about my work. We often talk about hers: the problems she has with her students; the number of exam papers she has to mark; the professor who thinks he has the answer to the world's problems but who can't stop himself flirting with, and sometimes bedding, the young female students. I know Pearl has a problem with my work but perhaps I'm too defensive, too willing to react to her barbed comments. I resolve to change my approach.

It's one of those days when there are almost no shadows. The sky is white and the city has no definition. The snow is dirty in the gutters. The bus takes me out past the lovely little church and the hospital, past the botanical gardens (even they look chill and forlorn today) and finally out to Sodermalm, the exclusive area where Pearl lives.

Pearl greets me warmly and ushers me into the kitchen, offering coffee and home-made plum cake. 'The boys will be back from school soon. They'll be pleased to see you.'

'I'll be pleased to see them too.' I smile at Pearl and she smiles back. She's proud of her boys. Why should she not be?

'Have you heard from Kaz?' Her smile dies away.

'Not yet.'

Pearl glances at her watch, her brow wrinkling like a used sheet. 'What time is it there? Perhaps I should call him.'

'It's late evening.' I don't want her to call right now, not while I'm here.

'I might have better luck.' She looks at me with ... what? Suspicion? Then she picks up her mobile.

I don't want to be around her when she speaks to Kaz. I don't trust myself, or him. I'm lucky: the front door opens with a crash and the boys come rushing in and I run to meet them in the hall. Oscar throws his arms around me and gives me a big hug. Lucas holds back. He's at a self-conscious age, I understand that, but he's quiet and doesn't smile and that makes me uneasy.

'How's Grandpa?' Lucas asks. He's standing awkwardly, hands in his pockets. The gesture reminds me of Kaz although Lucas doesn't look in the least bit like Kaz. He's tall and lean like Stefan, and has Stefan's blue eyes and fair skin.

'I haven't seen him today. Your Mum and I are going to see him later. How was school?'

'We're making a dinosaur,' Oscar says, hopping from one foot to the other. 'The whole class. It's so big.' He opens his arms. 'This big.' Oscar is small and dark and reminds me of Pa.

From the kitchen Pearl calls out, 'Hello! Aren't you coming to greet your mother?'

'We're talking to Auntie Mira,' Oscar calls back.

Maybe Kaz didn't answer his phone again. 'How was *your* day, Lucas?'

He blinks nervously. 'It was ...' Now the skin on his face reddens and he stares down at the wooden floor.

'He doesn't like school, do you, Lukes?'

'Who likes school?' I say, trying to make light of it.

'I do.' Oscar wrinkles his nose. He does that a lot. It makes me smile. 'I like it. Especially when we make dinosaurs. It's a T-rex, by the way. It's very fierce.'

'I saw a dinosaur in the museum the other day. Not a real one of course. It was made out of wire.'

'I remember it,' Oscar says. 'Can we go and see it again?'

'I'm sure we can. I'd like that. Did you know your Mum and I missed school for a while when we were around your age. It sounds great to miss school but we were sad about it.'

'Why weren't you at school? Were you ill?' Oscar sounds concerned.

'We had to move house after ...' I stop. Pearl doesn't like me discussing the past with the boys and I'm not sure what she's told them. They understand we escaped from a war but I have no idea what else they know.

I follow the boys into the living room. 'What's up with school?' I say to Lucas.

He shrugs. Just like Pearl used to do.

'He's being bullied, aren't you, Lukes?' Oscar flops down on the sofa and picks up the remote, although he doesn't turn on the TV.

'It's nothing.' Lucas walks over to the French windows and now I can't see his face. 'An idiot stole my lunch. That's all. It's no big deal.'

'Does Mum know?'

Lucas shakes his head and continues staring out through the glass, his shoulders slumped. The living room faces the garden. In the middle of the lawn there's a large weeping willow, dark and leafless. The boys' swing hangs from one of the branches; it looks rather lost in the snowy scene. I'm wondering what else to say to Lucas but then he turns, walks out of the room and up the stairs, leaving me alone with Oscar.

'May I sit down?'

Oscar moves over.

'What's going on, Oscar?'

'Lukes says I shouldn't tell, but I can tell you, Auntie. This bad boy keeps on taking Lucas's lunch. The bad boy never eats it. He just opens the box and throws everything in the hedge.

Weird, isn't it? Lukes got sick of it happening so he swore at the boy and said he'd tell on him. The boy punched Lukes and knocked him right to the ground. Lukes is scared but he doesn't want anyone to know.'

'When did this happen?'

'Yesterday.'

'You need to say something to Mum. This is serious.'

'I can't. Lukes'll kill me.' Oscar looks at me, pleading. 'Please don't tell her, Auntie Mira. Please.'

I'm caught. Like I was before, all those years ago. 'Do you think it would help if I talked to Lucas? Will he listen to me?'

'I don't know. Can I go now?'

'Of course.' He runs off upstairs and I return to Pearl in the kitchen. Her kitchen is enormous. It's painted white. All the fittings are white too. I find it a little stark but there are a few splashes of colour amid all that unsullied white: six blue flowered cups hanging in a row; a few of the boys' old drawings pinned up; a small blackboard where Pearl writes her lists; three succulents on a shelf.

'Where are my boys? They seem to have said hello to you and forgotten about their own mother.'

'They've gone upstairs. Lucas seems rather quiet.'

'He's upset about Pa.' Pearl's tone is clipped.

'Did you speak to Kaz?'

She shakes her head. 'No. He's not answering. I left a message.'

'Oh,' I say. 'About Lucas ... I'm wondering if something is bothering him at school and ... you know ... perhaps because of what happened to us.' I take a deep breath. 'Do you ever talk about the past with them? Maybe some of that trauma has passed down to them. It can happen.'

The moment the words are out of my mouth, I regret them. Pearl rolls her eyes. 'You and your pop psychology, Mira. The past is past. It's gone. I don't need to go over it again and again like you and Kaz.' She flicks her fingers at me.

'Okay,' I say, holding up my hands. Her words sting. 'He's my nephew. I'm concerned, that's all.'

Pearl nods but her mouth is set in a straight line. 'Why isn't Kaz picking up, damn him.'

'It's late there. Perhaps he's asleep.'

'Why do you think he hasn't called you back? Because he's a coward, that's why. He'll never change.' She hands me a tea and a slice of cake. 'I'm surprised the boys haven't come in for something to eat. They're usually starving when they get home.'

'I expect they'll be down in a moment.' I want to defend Kaz, but I don't want to prolong the argument and I'm not sure what defence I can use. Ever since he didn't come to Ma's funeral, his name has been mud.

We take our drinks into the living room and sip in silence while the sound of the boys' voices drifts down the stairs.

'Lucas sounds fine to me,' Pearl says after a while. 'I can hear him laughing. Can't you?'

Perhaps she's right. I'm being overprotective. I ought to let Pearl deal with it; allow Lucas to sort out his own problems.

Pearl crosses her legs and leans back into her soft white leather sofa. 'Stefan says if neither of us hears from Kaz by the end of the week, he'll hire a detective to track him down.'

'That's a bit extreme, isn't it?'

Pearl gives me a penetrating stare. 'We're doing this for Pa, Mira, not for us.'

'I know, I know.'

'Don't you want to see Kaz?' Now she's biting her fingernail. 'You were so close once.'

'I'm not sure I know who he is anymore. It's been such a long time.' This isn't a lie but it's a half-truth.

'I suppose.' She runs her hands through her hair. It's been styled again recently. And though she's not been at work today, she's still wearing a pair of expensive black woollen trousers and a pink angora sweater. But I notice a few grey hairs where there were none before.

'What are you staring at?' she asks.

'Your hair. You've got grey.'

Pearl frowns, but then her face breaks into a wide grin and she laughs.

'What's so funny?'

'I don't know,' she says, still laughing. 'Maybe the expression on your face. You looked so shocked, as if I'd dyed my hair pink or something.'

'As if.' The words come out hard.

'*As if.* Can you imagine? I think Stefan would ask for a divorce. I am considering a tattoo though.'

'Are you serious?'

'Yes, I am.' She laughs again and this time I laugh with her.

Later we go together to visit Pa. But he's sleeping and we don't stay long.

*

I'm exhausted when I get back to the apartment. It's been a busy day. There's still no sign of Mimi but there's no point in me looking for her now; it's late and dark and Mr Engman has promised to contact me if he hears anything. I run a bath and soak in it, and the phone rings just as I'm getting out.

'Kaz,' I say. 'I thought ...'

'I'm not dead.'

'You got my message then – and Pearl's.'

'Of course.' A pause. 'Can you call me back?'

'Okay. Give me a moment. I've just got out the bath.'

I hang the towel on the rail and slip on my dressing gown – the one Pearl bought me. For a moment I consider not returning the call. If I don't, he probably won't call back. But I have to do this. For Pa. For Pearl. For the boys.

Kaz picks up straight away. 'Sorry I had to ask you to call me. I know, I know … I have the usual cash-flow problems.'

'It's okay.'

'Is Pa really so ill?'

'I don't think he's going to make it, Kaz. His heart is failing.'

A short silence. 'That's not good news.'

'We need you here. Pa's been asking for you. He wants to see you. Pearl and Stefan will pay your fare. Pearl wants you here too, Kaz. You've never even met Lucas and Oscar, you must come otherwise it will be too late and …' The words come tumbling out of my mouth. I stop. Take a breath. Kaz is silent again. 'Will you?'

'You and Pearl must hate me.'

'We don't hate you,' I say, gently. 'Though it's not been easy. When you didn't come to Ma's funeral …'

'You know why.' He sounds like he's accusing me.

'Don't start.'

A hollow laugh. Like he couldn't care less. But when he speaks again his tone is more emollient. 'I'm sober, Mira. I've been sober for three months.'

'Really?'

'Yes, really. You think I'm a coward, always running from things but this time it's different. I mean it to continue that way. I've been going to therapy.'

I walk to the window and look down onto the square. A couple are embracing under one of the lamps. I don't think Kaz is a coward but I'm angry he's been running so long. Yet we're all still running, one way or another. 'Pearl has no idea. You hear me? She knows nothing and I mean it to stay that way.'

117

'I understand.' His voice is soft but the weight of what we did settles between us.

'Are you afraid it will all come out? Is that why you've never visited?' The couple pull apart. The man takes the woman's arm and they set off across the square.

'No,' Kaz says. 'That's not the reason. You're the one who's afraid, Mira.'

I say nothing.

'How long does Pa have left? What do the doctors say? What does Moe think?'

I examine my fingernails. They need trimming. 'He may have weeks or even a couple of months, no longer. Will you come? Please don't make me beg.'

'I don't see how he can forgive me.'

'You told him, didn't you?'

Another silence. Longer this time. Then I hear him sigh through the thousands of miles that separate us. 'Me not attending Ma's funeral ... that was unforgivable, I recognise that now. I was in a bad way back then, and only thinking of the next drink.'

I glance out of the window. The kissing couple have vanished. 'You're the one who won't be able to forgive himself if you don't come.' I make my voice flint.

'How can Pearl even think of paying for my flight after I let her down so?'

'Stefan and Pearl have money coming out of their ears. Swallow your pride, Kaz.'

'Give me twenty-four hours ... please, Mira. To sort my head out.'

'Okay. I'll call you tomorrow.'

When he's gone I pick up the mobile to call Pearl but I don't press the number. I'll give her the news in the morning. Before I settle down for the night I think of the doe in the dark forest the night we fled Lyrian, and I imagine what it would feel like to touch its soft damp muzzle. Then I remember Mimi, out in the dark and the cold, and a tear slides down my cheek and soaks into my lonely pillow.

13

The past: Isara Camp, Sufra.

Exile – displacement, exclusion – the state of being barred from one's native country, usually for political or punitive reasons.

The Standard English Dictionary/Neeland

We crossed the snowy field, carrying our heavy bags, but our hearts were heavier than anything we could ever pick up with our hands. As we walked, our feet crunched in the snow and the cold night wind scoured our faces. Then we came to a sea of tents set on a low, barren, plain. At the entrance stood long queues of people – exiles like us – their faces lined with fatigue and bewilderment as they waited to be allocated somewhere to stay.

It was a shock to see so many people. I don't know what I'd expected but it wasn't this. I can't remember them all now, but some of those people have lodged in my mind like a splinter lodges in the skin: the hunched-up man with vacant eyes; the tiny, crinkled woman, with tears spilling down her face; the child crying and clutching at the hem of its mother's skirts, the mother immobile, staring at nothing. Like everyone else, we waited, small and scared; we waited and filled in endless forms. Above our heads the silver-edged clouds bombed across the sky and the cold wind worried at the snow and made us shiver.

'When we're settled I'll find us somewhere to rent,' Pa said. 'Something nice. In town.'

'What town?' I asked.

'Isara,' Pa answered. 'It's not so far.'

I'd never heard of Isara. I presumed it must be a small place, but I was too tired to ask more.

'So many people already,' Kaz said. He sounded surprised.

Pa pulled up his coat sleeve and checked his watch. 'How slow it is. You'd think they'd have more officials to help.'

'Be patient,' Ma said. Moe was asleep in her arms.

Pa glowered at her. 'Patient? I've spent all my life trying to be patient … thinking things would change.'

'Shh,' Ma said. 'Not here, not now.'

And so we waited. Silent. Patient. Or if we were not patient, we did not share that with each other. What else could we do but wait? It was not as if we had any choice and the long winter night was halfway over by the time we were allocated a tent. It stood in a row of tents, ten minutes from the main gate. So this was to be our home. A place with no beds, electricity or running water. The kind of place that's fun for a weekend with your friends, but for weeks, months? I tried not to think about that. Pa had said it would be temporary, hadn't he?

I was tired beyond reason but I couldn't sleep. The blankets were thin and scratchy, the air freezing and the noises in the camp – the barking of dogs, the crying of babies, the yelling and cursing of a man nearby – kept me awake. However, amid that clamour were soothing sounds: children whispering and giggling together; a man calling for his dog in a soft voice; and later, a woman singing a sweet lullaby.

Just before dawn I crept outside. The moon had set and the stars lay scattered like tiny beads across the sky, untroubled by our human suffering. I didn't stay outside long: the air was chill and my hand ached, and my heart with it.

*

I woke to the faded grey light of a winter morning filtering in through the canvas. In my half-waking state, I expected to see the familiar furniture that inhabited our room – Pearl's bed with its floral coverlet, the carved mirror on the dresser, our two old wooden chairs – but all was gone. It was a sad shock when my eyes fell upon the row of thin mattresses, the five of us huddled under grey blankets. Instead of the welcoming smell of coffee brewing and the aroma of the beeswax Ma used on our furniture, there was only the damp and the cold, the smoke of fires, the sweat of human bodies and the stink of latrines. It had already been weeks since I'd woken up to those comforts of home, yet the brutal reality of this new, alien environment, made even the cellar feel like a lost paradise.

'Pearl,' I whispered, tapping her arm. 'Are you awake?' Pearl's thick, dark hair spilled out from under her blanket. Everything looked so dismal and grey in the tent but at least the sleeve of Pearl's sweatshirt made a splash of pink in the gloom. It reminded me of a flower blooming in a wasteland.

Pearl opened her eyes and wrinkled her face like the old apples in the cellar. 'I don't like it here. I want to go home. It's cold.' She was shivering. But she'd spoken again. That was the important thing. Perhaps now we'd left the bombs and bullets behind she'd go back to her normal self.

'It might help to get up and move about.'

She wriggled out from under the blanket and reached for her coat. None of us had changed out of our daytime clothes.

Our movements woke Ma. 'Are you going somewhere?' There were red creases on Ma's face and her eyes were bleary and swollen as if she'd been crying.

'We need the toilet.' Pa had put a bucket in the corner of the tent but I wasn't going to use that.

'Is Pearl going with you?'

'Yes.'

'Keep a close eye on her.'

I moved to the doorway. It wasn't a sturdy wooden door like ours at home with its lock and key but a sheet of canvas that let in the light and cold.

'Can you find me water?' Ma added. 'There must be some nearby. Take the bucket by the door. I'll empty the other one later.' We hadn't brought the buckets with us. They'd come with the tent, together with a single kerosene lamp, a two-ring gas cooker, and the mattresses and thin blankets.

Outside, the chill wind was still blowing. Pearl pulled her hat down over her ears and I huddled into my parka. This was our first proper view of the camp: the hundreds of white tents in rows, their skirts splattered in mud, the patches of snow like oversized sticking plasters. The camp was large and would soon grow larger; it seemed to stretch on forever on the flat, muddy plain. The sun had now risen above the horizon but it was obscured by a thick layer of cloud, and in the far distance a range of mountains stood moody and foreboding. To our left, beyond the main gate, I could just make out the distant huddled buildings of the town.

'Are those Grandma's mountains?' Pearl said.

'No. Those are in a different direction.'

There was a woman standing outside the tent next to ours – about Ma's age I guessed, though her face was as thin and worn as the blankets we'd been given – and she had a faraway look in her eyes, as if she were looking back to what she'd left behind. It was a look that I'd see time and time again in the camp.

'Can you tell me where the water tap is, and the toilet block?'

She blinked, then stared at me. Finally, she said, 'It's five minutes in that direction,' and she pointed in the direction we were walking.

'Thank you.' I smiled but she didn't smile back and Pearl tugged at my jeans and pulled me away.

I thought I'd try and cheer Pearl up by talking about Grandma. 'Do you remember when we played hide and seek at Grandma's and I thought we'd lost you?'

She smiled and nodded.

'You must be careful here. If you got lost in the camp it would be difficult to find you.'

'I will.' Her voice so small. Like a distant echo.

'I thought a wolf had eaten you at Grandma's.' I grinned and made a low growling sound but Pearl didn't smile; she gripped my hand tighter. 'It's okay, Pearl. I was teasing. There aren't any wolves here.' Though I knew it wasn't wolves we needed to worry about but the soldiers roaming our country, tearing it apart.

Pearl looked up at me and her mouth trembled; I thought she was going to say something but she didn't.

We found the water tap behind the latrines. Already a queue had formed – mostly women and a handful of kids. The women and girls chatted quietly among themselves while the boys jiggled about and made a lot of noise. Seeing those boys gave me hope. They looked happy. Not everything was bad in this place, it seemed, and anyway, we wouldn't be there long. We'd make the best of it.

As we waited our turn I examined the mountains. They certainly weren't Grandma's mountains – those lay to the east, behind us, beyond the border. I wondered if these mountains were covered in junipers and small pines, or if perhaps they were bare and stony, or if goats roamed them; but all they revealed was a smudged line, their pale grey shapes hardly distinguishable from the sky.

*

Our days soon settled into a routine. Each morning Pearl and I fetched the water, our teeth clenched against the cold, our breath steaming out into the morning air, everyone in the queue coughing and spluttering. It was as if the warmth had been stolen from us along with our home, and might never return.

Pearl always insisted on carrying the full bucket, even though she struggled with it, even though her feet slipped in the mud and the water slopped over the top. I was impressed with her determination and I told her so, over and over, but she rarely reacted. Most of the time when we spoke to her she'd nod, shake her head, or wrinkle her nose. If we asked a direct question she might give us a 'Yes,' or 'No,' but she'd never initiate a conversation and nothing brought her out of herself – not Pa's stupid jokes, or Kaz farting, not even Moe's giggles.

'We just need to give her time,' Ma said.

I wasn't so sure. Once, when I asked Pearl why she wasn't talking, she said, 'I am talking,' and pointed to her mouth. 'See?' Then she closed her mouth and didn't say another word for two days.

The camp was pretty miserable. The latrines leaked and stank, the shower block was as chill as a tomb and the water often ran out. Pa tacked up a curtain to make a screen and Pearl, Ma and myself washed inside the tent. The curtain had once been a bedcover; it was patterned with singing birds and pink flowers. It reminded me of the garden we'd left: the cooing doves and chattering sparrows, the thick creamy blossom that covered

125

our fruit trees in spring, and Ma bent over her roses in summer, coaxing them through the heat, the smell of their scented heads wafting into the house through the open door. I tried not to think of home too much because every time I did I was gripped by a vice-like pain in my chest. It was too terrible to think of what we'd lost. Sometimes the pain of that was almost greater than the pain of losing Tam.

Kaz also fetched water – Pearl couldn't carry enough for our needs – and he was given the task of queueing for bread, and the other meagre supplies we were allowed: rice and lentils, a little flour, the occasional tin of tomatoes or beans. There were no fresh vegetables in camp at the beginning, and there were certainly no luxuries of any kind. Once we'd thought nothing of running to the shops to buy more or less what we liked, and we'd never been short of fresh food as we'd grown our own. We hadn't been rich but we'd lived well, and we hadn't wanted for anything before.

Pearl and I helped Ma with Moe, and we were tasked with keeping the tent clean and tidy. In those first few weeks we had no school and so, after we'd eaten breakfast – which on most days was plain bread washed down with thin tea – we had little to do. Except think and worry. My burns had healed but I wasn't able to uncurl my fingers properly and my hand often ached. Because of my injury I couldn't draw pictures for Pearl or make paper houses like I'd used to; in any case we had little paper to spare. Nor could I brush her hair. Ma no longer had the time or the energy for creative things and although she would do Pearl's hair even that got forgotten some days. Pearl withdrew more and more. We all did. Even Moe was quiet.

Ma would break up the middle of the morning by preparing coffee. We'd sit and drink together, sitting on our thin mattresses, but it wasn't like the milky, thick and frothy coffee we'd had at home. Like the tea, this was as thin and grey as our blankets.

After coffee, Kaz and Pa would wander off, looking for work they claimed, but Ma said they sat in a tent with other men, smoking, and discussing the troubles of our world.

The weather continued dry and cold for some time, but one night a terrific snowstorm blew into camp and two children froze to death in an unheated tent. When Ma heard the news, she sat down and cried. I'd never seen her cry quite like that, not even after Grandpa died.

At first I stayed put, but then I took to wandering round the camp. I was bored and the tent felt oppressive, especially with Pearl so silent. Ma wasn't happy with me going out but there was little she could do to stop me. I offered to take Pearl out with me one time but Ma was definite in her refusal and I didn't argue. To be honest I was relieved because it wasn't easy spending time with Pearl. Being with her was like being with a ghost.

I soon came to know every corner of the camp: the main gate where hundreds of new arrivals streamed in every day and the trucks brought in supplies; the barbed wire fences; the Portakabins that housed offices and classrooms; the stalls that sprung up selling cloth, cheap tins, drinks and household items; the muddy road where boys hawked cigarettes and lighters; the places the kids gathered; the tent where the men sat.

In my wanderings, I saw many people and events, tragic and funny, private and public; things to humble me or make me smile. Each day at the main gate I watched the small boy who stood there in all weathers selling hot tea from a thermos; he was dressed in a dirty coat and torn jeans, his feet shod in sandals without socks. I watched washing blowing in the breeze, boys playing football on a patch of muddy ground, girls skipping. I witnessed a man slap his wife and a young woman weep over a photograph of a young man. I came across a child with eyes as blank as the canvas wall in front of him, an old man talking to his shoes, a young couple making love behind a curtain and a boy playing with a pack of home-made cards. And a burned tent, where a kerosene stove had been knocked over. I saw torn plastic bags caught up in the fence, and a dog so thin it could slip through the eye of a needle.

I saw cats, rats, shit, garbage, love, friendship and hate.

But I didn't make new friends. In Zazour I'd been outgoing and sociable but now I, too, began to withdraw. There were girls my age in the camp; I saw them giggling and gossiping together but I felt like an outsider – and I wanted Rey. I wanted her giggles and pink lipstick, her acid wit, and the two of us dancing in her bedroom to Beyoncé and Miley Cyrus.

I texted her again, and again. We had no electricity in the tent but there were places I could charge my mobile and buy credit. For a price. Always for a price. 'Where r u Rey? Where r u?'

Three weeks or so after we'd arrived in camp I heard a familiar ping on my mobile. I expected it to be Ma asking me to return to the tent, but it was Rey. 'We had to leave town. Taking north route out of here. Sorry. Wanted to contact you. Fone lost. This is sister fone. Hope u OK. Take care. Love u. XX Rey.'

'Where r u now?' I texted, but she didn't text back.

I ran to the tent. 'Rey's left,' I shouted. 'They're heading to Europe.'

'Is that good news?' Ma asked.

'I suppose.' I looked at Ma. She was bent over, her face turned away from me. 'Ma, what is it?'

She looked up. Silent tears were coursing down her cheeks. 'I haven't been able to reach Eva.' She and Eva had been friends since school, friends almost forever.

'I'm sure she'll turn up. Like Rey.'

'I don't know. Look what's happening to us. We're all being scattered like seeds.' Ma wiped her eyes. I noticed Pearl looking at us, her own eyes wide and dark.

'Did you hear?' I said to Pearl. 'Rey's going to Europe. Maybe she'll go to Rome and see the Colosseum or to Venice. I'd like to go to Venice, wouldn't you, Pearl?'

'Perhaps we should go to Europe,' Ma said.

'How would we get there?'

'I don't know but there must be ways.' Ma signalled with her eyes and I walked with her to the entrance.

'What about renting an apartment in the town?' I whispered. 'Pa said we would.'

'It's very expensive and Pa is worried about how long our money will last. We have to face facts, Mira. The war isn't going to end any time soon. Have you seen the number of new arrivals? Have you spoken to any of them?'

'No,' I said.

She leant in close. 'Terrible things have happened. The woman in the tent next to us she ... she saw her own daughter killed in front of her. The soldiers raped the girl first.'

I pulled away from Ma. I felt nauseous. 'We should talk to Pa and Kaz,' I said, no longer whispering.

'Where is Pa?' Pearl asked in the tiny voice she'd adopted, when she did speak.

'He and Kaz are looking for work,' Ma said. 'You know that, Pearl. That's what they do every day.'

Pearl wrinkled up her nose and huffed.

'Let's go outside and see if we can spot them,' I said. 'Come on, Pearl. You need to get outside for some air.'

'Don't go far. Please don't go far,' Ma said.

*

Kaz and Pa were usually back by late afternoon but that day they weren't back by nightfall, so I took Pearl outside again to look. While we waited, stamping our feet against the cold,

I noticed a thin black cat moving in between the tents, and I thought of the kitten we'd left back in Zazour and I wondered if he was still alive, hunting in the rubble of the house opposite. Perhaps our house would be rubble too. Pa hadn't had direct news but he'd heard Zazour had suffered more bombardment. More civilians had been killed and injured too. No one we knew – so far.

'Do you see the cat, Pearl?'

'I see it.'

'Cats can look after themselves. I expect it's hunting for mice.' I thought to say 'rats' but decided against it.

The cat crouched on the muddy earth. A pool of light from the tent spilled out, illuminating its black fur and the lines of its ribs.

'It's hungry,' Pearl said. She went inside to fetch a few crumbs of bread. All Ma could spare. She threw the crumbs into the mud. The cat didn't take them.

'Cats don't like bread,' I said.

'Why don't they?'

I was glad she was asking questions, almost like her old self. 'Cats are carnivores. Dogs will eat different foods but cats are fussier.'

'Oh,' she said. 'I didn't know.'

We sat together in the settling dark, the distant mountains no longer visible. Dogs yapped, people shouted, children cried, and smoke curled up from wood fires in the camp and the lights from the nearby town shone like stars. It was pleasant out there, Pearl and I together. Comfortable. Almost like the old days. Then Ma appeared in the doorway and called out, 'Come inside. It's late.'

'You don't need to worry,' I called back. 'The camp has watchmen. They protect us.'

'The watchmen don't have a thousand eyes.' Ma laughed

and I laughed with her. Laughter was in short supply. We had to catch at it like a soap bubble before it exploded and vanished.

It grew colder. Pearl began to shiver and we retreated.

'They're late,' I said to Ma.

'It's okay. Pa just texted. They're on their way.'

I turned my attention to Moe. He needed a nappy change – I could smell it. I laid him on the floor and he kicked his legs happily as I wiped him and gave him a clean nappy. The camp was short of disposable nappies and those we saw for sale were too expensive. Ma and I washed Moe's nappies by hand.

'What kept you?' I heard Ma say. I looked up. Pa and Kaz had finally arrived back. They looked tired. Pa had lost weight and the skin on his cheeks sagged like the pathetic sack of onions we'd just managed to purchase. Kaz, too, had lost weight and his woolly hair had grown both in length and girth; it was as if he hid behind it. After what we'd done we had kept our distance from each other as much as possible – we said what needed to be said and avoided eye contact.

'We were waiting to hear about some work,' Pa answered.

'What work?' Ma's voice was sharp.

'Drivers for supply trucks. Kaz and I got lucky. We start tomorrow. Sometimes we'll have to drive to the port at Amara.'

'Amara? That must be over a day's drive away,' Ma said. She didn't sound happy.

'I know. We'll have to sleep in the truck.'

'Is the pay good?'

Pa shrugged. 'It's okay. Nothing pays well here. Except smuggling.'

I saw Kaz look at Pa and something passed between them. When I asked Kaz about it later on he said Pa was worried about how Ma would react, and I believed him.

*

That night I dreamed of monsters with huge hands and long fingers that plucked at my ribs and made music with my bones. I woke up, shivering, my hand painful and aching. The rest of my family appeared to be sleeping peacefully. I lay on my mattress for a long while, listening to the sounds of the camp and thinking about Tam. I felt so lonely. We'd been so close as a family but now I felt as if we were splitting apart like Lyrian itself.

When I woke again, it was warmer in the tent and I heard the soft patter of rain falling on the canvas.

14

Present day: Sundsholm, Neeland.

Eka Al trained as a lawyer. He runs the Missing.com site, together with Murna, Hani and Sam. Eka specialises in exhuming dead bodies and remnant bones and reburying them. The rest of his time is spent processing missing persons' forms and writing reports on the deceased. 'It's hard to see so much death and suffering. But someone has to do this job. There are people all over the world still waiting for news of their families and loved ones.'

www.OurMissing.com/who we are

A miracle happens: Kaz agrees to come. A week later and I am waiting to meet him at the airport.

His plane is late. I drink first one coffee, then another, and a third. The coffee doesn't help my nerves, it only serves to make me more jittery. I pace up and down the concourse and flick through the magazines in the stationery shop. I buy a notebook I don't need and a sandwich I decide I can't eat. And I check my watch a hundred times, as if by looking at it I could make Kaz arrive sooner.

The airport is busy. A holiday weekend is coming up and people are arriving and leaving. Sundsholm airport isn't large but, all the same, thousands of people are passing through today. Despite the crowds, there's a sense of quiet and order here, unlike what's going on in my mind.

A man trundles a large black suitcase along. He looks familiar. I'm sure he's one of our countrymen but I turn my head when he looks my way in case he recognises me too. I don't feel like exchanging pleasantries, or making vain attempts to work out if we do know each other or are perhaps linked through mutual friends. We've all changed and grown older, and it's not always possible to know what side someone was on. At the beginning of the war we knew who the enemy was, but as the years moved on everything fractured – alliances, buildings, friendships.

The man passes. The danger is over. I watch his back recede into the distance. He walks slowly, like an old man, almost shuffling, and yet he looks to be about my age. Now I feel a sudden guilt. Perhaps I should run after him and ask what caused him to grow old before his time but I don't, and anyway, I know the answer. Pa, too, is old before his time. We – Pearl, Kaz and I – also grew up too fast. Moe was shielded from a lot of our suffering because of his age. He remembers nothing of that time, he says. Nevertheless, his decision to become a doctor was influenced by the war. I know because he told me so.

The electronic board flashes. The plane has landed.

A slight nausea overtakes me. It's just nerves. Isn't it? Each time someone comes through the door which leads out from the customs area, my heart zigzags in my chest. But Kaz will have to wait for his luggage; he won't be here yet.

Oh my God, is that him, the man in the leather cowboy hat and scuffed brown boots?

No, it's not.

My mouth has gone dry. Perhaps I should go and purchase a bottle of water but what if Kaz arrives while I'm in the shop? I decide against it.

There are people waving placards and taxi drivers waiting for clients. We're all waiting for someone. A young woman dashes into the arms of her boyfriend. A family comes by, their trolley heaped with suitcases. An elderly couple, he in a camel coat, she wearing furs and dark glasses, sweeps past. So many people it makes my head swim.

Twenty minutes. Half an hour. Forty minutes. Maybe he won't come at all?

A tall, thick man wearing boots that have seen better days appears at the barrier. Kaz doesn't use social media and his phone calls are intermittent and he's only once sent a photograph. He told me he'd put on weight, but he said nothing about his hair. The man, who is now walking in my direction has woolly white curls which resemble a sheep's fleece. But Kaz won't have white hair; he's only forty-eight. The man is coming closer. That wide nose … it's Kaz's nose, isn't it? No, that can't be him. I should leave now. It's not too late. I ought never to have agreed to this. So why did I? Because of Pa. For Pa. I think of him, lying in his hospital bed, his breathing ragged, his rheumy eyes dark with pain. I have to do this for him.

The man is scrutinising my face but saying nothing. Perhaps he doesn't know me. Oh my God, it is Kaz, I'm sure of it. I open my mouth and say his name but my voice comes out in a whisper and anyway it's drowned out by an announcement over the tannoy. Yes, it really is him. He's smiling and saying 'Mira, Mira.' He sweeps me up in his strong arms and he smells different, he smells of salt as if he'd brought the sea with him all the way from the other side of the world; then he draws back and he's grinning and I see him as he was before everything changed –

a young man running down the street, his red scarf flying, his arms waving as he if were about to fly, the snow falling silently in the street.

*

We don't say much in the taxi. Once, a car cuts up the vehicle and I curse and Kaz laughs and says, 'I never remember you swearing before,' and I laugh with him and think, *Well, this is going to be all right.* And it is all right, at first. We walk up the steps to my apartment and I put on the kettle and I ask if he's hungry; he pats his stomach and says, 'I'm always hungry,' and he laughs again, but this time his laugh is guarded and I see a dullness in his eyes.

'You've got a nice apartment, Mira. How long did you say you've lived here?'

I count on my fingers. 'Six years.'

'I can't remember where you said you lived before.'

'I had another apartment, though it wasn't in such a good position.'

'Yeah, you got it good here.' He pauses. 'You never lived with Ma and Pa?'

He knows my history but perhaps he's forgotten. I shake my head. 'For the first few months, yes. Pearl stayed with them until she got married and Moe left when he got his scholarship. I needed my own place, freedom to be my own person.'

'Freedom?' His mouth drops. 'Yeah, well. Sometimes freedom isn't quite what you expect it to be, is it?'

I walk over to the sink and fill the kettle. 'Coffee, or tea?'

'Tea. Weak. Or I won't sleep.'

'Didn't you take those tablets? You know, the ones that are supposed to cure jet lag?'

'No. I never take stuff like that.'

'Tea, you said?' He never used to drink tea, did he? Maybe I've forgotten. I suppose we've both forgotten things. 'Do you still take sugar?'

Kaz gives me a sheepish look. It matches the hair. 'Three spoons, please. Yes, I know I shouldn't but it helps me beat the drink even if it does rot my teeth.' He steps to the window. The light catches his hair, making it look almost as white as the snow outside.

'Your hair,' I say.

'This?' He runs his fingers through the silvery-white strands. The gesture reminds me of Pearl. 'It turned white almost overnight. Weird, eh?'

'Overnight?' I can't keep the surprise out of my voice. 'When?'

'After I broke up with Cindy.' He goes quiet, stays looking out of the window. 'I should have talked to you about that time. There's a lot I should have talked about.'

I make the tea and place it on the table. 'Sit down. I'll make you a sandwich.'

'Thanks.' He picks up the tea and takes a sip. 'When are we seeing Pearl ... and Pa?'

What do I say? He seems so enthusiastic. Doesn't he understand? He can't just walk back into our lives and pretend nothing has happened. All the same I feel awkward explaining. I'm angry with Pearl but something in me still feels the need to protect Kaz. Or I am just trying to protect myself? 'Pearl and Stefan have gone skiing in the mountains with the boys. They'll be back late this evening. We'll see Pearl tomorrow.'

'It's like that, is it?' Kaz leans forward and scratches at one eyebrow. Like Pa.

I open the fridge, ignore his words. 'How about a toasted sandwich? Tuna and cheese? Tomatoes.' Why didn't I make soup yesterday? Soup is much better in this weather. But, of course, I was trying to pretend he wasn't coming.

'Sounds good.' He yawns and stretches.

'The spare room is tiny but it's comfy. Go and put your stuff in there.' I point to the open door. 'You can sleep for a while after we eat.'

'At least you have a spare room.'

I nod. 'You sound different. I'm sure last time we spoke your accent wasn't so strong.' I smile. 'I can't think why I never noticed on the phone. Moe speaks different too. He's a true American. We're all international now.'

'You sound just the same.' He looks down at his mug of tea and falls silent.

I prepare the sandwiches and ask about his boys. It's easier to talk while I'm busy with my hands. Then I don't have to see how blank his face turns in the gaps between our conversations – as if a light has been switched off. But he's tired. He's travelled for twenty-four hours and it's a different time zone.

'It's been a while since I last saw them. Too long.' He bites his lip. 'They're not boys now. Darryl is at university and Alex has a job with an IT company in Perth. I've no idea what kind of job he does there. They both send Christmas cards, a text for my birthday. That's it. Not that I blame them. But you know all of this.' I look up. He won't catch my eye.

It's true; I do know but I was hoping things had changed. I wonder how much the boys know about his life and the war. A wave of anger washes over me. I'm chopping tomatoes with my left hand – the right hand never quite recovered – and now I loosen my grip on the knife and it drops to the floor with a clatter.

Kaz jumps.

'Sorry,' I say.

'Your hand? How is it?'

'It's okay. It's not that.' I'm close to tears. 'My cat has gone missing and what with Pa and everything …'

Kaz picks up the knife. 'Here, let me chop.'

'No. I'll do it. You look exhausted.'

'I'm sorry about your cat. How long has he been missing?'

'She ... a week already ... I think. It's hard to remember. So much has been going on lately.'

Kaz sits back down in the chair. I finish chopping the tomatoes, and place them inside the bread, along with the cheese. There's so much I want to say but now isn't the right time.

'How is Pa? Are we seeing him later?'

'We'll go tomorrow.' I put the sandwich in the toaster.

'Oh.' Kaz's face falls.

'You'll find him very changed.'

'Like me.' He grins.

'We're all older,' I say, grinning back at him. 'But are we any wiser?'

The sandwich is ready. I put in on a plate and hand it to him.

'Wiser? You know what I think ...' His smile vanishes. He takes a bite of the sandwich. I hover over the toaster, waiting for my sandwich, waiting for him to complete his words, but he does not.

*

Kaz is stretched out on the sofa, yawning again. 'Sorry. The jet lag is catching up with me.'

I don't travel. I've scarcely been outside Neeland since we came here. Pearl and Stefan are always going somewhere with the boys, although they've never been to Lyrian. 'Why didn't you go back?'

'You know why,' he says.

I almost argue with him but then I decide now is not the time to talk. Kaz is too tired. 'Do you want another tea? Flying dehydrates the body. You should drink as much as you can.'

I step into the kitchen and, while I'm preparing the tea, I stare out of the window, like I always do, although these past few days I've been looking ever more intently and frequently, hoping to see Mimi crossing the square. The old man in the ground floor apartment opposite is brushing away snow from the path. I don't his name. I don't know any of my neighbours, with the exception of Mr Engman. In Zazour we knew everyone on our street.

Kaz's eyes are closed when I come in with the tea, and he's snoring quietly. I watch him for a few minutes, then I return to the kitchen, pour his tea down the sink and drink my own. The man has swept half the path now. For an old man he's working pretty fast.

*

Kaz sleeps until it grows dark. I sit in the kitchen with my laptop, log onto the missing persons' site and trawl through the list searching for new names. I'm not just looking for news of Tam, I'm also searching for information on Kaz's other university friends but there's nothing new. Tonight I create another user name – my sixth – so that I can chat more freely on the blog. Thirty years cannot erase all memory of what happened in that war; people still take sides.

The blog too is quiet. I log off.

I peer out of the window but all I can see is my own reflection. I switch off the kitchen light and look out again. A cat is moving across the square from left to right. My heart misses a beat. A moment later the cat passes over a pool of light and I realise it's not Mimi. A woman on a bicycle comes into view. The two pass each other and are gone.

15

The past: Isara Camp, Sufra.

For people living in a refugee camp exile is not just geographic; it is emotional and heartfelt. And for many, it is more than this. It is trauma.

www.worldincrisis/nee.com

Living in the camp didn't bring us together as a family, it tore us into ever smaller pieces. We argued over trivial things: who was getting the best coffee cup, whether the temperature inside the tent was three or four above zero, if we should buy soap or shampoo. Pearl didn't join in our petty disagreements; she stayed silent as the stars I stared at night after night as I huddled outside the tent, shivering, until Ma called me in.

For weeks the weather had been frosty with bright blue skies but now a cold rain blew in, turning everything to mud, puddles and complaints. Water dripped off the canvas and damp crept into our bones. The clag from the paths stuck to our boots and splashed our clothes. The tent sprung a leak – we had to put a bucket underneath to catch the drips – and Ma grew ever more impatient. 'You promised you'd find us a place in the town, somewhere with a proper roof. We can't stay here. This place is impossible.'

'I'm looking into it,' Pa said. Most days Pa and Kaz left before we woke and didn't return until late, and sometimes they were gone overnight. That morning they were late in leaving.

Ma shook her fist. 'Looking into it? Like hell you are.' She'd never spoken to Pa like that before.

'I'm doing what I can, Sara,' Pa said. He was sitting on the ground, pulling on his boots, his back hunched, a stain on the pocket of his jacket.

'There are always other choices,' Ma said.

I wondered what choices Ma was speaking of, but Moe distracted me. He'd started crawling and had almost reached the entrance, but I grabbed him before he could disappear into the mud. Now he squealed and squirmed in my arms.

'Put him down,' Ma said, sharply.

I sat Moe in my lap and tickled his toes while Ma rearranged the few possessions we'd brought. When she'd completed that task to her satisfaction she picked up the cups and wiped them with a tea towel, even though Pearl and I had washed and dried them already.

'For God's sake,' Pa said. 'What are you doing?'

'What do you think? Tidying, cleaning. It's more than you ever do.' Ma slammed a cup down onto the wooden crate that served as our kitchen sideboard.

'Everything is tidy,' Pa said gently.

But Ma ignored him. She picked up a tin of beans and wiped that. She'd always liked to keep our house in Zazour tidy but in camp her tidying and cleaning had become obsessive. If our shoes weren't lined up she'd move them until they were in a precise line. Even the pots and pans had to be kept in a certain order, and she wiped everything three times over. It nearly drove us crazy.

I turned to Pa. 'Rey and her family are going to Europe. Ma is right. We should get out. Why don't we go too? There's nothing for us here.'

'It's not that easy.' Pa's face was sad. Like late autumn when the leaves are gone.

'Maybe it's better to drown than to live like this,' Ma said. Her earlier anger was gone and she seemed close to tears. Like the rest of us she'd lost weight, and her face looked pinched and old. She'd tied her hair back with one of Pearl's hairbands, but it was in need of a wash and trim. At home she'd always been particular about her appearance. She had visited the hairdresser every week and when she went out, she had always worn red lipstick and her black patent shoes. Here, she did none of that. She obsessed about the tent and neglected herself. But that's how we were. We'd all turned strange in our own ways and now we were becoming strangers to each other.

'I'll find somewhere but it's not cheap to rent in town. The locals are fleecing everyone.' Pa glanced at Ma and then at me.

'That's even more reason for us to leave,' I said. 'We're not welcome.'

Pa scratched at his eyebrow. 'Have you any idea how much it costs to leave, Mira, and how dangerous it is? The people who arrange these things can't be trusted. These are people smugglers who care only for money. They have no concern for safety ...'

'They send people across the Med in rusty old cargo ships, leaky fishing boats, even inflatables. I wouldn't be surprised if some of them even used colanders.' Kaz zipped up his jacket. 'They cram the people in and sometimes the boats capsize and people drown. Is that what you want? And why should we leave to go to a country we know nothing about? We'd be no more welcome there than we are here. We should stay and wait for things to get better.'

'Better?' I echoed. I hated how he'd spoken – the sarcastic tone, the way he thought he knew best. We'd had our arguments in the past but now we were cold with each other.

Ma stopped tidying and turned to me. 'Your father knows best, Mira. And you and Pearl are starting school tomorrow. That's something, isn't it?'

'We must all learn patience.' Kaz tapped his watch. 'We should go, Pa.'

Patience? Since when have you been patient, Kaz?

'What time do you think you'll be back?' Ma asked.

'Around seven,' Pa said, giving Ma a peck on the cheek.

After Pa and Kaz had left, I let Moe crawl to the doorway but I ran after him and picked him up before he went out into the mud. Now he giggled. It was all a game to him. He was too young to understand. I was happy to see my baby brother thriving and growing stronger after his illness, but I still couldn't help wishing I could turn back time to the time before he was born – to before all the bad stuff happened. And then Pearl suddenly spoke, in a loud clear voice. 'I want to go home,' she said. 'I want to go home and wear my blue dress and walk in the garden. Just for one day. Then I can die.'

Ma spun round and almost dropped the plate she was holding. 'You mustn't speak like that.'

'When *are* we going home?' The dark circles under Pearl's eyes were like bruises.

'When it's safe,' Ma said. 'Only then.'

Moe wriggled out of my lap again. He crawled to Pearl and she cradled him in her arms. She didn't speak again all day, and Ma and I were silent with her. What more could we say? Perhaps it was better to be like Pearl and only speak when necessary. Words only seemed to get in our way.

*

144

The following day Pearl and I went to school. Our lessons were to be mornings only. The afternoons were reserved for boys. The place hardly merited the word school. It was a large, chilly tent with matting to sit on. No books, chairs or tables, no laptops or screens. Two female teachers were standing at the front and there must have been at least seventy girls there.

'Welcome,' the older teacher said. 'For those of you who are new here today I'm Mrs Muhar and this is Miss Katina, who teaches the younger girls.' The younger teacher was bareheaded but Mrs Muhar was wearing a red headscarf.

Miss Katina smiled and bowed slightly. 'Welcome,' she said, in a soft voice.

I was sent to the back to sit with the older girls. Pearl sat at the front. We were each given a single notebook and a pencil. The girl next to me had burn scars on her face. I mumbled hello and she said hello in return and gave me a weak smile.

The first lesson was grammar and spelling. Then we had maths. I'd already covered the work in my school in Zazour and I was bored. I could write quite fast now with my left hand, though my writing did look like a six-year-old's.

At the end of the lesson Mrs Muhar walked up to the front and clapped her hands. 'I have good news, girls. The funds for a proper school building have finally been agreed. But we'll have to be patient.'

A buzz went through the students.

'Are you still going to be here then?' I asked my neighbour, the girl with the scarred cheeks.

'I expect so.' Her hands shook and she spoke with a lisp. 'We have no home to go back to. It's all burned. What about you? Why did you come?'

'The government bombed our town.'

She leant in close. Her breath smelled of peppermint. 'Do you think they mean to kill us all?'

145

'I don't know,' I said, picking up my pencil. We didn't speak again.

*

In the middle of the morning we had a break. I found Pearl sitting next to a girl with piercing blue eyes and a tangle of black hair.

'How did you find the lessons?' I said to Pearl. But I got no reply, not even a shrug.

'I'm Nadia,' the girl said. Her face was dirty and her hair looked like it hadn't been washed in weeks.

'Mira,' I said. 'And this is Pearl, my sister.'

'She already told me her name. She can talk, you know.'

I felt my cheeks flush.

'You have a bad hand. It got burned. You have a baby brother called Moe. Your big brother, Kaz, is studying architecture. Sorry – was.' She gave me a mean little smile. 'I know everything about you.'

'Oh,' I said, looking at Pearl again. She turned her head and I walked away.

*

Now we were given coloured pencils, felt-tip pens and a sheet of rough paper. 'There's no subject today,' Mrs Muhar said. 'You are free to be creative.'

A girl with only one arm was handed some kind of clay. Miss Katina, noticing my hand, asked if I too would like clay. 'I suppose,' I said, rather rudely. How could I explain to her that I wanted my paints and brushes, my inks, pens and drawing paper, and my hand working like it used to. I needed to design a house, one that nothing could touch, a house to withstand a

146

volcano, an earthquake, a bomb, even a tsunami. I didn't want to make a clay house, a place that could be broken as easily as a vase dashed to the floor. I didn't want that at all.

The girl with one arm pressed, squeezed and coiled the clay. The pot she created was really quite beautiful. I left my clay where it was and went to Pearl. She was drawing a fish.

'That's nice,' Mrs Muhar said, passing by.

'Pearl,' I said. 'Her name is Pearl.'

'That's a pretty name.'

'She doesn't like to talk,' I said.

Nadia scowled at me. 'What do you know?' She dug Pearl in the ribs. 'You can talk, can't you?'

Pearl said nothing.

'See,' I said. 'She doesn't want to.'

The teacher had green eyes like Tam's. 'I'm sure she'll come out of herself in a while.'

'She doesn't want to talk with her sister here.' Nadia placed an arm on Pearl's shoulder. I thought Pearl would resist but she leant into Nadia as though they'd been friends forever.

My hand twitched and I turned back to Mrs Muhar. 'She's been very quiet since we came here.'

'It's quite a common response,' she said. 'I do understand.'

You don't understand. You're not from our country. You don't know a damned thing. 'Right,' I said.

Pearl picked up her pencil and drew a second, larger fish, with a row of long and terrible teeth like a shark.

'You draw nicely,' Mrs Muhar said. 'With real expression. Not everyone can draw like that.'

'What about mine?' Nadia waved her drawing about. It was an exact copy of Pearl's small fish, though clumsily executed.

'Very good,' Mrs Muhar said.

I walked away. Else I might have done something I regretted. But I'd already done that, hadn't I?

147

*

'I see you've made a friend,' I said to Pearl as we walked back to our tent. It was still raining although not as heavy as before. The mountains were hidden behind veils of cloud.

Pearl nodded.

'You like her?'

Pearl nodded again.

I wanted to ask Pearl why she would talk to Nadia and not to us but I bit my tongue. 'Let's go a little faster, shall we? The rain is cold. And Ma will want help with Moe.' I reached for her hand but she shook me off.

I was surprised to see Kaz and Pa there. Perhaps there had been a change of plan.

'Can we talk?' Kaz whispered to me.

I followed him outside. 'What is it?'

He put a finger across his lips and steered me down the muddy lane that separated the rows of tents, until we were in an open space. 'Pa and I are going away. It's going to be a long trip this time. We haven't said anything to Ma yet.'

The rain had stopped. The blue peaks floated like distant islands above the layer of cloud and mist. 'When?'

'Tomorrow.'

'So soon?' I looked at Kaz but he wouldn't meet my eyes and it came to me then, what he and Pa were doing. 'You're going back to fight. The story about the supply trucks is just a cover isn't it?'

Kaz nodded his head.

'Why didn't you say something?'

'Pa doesn't want Ma to know. I thought if I told you earlier, you might blab.'

I felt myself grow hot, then cold. 'Like I've blabbed about what happened in Zazour? And it's not right to keep Ma in the

148

dark.' I looked across to the mountains again but they were no longer visible. A man cursed nearby, and a dog yelped.

'I'd give my soul for our country, Mira.'

'How can you leave us, you and Pa? Why can't you help in other ways?'

'People are giving their lives. I can't sit here twiddling my thumbs when others are fighting the regime and dying for our freedom.'

'Why does Pa have to go too?'

Now Kaz caught hold of my arm. 'Because he's needed. We're needed. For the cause.'

I shook him off. 'You don't think of our needs? Well fuck you, Kaz.'

'I know it's not easy living here but it's safe.' Kaz pressed his hand into his forehead as if he had a headache. 'Can you imagine what it's like for those left behind? The regime has been bombing Lyri, day in and day out. Parts of the city have been almost flattened. I have to do something for them too. Do you want me to leave people to die, helpless and alone?'

'Is that where you're going, to Lyri?' I had other questions I wanted to ask, other things I wanted to say but I did not.

We were both silent. The sounds of the camp drifted through the chill air: the cries and shouts, the rumble of trucks at the gate. Then he spoke. 'I don't know where I'll be going. But one thing I do know: this war won't be over any time soon. We're just at the beginning.'

I looked to the mountains but they were blotted out as if they'd never existed. 'And you fighting is the answer; is that what you believe?'

Kaz reached for my arm again but I stepped back. 'Mira … listen, please. I want peace too, but I also want freedom for Lyrian. We can't fight bullets and bombs with words.'

'So you thought Tam was talking shit?'

'How can you say that?'

'I'm sorry,' I said. And we hugged each other. The first time we'd had any physical contact since the day we met in the cemetery.

*

After we'd had our supper of rice and lentils, Pa stood up and said, 'I need to make an announcement.'

'What is it?' Ma's voice was wispy like the smoke that curled up from the camp's many fires.

'Kaz and I have to go away tomorrow. A longer trip.' Now Pa cleared his throat as if his words were sticking there.

Ma got up too, and took our plates. 'Tomorrow?' I could hear suspicion in her voice.

'A few weeks. Maybe longer.' Kaz wouldn't look at us. His eyes were fixed on his boots and he was chewing at his fingernails. When had he started that habit?

'Weeks?' Ma said. She set the plates down on the crate and picked up a cloth. Wiped her hands on it, over and over. 'Where exactly are you going?'

Pearl shot to her feet and shouted, 'I know! They're going to fight.' There were two red spots on her cheeks, like Ma's roses.

For a moment none of us said anything. We were too stunned by Pearl's sudden outburst to react.

'What?' Ma said, frowning and turning to Pa. 'Is this true?'

Pa reached for Ma's hand but she pulled away.

'Is this true?' Ma asked again. She looked across to Pearl, sitting in the corner, her knees pulled up. Then she looked at me. 'How does Pearl know?'

'I have no idea,' I said. Because I did not know.

'Do I have any say in this?' Ma folded her arms across her chest. She was trying to act defiant, like I had done with Kaz

150

earlier, but she knew she'd already lost. She gripped her forearms with her hands, perhaps to stop herself from crying but the tears were already there in the corners of her tired eyes.

'It's not the front line,' Pa said. 'There's no need to worry.'

'What do you think I do now? I worry from morning until night. I do nothing but worry.'

The rain started up, pattering on the canvas like a thousand fingers and Ma sank to her knees, her head in her hands. Pa walked over and placed his arm on her shoulders. No one said a word. We listened to the rain dripping off the canvas and plopping into the bucket. After a while Ma got up, sighed and said, 'Well, we'd better get you both prepared,' and that was it.

*

A morning. Warm sunshine. A woman singing. Sparrows chirping behind the tent, seeking crumbs. A faint smell of coffee, that thin coffee we now drank. Kaz chewing his fingernails. Pa pulling at the growth on his chin. Moe's small hand reaching out for Ma's skirts. Pearl's dark hair tangling down the back of her pink sweatshirt. Our empty breakfast plates scattered on the rug. Our cooking equipment, sleeping mattresses and clothes piled up in the corner. A whole family's existence in one small tent.

But we weren't going to be a family any more.

'We're not staying indefinitely,' Pa said.

Ma pulled at non-existent fluff on her long skirt.

'Define indefinitely,' I said, but neither Kaz nor Pa answered and my words just hovered in the air. Pearl gave me a funny little look. She picked up her doll and walked over to the corner of the tent where Kaz and Pa's packed bags lay, close to the screen of birds, and placed the doll on top of Kaz's canvas bag. The doll was wearing her blue skater skirt and a red-and-white striped top but she had no shoes.

'Is she coming with us?' Kaz's voice sounded broken. Broken like our country. Broken beyond repair.

'Yes,' Pearl said. There was a determined expression on her face, something I hadn't seen in a long while.

And then it was time for them to leave.

'I promise we'll be back,' Pa said, when we'd hugged each other but I wondered how he could make such an impossible promise. He reached into the pocket of his jacket and produced our old front door keys. 'Keep these safe,' he said, handing them to Ma. 'For when we need them again.'

Ma turned away; she was weeping. She had Moe in her arms.

I stood awhile watching Kaz and Pa slump along the muddy path, and all was quiet as if in a dream.

16

Present day: Sundsholm, Neeland.

'Disappearances are a sensitive social and political issue, but this is no excuse for inaction. Governments must generate the political will necessary to provide answers.'
Barbara D.A. Watson, Chairwoman - This is our World

Kaz is up before me. Usually I'm the early bird. He's lying on my sofa, dressed in a pair of red shorts, and a dark blue sweatshirt, his feet bare. The last time a man – any man – lay in my apartment was the day before Pearl took me to the psychiatric ward.

'Are you okay?' Kaz says. 'You seem a little … I don't know … distracted.'

'I was thinking about Mimi.' Except I wasn't. 'Are you hungry?'

He grins and pats his stomach. 'I'm always hungry.'

'What would you like – eggs, yoghurt, fruit?'

He waves his arms. 'Eggs sound good. But first I could murder a coffee …' He stops. He knows what he's said.

'Is scrambled okay.'

'Sure. Do you need help?' Kaz leans forward and places his large hands on his hairy thighs.

'The kitchen isn't big enough for two cooks.'

'Okay, I'll fling some clothes on then.'

He's not gone long. He comes back in a pair of jeans, frayed at the hem, and a faded red T-shirt. 'You've got this place nice, Mira. I'm impressed. My pad is full of junk. I ought to clear it out.'

'Why don't you?'

He shrugs and his shoulders hunch up like they always did; another gesture that reminds me of Pearl, that reminds me we're family. 'I'm too fucking lazy.'

He never used to swear, did he? But I swear too. Sometimes. 'Where are you living now?'

'A room.' He shuts up, doesn't elaborate.

'Wait till you see Pearl's house. It's like something out of the pages of a magazine.' Probably I shouldn't have said that. I wasn't thinking. I get the coffee going, break four eggs into a bowl and whisk them with a fork.

I hear Kaz sit, and his foot tapping on the wooden floor. Then he walks to the kitchen doorway. 'Pearl doesn't want to see me. I can't say I blame her. I was such a mess when I came back from Lyri. What do you think she remembers from that time?'

'We rarely talk about the past. That's how she wants it. She'll come round, Kaz. I mean you're her brother, for God's sake. We're family. That has to count for something.'

He smiles but his smile goes nowhere. 'Will Pearl's boys be there?'

'Lucas and Oscar? They'll be at school. You'll see them later.'

'What are they like?'

'Just normal, ordinary boys.'

'I wish I had more contact with my boys.' Kaz puts his hand to his forehead and looks at me sadly. 'You'd have been good with kids.'

I snort. 'You think?'

'Yes, I do,' he says, his face serious.

'Why don't you see your boys?' I ask, although I can guess the answer.

Kaz looks down at his bare feet. One toe is crooked and there's a deep red scar along the side of his left foot. He sighs. Looks at me now. 'It's obvious, isn't it? They still think I'm a hopeless alcoholic. Even though I'm not any more. I wish they'd give me another chance but how can I convince them I'm sober when they refuse to even meet me?'

'I don't know, Kaz. You'll just have to keep trying.'

He walks into my kitchen. On one shelf I keep a number of ornaments: a solid glass bottle, a small wooden ship and turquoise-coloured bowl made by an exile friend of mine. Not a close friend, but someone I knew well enough. Kaz picks up the bowl and cradles it in his hands. His hands are shaking and the bowl shakes too, as if a small earthquake were passing through my apartment. 'This is beautiful. Didn't Ma have a bowl like this?'

'She did. Pa bought it for her fortieth birthday.'

'I remember.'

'Someone I know made that – one of us. She died last year. Heart attack. But I'm convinced she died of a broken heart. Her sister-in-law went missing in the war. No one ever heard from her again.'

'I'm sorry.' Kaz replaces the bowl on the shelf. 'We've all endured so much loss. Do you still dream about that time?'

'Sometimes.' I busy myself with making the breakfast. Find a pan. Put a knob of butter in. Cut the bread. Pour his coffee. Hand it to him. I don't want to talk about 'that time' with Kaz. It's dangerous ground.

'Can I poke my head into your bedroom? You can say no. I'm only being nosy.'

'Go ahead. You can't exactly get lost in this place.'

When he comes back, he says, 'I really do like your style, Mira. Minimal but not too stark. My problem is I collect stuff. I can't seem to chuck anything out, even old newspapers. I never thought I'd end up like that.' He laughs. 'Crazy man, eh? *Crazy Whitefella* – that's what the Aboriginal people call people like us. Though when those guys look at me they see I'm not so white. Maybe I'm more like them than they realise. They're exiles too, but at least they're exiled in their own land ...' He stops, lowers his voice. 'Not so easy for them either.'

'No,' I say. 'It's not.' I turn on the heat. Pour in the eggs. Put the bread in the toaster.

'What's this?' He's back in the living room. A real jack-in-the-box.

I poke my head round the doorway. He's pointing to one of the framed photos that hangs on my living room wall.

'A photo,' I say. It's a black and white photograph of the reflection of a man walking through a blur of winter trees.

'For sure.' Kaz takes a sip of coffee. 'But what does it mean?'

'Who knows? I liked it. I bought it at an exhibition I went to. It wasn't expensive. I bought that at the same time.' I point to the photograph on the opposite wall which hangs above the carved oak chest. I purchased the chest in a bric-a-brac shop close to the refugee centre.

'I like this one better. God, how do you keep this place so clean?' He runs his fingers along the window ledge. 'Not a speck of dust.'

'Well, it's not exactly a palace.'

'I suppose,' he says. 'And you've no kids to mess things up. Sorry. I shouldn't have said that.'

'It's okay. It was a conscious decision.'

'Marriage and kids isn't all it's set out to be.' He rolls his eyes. Grins slightly. 'I drove Cindy crazy with my mess. If she ever threw so much as a newspaper away I'd get mad. No wonder she couldn't stand it. You'd think I'd have needed order too but no, I let everything slip.' He puts his hands on his stomach. 'I used to be in such good shape, too. Now look at me.'

'You can get back into shape. You're not that old, not like Pa.'

We fall silent. I go back into the kitchen to check on the eggs. 'Orange juice?'

'Yes, please. How is Pa?'

'Like I said. Up and down.'

I serve the breakfast. Kaz sits but he keeps jiggling his legs, and when he's not eating he drums his fingers on the table.

'Does Pa really want to see me or have you and Pearl used that as an excuse?' he asks.

'Pa gets confused sometimes; he muddles up the past and present. The heart attack damaged his brain. Lack of oxygen.' I tuck into my toast and eggs. I'm hungry this morning. That, at least, is a good sign.

'You haven't answered my question.'

I swallow, put down my knife and fork. 'He's been asking for you. Isn't that enough?'

We eat in silence. I stare out of the window, like I always do. The old man in the ground floor apartment opposite is brushing away snow from the path again. In the autumn he sweeps up the leaves, and in spring there's the blossom. Always something to sweep. 'We'll take a taxi to Pearl's,' I say, getting up to pour my coffee and a second cup for Kaz. We're expected around midday. Before then I might check with the man at the mini-market in case he's heard anything about Mimi.'

'I'm sorry about your cat. I hope she comes back soon.' Kaz points to his clothes. 'Will these do? For Pearl?'

'I'm not sure.' A moment ago I was angry with him. Now he strikes me as almost comical. 'Pearl is very particular. She might throw you out with the garbage if you turn up looking like that.'

'Should I put on a proper shirt? I did bring one.' He sounds alarmed.

I start laughing. 'Only one? I hope it's decent.'

He laughs with me. 'Is she so particular? I don't remember that about her.' But his laugh soon fades. 'I remember how she stopped talking in camp. None of us knew what to do.'

I examine his face. The lines that were not there the last time I saw him. His skin darker and rougher. His eyes rimmed with red. What does he remember? What do any of us remember really? 'You weren't around so much.' I turn away from him and look out of the window again. At the sweeping man. The elegant buildings. I sigh. Turn back. 'Would you like toast and jam too? I have apricot. Like Ma used to make. Only it's not quite so good.'

Kaz picks up the coffee. Puts it down again. His hands are still trembling. 'I remember Ma's jam ... the apricots from our own trees. It was a good life in some ways ... in spite of ...' He trails off. 'Only one piece of toast, Mira. I ought to try and lose some weight. Drink piles on the kilos. That and all the junk I eat. God, what must you think, seeing me like this, a fat old tramp?'

Anger bubbles up in me again. 'Why did you cut us off like you did? Don't you think you owed Ma and Pa?'

His face pales a little. 'I was ashamed. Of my drinking. My broken marriage. Losing the kids. Losing my job ...'

'We offered to help. Then you stopped answering my calls and letters ...' A door slams. My neighbour. The wind has caught the door, I imagine. I hear her feet on the stairs, receding. 'Why didn't you come to Ma's funeral? That was unforgiveable.' Now I've said it.

'I was such a fucking mess. You've no idea how much of a mess I was in. You think it's easy telling people that? How you've failed at life? Gone sick in the head.' He leans on his elbows and peers out of the window. 'How do you stand it here in the winter? It's past nine and it's hardly light.'

I think about my own sickness. How I too have felt like a failure. But I was here for Ma and Pa and he was not. 'You get used to the winters and there are compensations. In midsummer it's light almost twenty-four hours a day.'

'That must be odd.'

I cut two slices of bread and place them in the toaster; one for Kaz, one for me. I'm surprised at how hungry I am this morning. Usually nerves cut my appetite. 'What are your plans? I mean, after you go back. Are you going to try and find work?'

'Yes, I'm ready for that now. I'm thinking of retraining. I'd like to be a youth worker. What about you? What's going on in your life?'

'Me? There's not much to say. You know most of it.'

'I don't think I do, Mira.'

While we eat the toast and jam, I tell him about my job. About Tomas. About my failed romances, although I don't admit to sleeping around. But I don't tell him about my stay in hospital or why I gave up my full-time job and he doesn't ask.

'It's a shame there's no one special in your life.'

I shrug. 'I'm not interested. A man would just complicate things.'

'We messed up, didn't we, you and I.'

Now I glare at him. 'No, we didn't. We made mistakes, but it wasn't us who messed up. The regime messed it up for us. That's the difference.'

Kaz stirs another spoonful of sugar into the remains of his coffee. 'We made choices.'

I leap up from the chair, almost knocking over the cups. 'Choices? What do you mean?' Because I don't want to think what we did was a choice.

'All right, all right,' he says, holding up his hands. 'Let's not go there.'

'I'm searching for Tam,' I say. 'There's an online site in Lyrian; for missing persons.'

He blinks. 'What? All this time later?'

'They're always digging up remains. I need to know. It's important to me.' I turn to the window but I don't look out. I close my eyes. And I see Tam walking towards me waving his home-made flag as if it were only yesterday.

'You loved him, didn't you?'

'I was fifteen,' I say. 'Just fifteen.'

*

Pearl and Stefan own a traditional wooden house, built in the nineteenth century for a wealthy merchant. Once, it stood on the boundary between the old town and the countryside – Pearl has a photo of the house, as it was back then – but now the house is swallowed up by the modern city and lies in the middle of suburbs.

'This is grand,' Kaz says, as we approach Pearl's front door. 'And a nice area by the looks of it.'

'Lawyers can afford grand houses,' I say.

The doorbell is an old-fashioned pull. We stand under the shelter of the porch, our breath steaming in the cold air, waiting for Pearl's footsteps. We seem to wait a long time but at last the door opens and there she is. She's dressed in a smart blue woollen dress but she's wearing traditional felt slippers on her feet. She'd never come to the door in slippers unless she knew it was a family member visiting. But she only gives me a cursory glance and her smile is half-formed and, when she turns to Kaz, her voice is frayed, as if she'd not slept well. 'So, you finally made it,' she says.

A car passes on the road, its tyres swishing in the slushy snow.

'Are we late?'

'Late?' She frowns, then remakes her hostess face. 'No, no. Come in.'

I kiss Pearl on both cheeks and take off my coat. Soft music is playing from inside the house. I smell onions and polish.

'Pearl,' Kaz says. He's still by the door, his arms limp at his sides.

Pearl is standing stiff and upright, as if she were strapped to an ironing board. 'Goodness,' she says. 'You do look different.'

'It's been a long time.'

'It certainly has.' Then, quite out of character, Pearl marches off down the hallway, forcing me aside.

'Here,' I say to Kaz. 'Give me your coat. I'll hang it up. Take off your boots too. You can leave those by the door.'

'She doesn't want me here,' Kaz whispers. His cheeks are burning and it's not just from the cold.

'You can't expect it all to go like clockwork,' I whisper back. 'Be patient, okay?' He nods and hands me his coat. We take off our boots and I find him a pair of slippers – Pearl keeps felt slippers of all sizes for visitors – and we go into the living room. Nothing is out of place. The cushions are plumped up on the sofa. The floor gleams with polish. A vase of hyacinths and narcissi stands on the walnut sideboard.

'Take a seat,' Pearl says, as if Kaz were here for an interview.

Kaz lowers himself into the armchair where Stefan usually sits. 'You have a lovely house.'

'We work hard for what we have.' Pearl's voice is brittle and she's biting her thumb. When she sees me looking at her, she says, 'Lunch won't be long. I'll get us a drink,' and she waltzes out of the room without asking us what we want. I hear her in the kitchen banging doors and Kaz looks at me and I look at him

161

and I open my mouth to say something but he holds up his hand and I stay silent.

Pearl returns with a bowl of olives and three glasses filled with orange liquid. She places the tray on the low coffee table and sits on the large white leather sofa, crossing her legs. I've taken one of the remaining armchairs.

'Mango juice,' she says, her voice still brisk. 'Mira says you don't drink anymore.'

'That's right; I don't.' Kaz picks up a glass and takes a sip. He puts it back down. The clock ticks in the corner, a board creaks upstairs. The silence between us is thick and suffocating. Then Kaz says, 'I'm not going to pretend, Pearl. You know I've had a problem with alcohol but I'm dealing with it. I'm sober now and I intend to stay that way.'

'Really?' Pearl doesn't touch the olives or pick up her glass. 'Isn't that what they all say, *not again*? Her mouth curls at the edges.

'At least he's trying,' I say. 'Give him a break.'

A smell of warm bread wafts in from the kitchen. My throat tightens. The smell of warm bread always reminds me of our house in Zazour.

'Give him a break?' Pearl throws up her hands. 'He ran away, Mira and I think he's still running in spite of what he says.' She inclines her head in Kaz's direction. 'As soon as Pa is gone he'll be off again and …'

'Pearl,' I say. 'Please.'

'It's true, isn't it?' She fixes her gaze on Kaz. 'You didn't come when Ma died. Why come this time? Money? Is that it? Because Pa hasn't got any, you know.'

Kaz picks up his glass again and twists it round and round. 'I don't want money, Pearl. I'm grateful you and Stefan paid my fare. It's true I couldn't afford it myself. But I came to see Pa and I came because … because you asked me to and because I messed up and I want to make it right.'

'Oh, you messed up, Kaz. No arguing with that.'

I peer into my glass. The mango juice smells of honey and summer, but how far away summer feels right now.

'I'm sorry,' Kaz says.

'Sorry isn't enough.' Pearl picks up her glass of juice and slams it back on the coffee table. She jumps up and disappears out through the living room door. I go after her. She's leaning against one of the kitchen units, crying. I don't want to see her like this but I understand: I feel it too. All these emotions, the anger, the sadness, the relief, jumbled up together.

I wrap my arms around her. She doesn't resist. I smell her scent and feel the softness of her body. 'Would you like us to leave?' I ask.

She pulls away. 'No. Of course not. It's just ... oh, I didn't want it to be like this. I imagined this happy get-together and I'm the one who's ruined it.' A tear rolls down her cheek. 'Get me a tissue, will you please? A piece of kitchen roll will do.'

Next to the kitchen roll is a pinboard where Pearl keeps lists and appointments. Two drawings the boys made years ago are still pinned up there. I examine them with different eyes today. The smaller drawing is of a red tractor and a large yellow sun; Oscar drew it in his first year of primary school, and the man on the tractor is Stefan. The other drawing is one Lucas made when he was nine and it's almost an exact replica of a drawing Pearl made in Isara Camp. I wonder where Lucas got the idea from. A boy is standing in a garden among flowers and trees but the boy's face is obscured with thick black lines like prison bars.

I turn to Pearl. 'Kaz is trying. Give him a chance. And you haven't ruined anything. Just a bad start, that's all.'

'I know,' she says, blowing her nose. 'But I can't help feeling angry.'

She throws the used paper into the steel waste bin. I think she's about to say something else but Kaz appears in the doorway. 'Can you learn to forgive me, Pearl?' His voice is sad. It reminds me of the day Tam died, and other days: too many days of sadness. 'Maybe you'd understand better if I was honest with you.'

Pearl looks Kaz square in the face. 'Honest? In what way?'

I lean against the kitchen unit. The clock ticks. Something bubbles on the stove. I dig my nails into my skin.

'I killed a man,' Kaz says.

My heart stills.

There's a sudden hiss: the pan of soup bubbling over. Pearl takes it off the heat. 'Of course you did.' Her voice is matter-of-fact. 'We were at war. Do you think I never guessed?'

'I didn't have to kill him.'

Kaz, please. Don't say anything you'll regret.

'It was almost thirty years ago, Kaz. Why do you feel the need to keep on with the guilt? Isn't that a kind of masochism? I mean, you went back to fight. You were the one who made that choice.' Pearl wipes up the burned soup from the hotplate and I look across to Kaz, my eyes pleading with him, *Not now, not now*, but his eyes are fixed on the wall.

Pearl gestures to a plate of meat and cheeses. 'Take those into the dining room, will you? We'll eat at the table. Kaz, you get the bread. It's heating in the oven. Here. Take the gloves. The metal tray will be hot. I'll bring the soup.'

Kaz looks at me. I shake my head at him, a small shake, and anyway Pearl is busy pouring the soup. He nods, and the moment is over.

*

It's a good soup, thick and warming.

'I didn't tell you, did I?' Kaz says, looking at me.

I pick up a slice of bread, and almost drop it. 'Tell me what?'

164

'What happened on my way to the airport?'

Relief floods through me. 'No,' I say. 'You didn't.'

'Almost hit a kangaroo. The roo had gone troppy—' He says the word in English.

'Troppy?' Pearl says. 'What the hell is that?'

'Someone gone crazy with the heat. Tropical.' Kaz waves a finger at us. 'Know where the word "roo" comes from?' He doesn't wait for us to answer. 'The story goes like this. White guy asks the animal's name. Black guy answers "kangaroo," which in his language means, "I don't know, mate."'

We fall about laughing. We forget that Pa is in the hospital, dying. We forget our differences and it's like that day in the snow, the three of us chasing each other, not a care in the world.

17

The past: Isara Camp, Sufra.

Grieving is a personal and highly individual experience.
Healing happens gradually; it can't be forced or hurried –
there is no 'normal' timetable for grieving.

www.takecare.org.nee/grief

I woke, the river still in my head. I'd been dreaming it but in my dream the river was awash with headless fish, and their skins gleamed cold and silver in the darkness.

Pearl and I went to fetch water, like we did every morning. The snow-capped mountains shimmered in the cold early light. The mud and puddles were frozen, and splintered as we walked on them.

'Will we see Grandma again?' Pearl reached for my hand.

'I don't know.'

'Grandma is strong.' Pearl looked up at me, blinking against the brightness of the sky.

'We're strong too,' I said, and we quickened our pace.

When it came to our turn to fill the water container Pearl

insisted, as always, on doing the task alone. She heaved the plastic container onto her shoulder and staggered back along the frozen path. Her muscles were bigger and she'd grown taller, but she'd lost weight; there wasn't an ounce of fat on her.

Halfway back to the tent, she spoke again. 'Will Kaz and Pa come back?'

'Of course they will.' I was glad Pearl was talking, even if it was painful to speak of such things.

'I want to go home.' Pearl put down the water container and started to cry.

I hugged her tight. How good it was to feel close to her again.

*

Our teacher meant well but she wasn't from our country. War hadn't touched her like it had touched us.

She asked us to write about our experiences. My writing hadn't improved – I was still learning to write with my left hand – and my words scrawled almost illegibly across the page. The girl next to me, with the scarred face, asked if she could help but I said I could manage. When Mrs Muhar came by she promised she'd try and get me a computer tablet to write with.

Pearl was at the front with Nadia. Always with Nadia. Pearl was bent over her page and didn't notice me walking over. Nadia hadn't written a word – I don't think she knew how to write – but Pearl had filled her page.

I snatched up the paper. I wanted to see what she had written. The words were beautiful but they broke my heart.

'Our life was good. I had a kitten and my family and lots of friends in my school. I had my doll and a garden with fruit trees and flowers. Then the war was happening and we ran out of everything. It snowed. It was very cold. There were tanks in our town and guns. Planes were dropping explosives. My friend's house tumbled on her and she was killed. We left our house at nine o'clock. It was dark. When we were coming along the road the car was sinking in the snow. I am always afraid when the sun goes down. I dream someone is coming to kill me.'

Nadia turned on me, her eyes like knives. 'What did you do that for? You should ask before you take.'

Nadia's paper was empty but for a small circle in the top right-hand corner which looked like the sun. I pointed to it. 'Why do you draw the sun and nothing else?'

'My Ma was killed,' Nadia said, quite without emotion. 'She got killed when the house came down. Our granny looks after us now.' She didn't mention a father. Maybe he was gone too. She jabbed at the yellow blob. 'That's the bomb. It comes down from the sky like the sun.' She scratched at her dirty hair. 'You're not the teacher. You shouldn't creep up on us like that. Give Pearl her paper back.'

'I'm giving it her back,' I said.

'What's going on?' Mrs Muhar had appeared, her usual mild tone replaced with annoyance.

'I was checking on my sister,' I said. Even to my own ears it sounded the lamest of excuses.

'She was stealing,' Nadia said. 'She stole Pearl's paper and read it.'

Mrs Muhar blinked and I saw that her eyes weren't green like Tam's eyes. They were more like the river where the weeds grew.

'I wasn't stealing,' I said. 'I was only looking.'

'May I?' Mrs Muhar said, inclining her head in Pearl's direction and ignoring our stupid squabble.

Pearl smiled and handed over the paper. 'Thank you. This is very moving. May I read it out in class later?'

'Yes,' Pearl said, her voice clear as the day outside.

'I hope you'll soon be able to forget the bad things that have happened,' Mrs Muhar added.

I doubted it. I doubted it very much. But I gave the teacher my best smile and returned to my place.

*

Pa phoned after lunch. 'Hi, Mira. How are you? Was school okay?' He sounded almost upbeat.

'It's all right. Where are you?'

'Just over the border. Is Ma there?'

'She and Pearl have gone to queue for food. There's been a delivery. I'm looking after Moe.' He was asleep on my lap, his mouth half open. 'I thought you might be going to Lyri.'

'We're in Hadiz.'

'Hadiz? Why there?' Hadiz was a sleepy little place, about thirty miles east of Zazour. I'd never been. No reason to.

'I can't say. Operational reasons.'

'It sounds quiet.' I strained my ears to catch at noise in the background but I could hear none.

'For now it is. I'll put Kaz on. He wants to speak to you.'

Kaz came to the phone but neither of us had much to say. Since that day in the cemetery we'd become almost like strangers. Then Moe woke up crying and I ended the call.

When Ma returned with Pearl, I said she'd only just missed Pa's call. She called him but he didn't pick up. Nor did Kaz. I said they were probably busy. After, she called Grandma, but again, Grandma didn't answer.

'I'm afraid for her,' Ma said, fretting and chewing at her nails. The skin was red and inflamed there from her constant chewing. 'It's been weeks now.'

'The line might be down,' I said. Grandma didn't have a mobile. She said they were too complicated.

169

'But if the line was down the phone wouldn't ring.'

'I suppose not. She could have gone to Lydia's, couldn't she?' Lydia was one of Grandma's close friends. She lived in the nearby town, five miles down the road from Grandma's village. 'I've already thought of that, Mira. Lydia's number is dead.' Ma sighed and put the mobile down on the bench. Hardly a bench. A plank of wood Kaz had dragged back from somewhere.

'We mustn't give up hope,' I said.

Ma picked up the metal box where she kept the house keys Pa had given her, and a handful of photographs from home. She opened up the box and laid the photographs out. At home we'd had mountains of photographs, carefully placed in dated albums, but these were all we had left. 'Come Mira, come Pearl. Come and look.'

Ma pointed at a picture of Pearl and me in the garden. I must have been around ten years old, and Pearl four. Ma's roses were blooming and everything looked so green and happy. Pearl had a big grin on her face and her hands were dirty. I was smiling too. I'd almost forgotten what it was like to smile. 'Do you remember that day?' Ma asked.

Pearl bent forward. Her hair, which she'd untied after school, brushed against the photo. She sprang back, almost fearfully, and scraped her hair back with her hands but all the while she was scanning the picture with her eyes as if it contained a secret she needed to decipher.

'You'd been helping me plant beans,' Ma said. 'That's why your hands are so dirty. I don't suppose you remember. You were only little.' She picked up another photo, of herself, posing, her chin resting on her hand, looking at Pa I imagine. Pearl was stood behind, hands crossed on her chest, frowning at the camera. Ma held it up for us. 'I look so young there. Not a grey hair or a wrinkle to be seen. Oh, how time flies.'

'You still look beautiful,' I said.

'Really, Mira, how you flatter me,' but she smiled all the same. Now she picked up a portrait of Pa. He wasn't smiling but his eyes twinkled, as if he'd just thought of a good joke. Ma gazed at Pa's image, then she placed the photograph against her heart, before putting it back in the metal box. 'Where's that one of Pa and Kaz together?' she said. She gathered up the photos and shuffled them like a pack of cards, and a distant, blank expression settled on her face. I glanced at Pearl, but she had her head down like a dog that's been kicked too often.

'They'll be back in a few weeks,' I said. 'Pa sounded quite cheerful on the phone.'

'We must hope for that.' A frown settled on Ma's face, until she almost resembled Pearl in the photo. 'Here's the one I was looking for.' Her expression relaxed. 'It was only taken last summer. How could we have imagined what would come to pass? That summer seems a lifetime ago to me now.'

I looked at the photo: Kaz and Pa in our courtyard. Pa squinting against the sun. Kaz with his hand on Pa's shoulder. A snapshot from an era that had passed forever.

'Pearl has a friend,' I said. 'Don't you, Pearl?'

'That's good,' Ma sounded distracted. I wondered if she'd even heard me. Moe woke from his afternoon sleep and began to cry, and Ma put the photographs away, and I fetched Moe a clean nappy and when he was cleaned up and happy again I had an idea.

'Can we have a make-up session, Pearl and I?'

'My bag is behind the couscous,' Ma said. 'What use do I have for make-up here?'

I got the make-up bag and set up the mirror on the bench, and Pearl took out Ma's lipstick and dabbed it on her lips. 'That looks pretty,' I said.

Pearl peered into the mirror. 'Oh yes, it does,' and she smiled. Moe crawled over to see what we were doing and Pearl placed two red lipstick circles on his cheeks. When he saw himself in the mirror, he giggled and we laughed.

We'll be all right. We'll pull through. That's what I was thinking, even if it was just for a moment.

*

An hour later Pearl and I walked up to the main gate. Not for any particular reason. She wasn't talking but it felt like we were friends again. There was quite a crowd gathered at the gate. When we got close, we spotted a small film crew – a blonde-haired woman wearing tight black trousers and a smart fur-lined coat, and three men with scruffy hair and thick, down jackets. In the weeks that followed, film crews would be as common as the litter that lay scattered about camp, but this crew was the first and I think we were surprised – and perhaps a little awed – to see them there.

'Maybe they'll film us,' I said, suddenly excited by the idea. The crew was recording a girl about Pearl's age. She was chattering away like a sparrow.

'How did you reach the camp?' The interviewer spoke in our language, but she kept making mistakes.

I elbowed Pearl. 'That woman sounds like a frog with a sore throat.'

'We came in the bus,' the girl said. 'It was a long way and I was with my mother and my four sisters ...'

I elbowed Pearl again. 'Why don't you say something?' Pearl was wearing her pink quilted coat and she still had traces of make-up on her eyelids. I thought her quite the prettiest girl there.

Pearl shook her head.

'What do you miss the most?' the woman continued.

'My friends.' The girl speaking had big hazel eyes and thick brown hair made up in a single plait, but she couldn't match Pearl.

'Don't be shy.' I pushed Pearl forward, but she stuck out her foot and refused to budge.

'I miss the flowers,' a boy piped up. He was waving a photograph. I couldn't see what it was.

'Chocolate,' an older girl chimed. 'We want chocolate.'

'Chocolate?' The interviewer's voice sounded false. I knew she didn't care for us. All she wanted was a story. 'I'd miss chocolate too.'

'Don't you have chocolate?' the boy waving the photograph asked, his voice plaintive. 'We'd like chocolate.'

'I'm sorry. I don't.' The woman smiled her fake smile and directed another question at the girl. 'What would you like to be when you grow up? What are your ambitions for the future?'

Who did they think they were, she and her crew, poking their cameras in our faces? And I'd have given anything for a bar of chocolate. I'm sure the kids gathered round wanted the same. There was a hunger in their eyes. 'An architect,' I called out. But the woman didn't even look my way.

'I want to be a teacher,' the first girl said, smiling for the camera.

'An engineer,' the boy with the photo pitched in.

Another boy at the front, a skinny thing with legs like a stick insect, shouted, 'A doctor. I wanna be a doctor so I can cure the injured kids.'

'That's excellent.' The woman's smile was fixed to her face like a clown's mask. 'How do you find life in camp? Are you going to school? Are you making new friends?' The crowd had grown in size and I hadn't spotted Ma at the edge, Moe in her arms.

'We're not chimpanzees in a zoo,' a boy shouted from the back.

The woman's face turned as pink as Pearl's jacket. Now she turned her attention to an older boy, a cocky kid I'd noticed

173

hanging around our part of camp. 'What about you? What brought you here?'

The boy wrinkled his nose. 'It's shit, that's what it is. You think we came here by choice, lady? The regime bombed our town, dropped all sorts of junk. They've killed whole families, babies and all. Even our pets have been killed. My town has been flattened. Nothing left but ghosts. Why don't you go and ask the regime in Lyrian why we're here in this fucking dump instead of bothering us with your questions?'

A silence fell on the crowd. I looked up at the sky. Dark clouds were passing. Like something a child might have scribbled.

'I see,' the woman said. Her cheeks were red and she was playing with her bottle-blonde hair. 'I was trying to find out how you've adapted. There was no need to be rude.'

'Adapted,' the boy sneered. 'How do you think you'd adapt to living in a tent with no running water, nothing to do all day but wait for a future that never comes?'

I clapped my hands. 'Why don't you find us some proper help instead of taking pictures? We need schools, clinics, better wash facilities ... and chocolate and crisps!' The camera fixed on me. 'Shame on you!' I clapped my hands again and some of the kids did the same. It wasn't like me, to shout and stand out in a crowd but I was so angry I couldn't stop myself.

Pearl didn't clap. She flapped her arms up and down and a thin sound came from her throat, like an engine starting up. Then she screamed, a full-on, high, wailing scream, and there was Ma, running, and all the film crew turning their heads to see what the commotion was.

Ma almost threw Moe at me. She flung her arms around Pearl and held her tight. 'We've all lost someone,' Ma shouted. The film crew was still staring at us. 'Go away. What can you do for us? No one cares for us.'

Pearl buried her head in Ma's dress and we turned our backs on the film crew and went back to the quiet of our tent. I thought Ma would be mad at me but she wasn't.

*

I called Pa. I told him about the film crew and me shouting and Pearl getting upset. He said it would be okay. That's what he always said. But when I asked to speak to Kaz, Pa said he wasn't there.

'Where is he?'

Pa didn't say anything. I shouted at him too. 'Where is Kaz?'

Ma had gone with Pearl to the washroom. Only Moe was with me.

'He's gone to Lyri; to the front line,' Pa said. 'Please don't tell your mother. She'll worry herself sick.'

'You said you weren't going to the front.'

'I'm not, Mira. It's just Kaz. He's young and fit. Not like me.'

'It's so dangerous, Pa. What if ...' I couldn't say the words and I was thinking, *It's all my fault. I know why Kaz has gone and now he's going to die because of me.*

'It's dangerous everywhere, Mira.'

Panic. A monster squeezing the oxygen from my lungs. 'Please come back, Pa. We need you here ... Won't you come back ... Won't you?'

Silence.

'Pa ... are you still there?'

'I'm still here. Kaz knows how to look after himself.'

Look after himself. How hollow Pa's words sounded. No one can dodge a bomb that falls, or run from a sniper's bullet, or avoid a mine hidden in the rubble. War is mostly luck. You either survive or you don't. There's no logic. Tam got shot and he was one of the best.

175

After my conversation with Pa, I called Grandma again. I had this mad, stupid hope that she'd answer. She didn't. I listened to the distant sound of her phone ringing, and I imagined what I'd say if she picked up. I'd tell her everything. *Everything.* The beautiful, the terrible and the sad. She'd listen and give me words of wisdom because that's what she always did. She'd understand why. She wouldn't judge. But the phone rang on and on, like a church bell ringing for the dead.

I kept my promise to Pa. I didn't breathe a word to Ma about Kaz. She knew in the end of course.

*

Another night in camp. Once, Pearl cried out and I rolled over and held her hand until she settled again. Moe whimpered and I heard Ma soothing him. Later I heard Ma crying, her muffled sobs like the soft calls of birds.

'Ma?' I whispered. 'What's wrong?'

'I can't stop thinking of home, Mira. I'm thinking of the seeds I'll never sow in the vegetable patch and the apricots and figs that will fall and rot next summer. We won't be home by then, I know it.'

'Maybe next year. Maybe then.'

'I wish I'd brought our quilt, the one your Grandma stitched, but it was too heavy. Now I'll have nothing of hers.'

'We'll get new things.'

'I don't know, Mira. I feel like the sand's running out through the glass. That it will never run back in again.'

I didn't how to answer. When I heard Ma's breathing quieten, I put on my coat and crept out of the tent to look at the stars. Whatever happened, they'd still be there after we were all gone. Though one day they too would burn out, leaving the universe dark and empty.

18

Present day: Sundsholm, Neeland.

Revenge cannot undo harm, but it can restore the balance of suffering between the victim and the offender.

www.issues_talk.com/revenge

'That went all right,' I say to Kaz when we get back to the apartment. 'Though it's a shame you didn't get to meet the boys today.'

Kaz rolls his eyes. 'I thought it was fucking awful. I mean ... for God's sake ...'

I slip off my boots, walk into the living room and sit down on the sofa. How tired I feel. Yet with Kaz here I'm sleeping better. I expected the opposite.

Kaz sits down in my blue armchair, his legs dangling over the side. 'It was fine,' I say. 'Except the moment I thought you were going to blow it for me.'

My brother gives me an odd look. 'What? Telling Pearl I killed someone?'

'Not *someone*, Kaz. Who else have you told?'

He shrugs. 'About that? No one. I only talk to my beer cans these days.' He laughs but the laugh passes as fast as a cloud on a windy day and then he closes his eyes as if he is remembering. When he opens them again, Kaz has a faraway look on his face, like the people I saw in the camp. An emptiness. Life drained out.

'You're lying. You told Pa.'

Kaz's face pales almost to the colour of his hair. 'You've talked to him about it? Why didn't you say?'

Now I'm pissed off. Big time. 'For your information, Kaz, we didn't *talk* … it wasn't a discussion. Pa just told me he knew. I walked away. I was so shocked.'

'I never imagined Pa would say anything.'

'Why wouldn't he? I'm amazed he's kept it a secret all these years.' I pick at the threads on the cushion next to me. I feel like punching Kaz. 'I trusted you. I've kept my silence and you promised. You promised.' My heart is drumming in my chest like a lunatic.

'Pa won't say anything to Pearl or Moe, I know he won't.'

'Oh, you know, do you? Are you certain of that? When did you tell him?'

He puts his head in his hands. 'Just before you all left camp. I'm sorry, Mira.' Now he looks up. How dark his eyes are: like bullet holes in his head. 'I thought I might never see him again. Or any of you. But I've not told anyone else: not Cindy, not the boys, no one.'

I feel like I'm spinning. First one direction, then another. Never coming to rest. I lean forward on the sofa. I dig my nails into the palm of my left hand. I can't do that with the other hand. It has no strength. But I have strength. I can do this. 'I'm going to make it absolutely clear, Kaz. There's no way you are going to walk in after thirty years and ruin my life. If you tell Pearl, we're finished.'

'She's not a little girl, Mira, and I didn't just "walk in", as you put it, I was invited.'

'I'm the one who has to live here.'

'Even so. You carry the weight of it too, I know you do.'

'I said no. It will only do harm. The consequences could be very serious ... for both of us. Just because it was all that time ago, doesn't make it all right. We could be prosecuted. Have you considered that?'

Kaz shifts in the chair and it creaks a little under his weight. Across the square, the church bell tolls seven. 'Maybe it's a chance we have to take. Do you think Pa ever said anything to Ma?'

'It's possible, yet I doubt it.' I think back to when Ma was diagnosed with the cancer that killed her. How once she said that she and Pa had no secrets. But I didn't believe that. We all keep something of ourselves back.

'About Ma's funeral. I don't blame you all for being angry at me for not attending. I've been a selfish bastard. I want to make it up to you but I'm not sure how.' Kaz gets up and starts pacing round my living area, not that there is much scope to pace, and he takes up so much room. 'Oh God, Mira, I don't know how to live with it, any of it. What should I do?' He's almost shouting now.

'Keep your voice down, Kaz. I have neighbours.'

He sits down. He's shaking and won't look at me. It was a mistake, him coming here. I thought I'd put the past behind me, but the past will never let me go. But now we have to go and see Pa. I tap my watch. 'It's time we went to the hospital. Pearl's expecting us.'

'What if Pa says something to Pearl?'

'He won't. He'll have forgotten.' But I'm not sure of that any more, not sure at all.

*

Pearl is at Pa's bedside. Pa is awake, sitting up in bed. There's a beaker of water on his table and a tablet open to the news. I'm surprised to see he's been reading the news. He used to read the paper from cover to cover every day, and Ma would do the crossword, but he stopped reading a while ago. I wonder who opened the tablet. I doubt it was Pearl. Perhaps it was Kerstin, the nurse, or one of the other patients. Pa won't remember what he's read; his short-term memory is impaired. But his long-term memory is almost perfect.

'Here we all are.' Pearl's voice is bright but her eyes are swollen as if she's been crying. 'Look, Pa!'

Pa stares at Kaz, blinks, looks again. For a moment I wonder if he won't know this middle-aged and overweight man with his white hair, but a smile breaks out across Pa's face and he says, 'Kaz, my dear boy. Good to see you.' As if Kaz had only been gone a few months, not those years and years.

Pearl taps me on the shoulder and whispers, 'I'm surprised Pa knows who Kaz is after all this time.'

'Pa. Dear Pa.' Kaz reaches over and gives Pa a gentle hug. 'It's been too long.'

'Has it? How long? I can't remember.' Pa scratches at his eyebrow. He always does this when he's trying to catch on to something that he's lost.

Pearl and I exchange glances. She leans close to me. 'The prodigal son returns.'

I nod but I'm shaking inside. Can't Pearl see how nervous I am? Perhaps not. It's amazing what we're able to conceal from each other.

'It has been quite a while,' Kaz says. His understatement is almost comical but Pearl and I aren't smiling. 'It's good to see you, Pa. How are you?'

'How am I?' Pa grins. His mouth is cracked and sore. I must ask the nurse for something to help this. 'I'm rotten, Kaz, quite rotten.'

'You don't look so bad,' Kaz says in a light-hearted kind of manner, but he's not feeling light-hearted; none of us is. His legs are twitching again, and there are beads of sweat on his forehead.

I fetch another chair from near the window, and nod to the other two patients. They have no visitors this evening. I sit down. 'I hardly recognised Kaz at the airport,' I say to Pa. My voice sounds falsely upbeat, like the interviewer in the camp, a woman I've never been able to forget. I wonder what she's doing now, if she's even still alive. 'How changed he is. Look at his hair. You'd think he'd been out in the snow for the past few years. Though I don't think they have snow in Australia.'

Pa peers at Kaz. 'Changed? We're all changed. At least Kaz has hair. I have almost none left these days.'

There's a strange smell in the ward, like decaying leaves. Usually the ward smells of disinfectant and lavender oil. 'How are you feeling today?' I ask Pa. 'You look a little brighter.' Anything to distract.

'What do you think?' His forehead puckers in a frown but then he raises a thin, papery hand and says, 'But I'm happy to see you all.'

'We're not all here,' Pearl says, almost irritably. 'Moe isn't with us.'

'Moe will be coming soon,' I say.

Pa smiles but this time there's no spark in his eyes. 'I'm dying. That's the reason you're here.' He raises his hand again. 'Don't try and tell me otherwise. We have enough secrets in this family.'

What does he mean, secrets? But he only says, 'I wish your mother could have seen us together like this.' He looks at Kaz, but Kaz is studying his boots and does not react.

'The nurse says you ate some dinner,' Pearl says, tugging at a sparkly earring. Diamond, I think. New. Perhaps Stefan bought them for their wedding anniversary.

'The food isn't good.' Pa wrinkles his nose. He has a feeding tube and I've only ever seen him eat the smallest of morsels and I wonder if Pearl's statement is true or if the nurse exaggerated. Kaz must be shocked, seeing Pa all skin and bones, but if he is, he's not showing it.

'Hospital food is never good,' Kaz says, looking up from his boots. Relief spreads through me. We're on safer ground now. Next our conversation moves on to Kaz's flight and the snowy weather. After a while, Pearl and I leave Pa with Kaz and walk to the hospital cafe. We don't want to tire Pa and we have practical issues to discuss. I'm uneasy leaving Kaz alone with Pa, but to stay behind might make Pearl suspicious.

In the fluorescent light of the cafe, Pearl's face looks tired. We wait at the shiny counter; it's always busy at this time in the evening. Ahead of us in the queue there's a heavily pregnant woman and a family of five. The man is tall and skinny, with blue-black skin. His wife is small and fair skinned with that white-blonde hair you only see in this part of the world. When we first arrived in Neeland, interracial marriages were almost unheard of but now they are common.

Pearl buys me a coffee, and a mineral water for herself. 'Kaz seems to have perked Pa up. I wasn't sure how he'd react, whether Pa would even know him.'

'Yes,' I say. I pick up my coffee and take a sip. Suddenly I don't feel like drinking it.

'How are things with Kaz? Has he said much?' Pearl's gaze is like a beam from a lighthouse. She has an uncanny ability to sniff out secrets and scandal. But not with me. She thinks she knows me, but she doesn't. She has no idea.

A baby starts to cry. His mother picks him up and tries to

soothe him. 'We haven't talked about the past, not really. He's definitely not drinking and he seems adamant his sobriety will last, but who knows.' I stop. I'm not quite sure what I want to say. 'It's weird having him around after such a long time.'

Pearl fiddles with her earring again. 'It makes me happy to see him and Pa getting along. I could almost forgive him.' The baby wails. Pearl turns her head and makes a face. 'Those days, eh? You remember how Lucas used to screech endlessly?'

I nod and smile.

'Oscar was easier. They say the second is often easier.' Now she's biting her thumbnail. 'I never understood why Kaz and Pa had to leave us in the camp and go off and fight.' Her lip trembles. She picks up her glass. Puts it down again. A tear runs down her cheek and another. This isn't what I expected.

I fish in my bag for a tissue. No one is looking at us. A woman weeping in a hospital is nothing out of the ordinary. I pass Pearl the tissue and turn my gaze to the large plate glass window. Below, the lights of the city pulsate in the darkness. *I know why Kaz chose to fight, Pearl. If you knew the whole truth, I doubt we'd even be sitting here together.* I say nothing. I don't trust my words, any of my words. Perhaps that's how Pearl felt all those years ago – that words were not to be trusted. I almost think to ask her about it. I don't. Of course I don't. The past is dangerous territory. Pearl is right. It's best we don't go there too often.

*

Pa has fallen asleep and Kaz is sitting in the chair with his eyes closed. He startles when we appear.

'He won't wake up again, not until the nurse comes for night duty.' Pearl turns to me. 'Why doesn't Kaz come and stay with us tomorrow? We have much more room in our house. What do you think, Kaz? You can get to know my boys and my husband, Stefan.'

'Thanks,' Kaz says. 'I'd like that.' He glances at me for approval. I shrug and zip up my coat and we walk down the long corridor and out into the car park.

*

Kaz and I are sitting in my kitchen again. Talking. It's late. Maybe it's too late for talking. For any talking. The church bell has just struck one and the square is deserted – not even a cat moves across it – and I shiver, thinking of our town, how empty it was that day Kaz and I walked together in the snow.

We have to tell her, he's saying and I'm saying we don't.

Now he sighs and leans forward, his chin in his hands. 'It's poison, Mira. Like a splinter that needs extracting.'

'I said no.' I pick up my tea but it has gone cold.

Kaz's lip trembles. 'I can't live like this anymore.' He starts to cry.

I get up and put my arms around him. It's strange hugging him after all these years. We never hugged much when we were kids. His body is soft. He smells faintly of sweat and cheap aftershave. 'I'm the one to blame. I thought of the idea,' I say.

'We're both equally to blame and if there is blame ...' He pulls away. 'I've done worse, much worse, Mira.'

'What have you done?'

A loud knocking on the front door stops me in my tracks.

'Are you expecting someone?' Kaz asks. His face has turned paler than the snow outside.

'No,' I say. 'And normally people use the intercom; someone must have let them in through the front entrance.'

'I'll come with you to the door. Just in case.'

184

My heart is beating fast. I'm almost expecting the police or someone from the justice department. But it's only Tomas. With snow on his woollen hat. 'Sorry, but I have nowhere to go. I cannot stay in that place.'

'It's okay, Tomas. Come in.'

When Tomas sees Kaz, he steps back into the hallway. 'Who this?'

'My brother, Kaz.'

I make us all a hot drink. I find biscuits. Kaz gives me a curious look but I shrug him off. I'll explain everything in the morning.

19

The past: Isara Camp, Sufra.

'The exact numbers of people missing throughout the world today is not known, although we estimate that it runs into the hundreds of thousands. The lack of accurate figures is a problem. However, numbers on their own can never convey the depth of suffering endured in each individual case.'

Barbara D.A. Watson, Chairwoman - This is our World

The days passed, one much the same as the other. A fortnight went by, a month, then two. Some days we heard from Pa, sometimes he didn't call in a week. Kaz rarely got in touch. He told us not to call; that it could be dangerous for him – and us. Ma disagreed but she had to concede, we both did. Then a time came when we stopped hearing from him altogether.

The rains ceased and the camp dried out. No longer did we have to negotiate our way along muddy paths, or sit, shivering, night after night. For a brief time, the air was mild and the earth soft and green. But soon the weather turned hot and windy and the earth turned to a fine dust that covered everything and got into our hair, our ears and eyes, a dust to grit the teeth and drive us crazy. Snakes and scorpions arrived with the heat. Pearl was terrified of the scorpions but Nadia didn't care; she stamped on them and laughed.

In Zazour, spring often lasted into the month of June. How I missed seeing the blossom flowering, the myriad white flowers dotting the pavements like confetti. But we'd heard reports that many people had fled our town; that the marketplace had been bombed, killing over twenty.

A nagging wind tugged at our tent all night long and the flapping of the canvas kept us awake. But one night, I woke to silence. Nothing moved. No one called. I lay on the mattress, my ears alert like a dog's. I could hear only my own heart beating. As if the camp had vanished in the night.

*

'How did you sleep?' I asked Ma, as I wiped away the sweat from my forehead. The sun was up and the temperature was rising fast but Pearl still slumbered, her bare arm laid across the blanket.

'The life of the dead is preferable to this,' Ma said, blinking and sitting up. She'd aged in the time we'd been in camp. Her dark hair was now streaked with silver and her skin had turned dry and blotchy. 'I never sleep well. I can't stop myself worrying. The only one I don't worry about is Moe. He seems happy enough.' She glanced at Pearl. 'Does she ever talk to you?'

'The odd word. If I'm lucky.'

'But she chatters to this friend of hers, am I right?'

'Nadia ...yes.'

'Why won't she talk to us?' Ma scooped her hair back from her face and tied it back with an elastic tie band. The effect was rather severe.

'I wish I knew.'

'Do you think we should get her some help? Someone to talk to?'

'But who? There aren't even enough doctors to cover our basic needs let alone specialists to deal with trauma. She'll come round ... in time.'

'You think?'

I didn't know what I thought. Probably I didn't want to think at all. I shrugged and pulled on my jeans and T-shirt. 'I'll fetch the water this morning,' I said, and I headed outside. The wind was still blowing dust across the camp, whipping up the litter, stinging my eyes and obscuring the distant mountains. I felt like we'd been abandoned, as if we were no more than the plastic bags caught on the barbed wire fences, or the dust itself.

*

I started asking questions. I asked if anyone had relatives who'd gone north to Europe, or if they themselves were planning to leave. Few people had left in those early days of the camp: most were still hoping to go home. Some looked at me as if I were a traitor, or as if I what I was suggesting was indecent. Others said they might consider travelling but not one person gave me a scrap of useful information.

I said nothing to Ma or Pearl. But the idea of leaving became an obsession with me and I began counting the days like a person waiting for deliverance from prison.

A week later, on my way back from school with Pearl and Nadia, I spotted the boy who'd sworn and shouted at the interviewer. I'd seen him about before but he'd always been in the company of older boys, the kind of boys I avoided. That day he was alone. I slowed my pace. Pearl was whispering something to Nadia, their heads almost touching. 'You and Nadia walk on. I won't be long.'

Pearl sent me a bad look.

'Is he your boyfriend?' Nadia asked, nodding in the boy's direction.

I felt my cheeks redden. 'I don't have a boyfriend and I don't want one.'

Nadia put her head to one side and folded her arms across her thin chest. 'I bet you're gay.'

'Just because I don't want a boyfriend doesn't mean I'm a lesbian.'

Pearl giggled.

'Get lost,' I said. 'It's none of your business.'

'Someone's in a mean mood,' Nadia sneered. 'Are you about to get your period?'

Pearl was no longer giggling but there was a horrible sneer on her face. 'What are you smirking for?' I spat out the words. When she didn't answer, I turned on Nadia. 'What the fuck is wrong with her?'

'She doesn't like you.' Nadia stuck out her tongue and moved it from side to side in a crude gesture. 'If you're not a lezzie, why don't you kiss him? Or are you too scared?'

'Piss off.' I raised my hand at her while the boy looked on, amused.

'All right,' Nadia said, backing off. 'We know when we're not wanted, don't we, Pearl?' She wagged her finger at me. 'If you get a baby, Grandma knows what to do. But it costs. Or you get can married. You're old enough to get married.'

'I'm not old enough. I'm only fifteen.'

'You'll be sixteen soon. Pearl told me. I know loads of girls married at your age. Some of them get married at twelve.'

'Liar.'

'I'm not a liar. There's a girl in the next tent expecting a baby next month. She's fourteen.'

'That's gross.'

'The girls get money. That's why they like the old men because the old men pay best, see.' Nadia flicked her fingers at the boy, who was still staring at us, almost open-mouthed. 'I wouldn't put your hand down her knickers cos she might bite your balls off.' She giggled, and Pearl giggled with her. 'Come on Pearl. Let's go.' She took Pearl's hand and they disappeared behind a tent.

The boy was openly laughing now. 'That one's grown up fast.' Then his face turned serious. 'A lot of the kids do here. It's no place for kids.'

'She's my sister's friend, not mine.'

The boy pushed up his mirrored glasses and lit a cigarette. When he saw I wasn't moving, he gave me a hard stare. 'What is it you want?'

'I want to go to Europe. If I stay here much longer I'll go stir crazy.'

He kicked at the dust and laughed again. 'I'm surprised you're not crazy already. Everyone else here is. Seen those kids playing war games? They're crazy.' He tapped his temple with his finger. 'And that guy talking to himself ... know what he's saying?'

I shook my head.

'He's asking for his son and daughter. He thinks they're somewhere in the camp. Every day he asks. But they're both dead, stone dead, killed in the street by a car bomb. Left in bits. Like old bloodied rags.' He took a puff on the cigarette. 'Want one?'

'No thanks.'

'Just you, is it, wanting to go?'

'No. There's my mother, my little sister – the one you just saw, not the other one – and my baby brother.' I thought about Pa and Kaz. My throat tightened.

'My father is gone too.' The boy's voice had softened.

'Gone?'

'Killed in a rocket attack last month.' His right hand flew to his chest but when he saw me looking he removed it.

'I'm sorry.'

He shrugged. 'Don't be. It happens all the time. It's the new normal.'

The new normal. I understood what he was talking about. It was when you didn't even turn your head seeing kids walking on crutches or missing a leg. When you saw men weeping in public and women scrabbling for food, shoving each other out of the way. When you accepted living in a tent and sleeping on a thin mattress and having less than half an education and no books and no new clothes and nothing to dream about. That's what he meant.

'My brother and father have gone back to fight,' I said.

Another normal.

The boy pulled down his sunglasses. 'You're leaving without them?' He didn't sound surprised.

'Yes … I mean …'

'I should go and fight.' He puffed on the cigarette and blew a smoke ring. The ring floated into the air and vanished. 'But I don't want my guts ripped out, my legs blown off, my brains blasted all over the street. Some people would call me a coward. At least girls don't feel like they have to. Fight that is.' He stopped. Dragged on the cigarette.

'No. I suppose not.'

He blew another smoke ring. 'I know someone but it's not cheap. Only life is cheap here.'

I asked the price, and he named a fee and I tried not to gasp at the amount. I wasn't sure we'd be able to get that much money together, or if Ma would agree, but I had to try.

'Still interested?' The cigarette had burned out and he held the butt between his two fingers. I could feel him staring at me through his dark glasses.

'I didn't come here just to chat.'

'All right. It's a deal. When you're ready come and find me.'

'I don't know your name. Mine's Mira.'

'Mira? Nice name.' He dropped the cigarette end and squashed it with his training shoe. There was a hole in one of the toes. 'I got rid of my old name when I came here. It's safer to be someone else. Now it's Fixer. I fix things, see? I live here.' He pointed to the sagging tent behind him, its roof covered in a blue plastic sheet; a dirty, patterned rug hung over the entrance for shade. 'You know where to find me.' He sighed, and I thought how vulnerable he looked in that moment, the pose all gone. 'Don't take too long to make a decision. That's my advice. I'm thinking of going myself. Maybe we'll take the same boat, eh?'

'Maybe.'

He pulled down his sunglasses and disappeared inside.

*

I found Ma stirring a pan of lentils. 'Where's Pearl?'

'Isn't she here?'

Moe staggered in my direction. He'd started to walk but he hadn't yet got good at it and he fell down before he reached me and started yelling. He could yell pretty loud for such a small boy with wheezy lungs. I picked him up. 'Goodness, Moe,' I said, rubbing my nose against his, 'You weigh a ton.'

'Mira,' Ma said sharply. 'Where's your sister?'

'I left them five minutes ago. They were walking so slowly. Pearl was with Nadia. Maybe she's gone there.'

'Well go and find her. Lunch is ready.' Ma wiped her forehead with the back of her hand. 'God, it's so hot today. I miss my old kitchen. I don't know how I could've ever complained about it.' She waved her hands in the air. 'This isn't a kitchen.'

'Has Pa called today?' I didn't ask about Kaz.

She shook her head. 'Not yet.' Ma took the pan off the heat. 'Scoot. We don't want anyone else to go missing.'

I gathered Moe in my arms and set off for Nadia's. As I had guessed, that's where Pearl had gone. She was standing at the far end of the tent, her back turned to Nadia and the little brother. There were three other kids there, skinny creatures in tatty dirty clothes and with bare feet, but I couldn't see the grandmother. The tent itself was a mess, everything spilling out: pots and pans, unwashed plates, an old bucket leaning on its side. We kept our tent tidy.

'What's the time Mr Wolf?' Nadia called out.

'Two o'clock,' Pearl said. 'One ... two ...'

Nadia and the other kids took two steps forward. Pearl turned her head. 'You're dead,' she said, pointing at the youngest and smallest. 'I saw you moving.' When she spotted me, she closed her mouth tight.

'Lunch is ready. Ma wants you back now,' I said.

'Oh, it's you again.' Nadia glared at me; fury in her eyes. 'Didn't it work out with the boyfriend?'

'We got married.' I patted my stomach. 'The baby's due next week.'

The kids giggled and nudged each other.

'Ha, ha,' Nadia said. 'Very funny.'

'Isn't it? Come on, Pearl, or Ma will get mad.'

Pearl didn't argue. She came with me and said not a word.

*

In the afternoon, we went to the clinic. Moe needed a vaccination and Ma wanted someone to check his chest. He wasn't coughing any more but he was still wheezy. And I needed my hand examined. It wasn't painful – though it ached at times – but the fingers were useless. Pearl said she wanted to go and play with

Nadia. But Ma said no. Pearl didn't speak another word after that.

The clinic was in a large tent. Inside, there were a few hard chairs and three screened-off areas for the doctor and the two nurses. All the chairs were taken and so we sat on the floor, just as we did at school. The place was crowded and noisy: kids crying and running around, women gossiping, and a few older men chatting at the rear. Others were silent. Like Pearl. Like the old grandmother with wrinkled skin who kept pulling at her bony fingers. Like the trembling boy who clung to his mother's skirts.

I plucked at Ma's sleeve. 'We should start thinking about leaving. There are so many people in camp now. It's only going to get worse.'

'Maybe,' Ma said, cautious as ever. 'Your father was talking about renting a place in town … when he gets back.'

'And how long will it take him to find somewhere when he comes back?' I nearly said 'if', but I didn't want to upset Ma. 'The rents are going up. I'm talking about us leaving altogether, going abroad. Rey and her family have gone. Others have gone too.'

'Have you heard from Rey?'

I felt my heart grow heavy again. 'Not a whisper, Ma.'

Ma sighed. 'I'll have to talk to your father.'

'Well, talk to him or I will. I'm not staying in this hellhole.'

Ma waved her finger at me. 'Enough, Mira. Now is not the time or the place.' She twisted the gold bracelet on her arm, the one Grandma had given her when she got married. I wondered if she would agree to sell it.

We waited and waited, until at last one of the nurses called Ma's name and took us into a small screened area. It wasn't like our surgery back in Zazour with its modern equipment and clean tiled floor. Here, there was just a small fridge, a couple of chairs and a narrow bed covered in a plastic sheet.

The nurse was brisk but efficient. When the needle went in, Moe opened his eyes wide but he didn't cry.

It was another hour before we got to see the doctor. His area wasn't much better equipped. The doctor said Moe was fine, though we should keep an eye on him. As for me, he said I might need further surgery but he couldn't offer it. Not then.

'I wonder if you could check my younger daughter's throat,' Ma asked, pushing Pearl forward. I expected Pearl to resist but she didn't.

The doctor pressed his hands against Pearl's neck and peered inside her mouth with a small torch. 'I can't see any sign of infection or swelling. Has she been complaining?'

'She hardly speaks,' I said. 'But she talks to her new friend.'

Ma coloured up but Pearl sat on the chair, still as a statue, her face blank.

'Her muteness is probably due to psychological factors. Perhaps she feels safer with her friend. There's so much need here but we can only offer assistance to the most severe cases.' The doctor turned back to Pearl and smiled. He had a kind face but there was an angry scar on his forehead. 'So you have a new friend?'

Pearl didn't say anything but she gave the doctor a little nod.

'Try and be patient with her,' the doctor said, addressing Ma. 'I'm sure the problem will pass.'

Ma smiled politely, and we left the clinic. The doctor had meant well but he had offered nothing of substance. On the way back to the tent, my frustration spilled over. 'Why are you doing this?' I yelled at Pearl.

'Shh,' Ma said. 'You heard what the doctor said.'

'I don't want to go away,' Pearl said, angrily. 'You can't make me.'

'Well, well,' I said. 'Isn't it amazing how you suddenly get your voice back when you want something?' I felt people's eyes on me but I didn't care.

'Mira, that's quite enough,' Ma said.

'It's true. Why pretend otherwise.' I kicked at the dust with my foot. Then I shut up. There was no point arguing. I was a hypocrite. I had no right to sit in judgement. We were all living a pretence. Perhaps that's what we had to do. To survive. Yet Pearl's silence hurt. It hurt like a knife. And when I thought of that I almost choked.

*

The following morning, I woke early and went outside, alone. The sun rose yellow as a sunflower. The wind was gone, and in the distance the mountains were pale and delicate, like a Chinese watercolour painting. Everything looked perfect, but it wasn't. I felt trapped. Like a fly in amber.

I was still sitting there when Pearl walked out with the water bucket.

'I'm not coming with you today,' I said, still mad at her. 'Get Nadia to help or go by yourself.'

I was jealous of Pearl's friendship, but something else was bothering me. Like many of the kids in the camp Nadia had probably witnessed stuff she ought never to have seen. Now I wondered what she'd told Pearl. My sister was always drawing houses; not happy, sunlit houses, but shuttered and exploded houses. Houses inside bird cages. Houses with thick bars at the windows. Houses struck by lightning, storms and floods. Houses with monstrous eyes on the walls. Houses dripping blood. I'd always imagined she'd made these drawings in response to what had happened to the family opposite ours but now I wasn't so sure.

After Pearl returned with the water, we ate our meagre breakfast and went to class. We picked up Nadia on the way. She had her youngest brother in tow, a small, thin boy with sores on his mouth and a mass of uncombed black hair. I don't recall the boy's name, but I remember how he picked at those sores and how he was missing the middle finger of his left hand. And how he trembled. Like a leaf in a storm.

'Why does he shake?' Pearl asked Nadia. She spoke the words quietly but not so quiet I couldn't hear.

'He got like it after they bombed the house,' Nadia said in a matter-of-fact voice.

'That's funny,' Pearl said in response. It was as they were discussing a cake recipe together.

At school Nadia and Pearl sat together at the front as usual, heads together. I don't know where the brother went. I sat at the back. The girl with the burned face wasn't there and at break I got talking to a girl my age from Kanya, a village close to Zazour. The girl was friendly, but I missed Rey and I wasn't in the mood for chatting.

'How was your morning?' I asked Pearl when our lessons were over. When she shrugged and said nothing, I saw red again. 'TALK! Stop pretending.'

'She doesn't want to talk to you,' Nadia said, grabbing Pearl's hand. 'You squeal like a pig. Oink, oink.' She turned to Pearl. 'You walk with me.'

I watched them go, even though I'd promised Ma I'd keep Pearl close. Then I marched off angrily in the opposite direction. The camp had grown considerably since we'd arrived. It was almost like a real town. There was the school, the clinic, the administrative offices, and rows of stalls that sold cigarettes, cheap household goods, even fruit and vegetables – if you could afford such items. But it had no parks, houses or tree-lined squares. No singing river. No reeds, bridge, fish or heron.

A group of kids passed and a boy shouted, 'Watch out, cow-face or my Kalashnikov will blow your face off.' He waved a stick at me. I told him to shut up and go away but he laughed.

Further on I came across a barefoot boy running around with a plastic machine gun. He couldn't have been more than five or six years old. He pointed his gun in the face of another boy. This boy fell to the ground and played dead. The barefoot boy poked the gun into the other boy's chest and then kicked him. The boy playing dead jumped up. 'You're not supposed to do that,' he said. 'It's not in the rules.'

'There are no rules.' The barefoot boy poked his toy gun into the other boy's thin chest. 'I'm taking you to prison. The guards will hang you up from your feet and beat you till you die.'

I was about to protest, but when the boys saw me looking they ran off.

Large numbers of kids were always gathered in the area close to the boundary fence. A group of boys was playing football, kicking up the dirt. In another corner a huddle of girls took turns with a skipping rope. I leant against the fence and watched the football. The game was moving fast and there was plenty of shouting. After a while, my eyes were drawn to two boys carrying a sheet of corrugated iron. One wore a grubby blue sweatshirt, the other, in green, had a mop of bright red hair. A third boy, younger than the others, was lying on the corrugated iron, eyes closed, his hands clasped across his chest.

The girls who'd been skipping, wandered over.

'Is he shot?' one asked.

'Yes,' the boy in the grubby sweatshirt said. 'He's shot and he's dead. We're burying him now.'

'Is he a martyr?' another girl asked.

The red-headed boy nodded and off they walked, the girls following behind in a line, their heads bowed; a silent funeral procession.

The wind had got up again. It blew dust devils, tugged at the lines of washing and chased the litter round and round in circles. I felt a tap on my arm. I spun round. At my side was ragged looking girl with dark, curly hair – like a younger version of Nadia. She carried a doll in her arms, but its chubby, plastic legs were covered in red marks. 'Those are bullet holes,' she said, looking up at me.

'You need a bandage,' I said. 'Do you have a handkerchief? You could use that.'

The girl shook her curls. 'It's too late. She's dead. She bled to death, see? I'm going to bury her with the boy.' She pointed in the direction of the boys carrying the bier. 'That boy is dead too.' And off she ran, her cheap pink plastic sandals sending up dust that flew into my eyes.

What is this place, I thought, that puts wool in my sister's mouth, and has children playing war games and drawing pictures of bombed houses?

A cramp gripped my belly. I should go back: Ma would be worrying.

I walked to the main gate. A truck revved its engine close to where a woman soothed a crying child with soft words. I went on. Past a child on a makeshift swing and an old man with haunted eyes. Past the cigarette seller and two boys on ancient bicycles. That's what I saw, and a thousand other images I no longer remember.

*

'Where's Pearl?'

'She's gone to Nadia's.'

'For goodness sake, Mira. You're supposed to keep an eye on her.'

I stood in the middle of the tent, my arms folded across my breasts. The cramping in my stomach had worsened. 'I'm not her keeper.'

'She's your sister. She's only nine.'

Another spasm had me clutching at my stomach.

'What's with you?'

'My period's coming on.'

Ma sighed. 'Sort yourself out first, then go and get Pearl, will you? I have some pads left but we need to get some more – if there are any to be found.'

*

Nadia's grandmother was sitting in the middle of the tent; Nadia's brother was with her, and several other children of varying ages, all dressed in clothes that looked like they needed a good wash. An older girl stood by the stove, stirring a large pot. A smell of stale sweat and spices mingled in the overheated air.

'Where's Nadia?' the grandmother asked.

'I thought she and my sister were coming here.'

'They're not here, as you can see.' The grandmother gestured with her gnarled hands. 'I haven't seen Nadia since she left for school this morning.'

A wave of nausea passed through me. 'Do you know where they might have gone?'

The grandmother shook her head. 'Nadia's a stubborn little creature. She's gone missing before but she always comes back.'

'Missing?'

The girl at the stove stopped her stirring. She was desperately thin, with black eyes like stones and thick, tangled hair which resembled Nadia's; perhaps she was an older sister, or a cousin. 'Last time Nadia was gone for three days. Nanny got very cross.' She spoke with a slight lisp.

'That's right,' the grandmother added. 'We've no idea where she went. She wouldn't say, not even when I tried to thrash it out of her, the little vixen.'

I fled, into the hot, dusty afternoon.

20

Present day: Blau Lakken, Valsby.

It is essential to establish whether recovered bones are of human or animal origin. Whereas the answer to the question may be obvious when a full set of skeletonised remains are present, a great deal more expertise is needed when only a few or even a single bone is found.

OurMissing.com/identification processes

Kaz said he'd walk to Pearl's house. I protested that it was too far, but he said he needed to walk, to clear his head. I wanted to install GPS on his mobile but he said he'd rather just wander and anyway, he knew the general direction and wouldn't get lost. We almost had an argument about it.

Tomas left early. He wouldn't even eat breakfast. Said he was in a hurry. I made him promise to call into the office before midday, but he hasn't turned up yet. I've called several times but he's not picking up.

All morning I make enquiries in between seeing my other clients, but I don't find Tomas anywhere to stay. I can't allow him to sleep out tonight. It's far too cold and he's vulnerable. Anything could happen. But I don't tell anyone here he stayed with me last night. We're supposed to maintain professional relationships with our clients.

At lunchtime I ask Anna for the afternoon off. 'I need to go and see my father,' I say.

'Has he taken a turn for the worse?'

I hesitate. I should tell her the truth, that I'm tired and can't concentrate, but I decide to lie; but then, I've lying my whole life. 'There's something I have to discuss with him. It can't wait.'

'You go,' she says but she gives me a sideways glance and I wonder if she believes me.

Back in the apartment I make myself a coffee and click on to the Missing site. There's nothing new. I check my personal mail. No message from Eka. And no one on the blog. Nothing on Mimi either. No calls. No messages. It's lonely in the apartment without Mimi and now I'm thinking the worst. In this weather cats and dogs can freeze to death overnight – people too. They say that no news is good news but I'm not sure that's true. I feel like I'm living in a twilight zone, where nothing is certain and even the shadows can't be trusted.

I sit by the window. Every now and again a flurry of snow dances across the square, blown by the icy wind. I close my eyes and focus on Grandma's lake but the image I conjure up is fuzzy and unclear and I can't hold it. Instead, the Blue Lake at Valsby floats into my mind. It's a lovely place, forty minutes north of the city and perhaps the only location I cherish in this country. With my hand curled around the coffee cup, I summon up the long summer days I've spent there, alone and with family: the bees drowsily humming in the honey-scented heather, the warmth of the lichen-studded rocks, the swallows diving for insects, their wings almost touching the clear blue water.

I open my eyes. I pick up my mobile.

'Driverless or accompanied?' the woman at the taxi office asks.

'I'm going out of town.'

'In that case you'll have to have a driver. Where to?'

'The Blue Lake at Valsby.'

'Are you sure? There are no houses out there and ... well, it's snowing. I'll have to ask if he's okay with it.'

'Please,' I say. 'It's important.'

I hear the operator talking to someone on the other line. When she returns she says, 'He'll be with you in twenty minutes.'

'*He*,' she says again. These days the daytime drivers are often women. Still, I don't give it much thought.

I pull on my thick fur-lined boots and down jacket, and dig out my gloves and the striped woollen hat Lucas and Oscar gave me last Christmas. I'm already waiting outside the building when the taxi pulls up. The driver turns his head when I step into the back of the cab; he is a handsome man with high cheekbones, a grizzled beard and bright blue eyes. Not my type though.

'Blau Lakken?' It's a question, not a statement. The driver is frowning. He has deep wrinkles on his forehead. Like a man who's spent much of his life outdoors.

'Didn't the operator tell you?'

'I thought perhaps there was a mistake.'

'No mistake,' I say irritably. 'Why? Is it a problem?'

'No problem.' He turns away from me and switches the taxi into drive-mode.

In ten minutes we've reached city's hinterland. We pass a row of large, metal storage sheds and a series of small farms. The farm buildings are mostly traditional in style, built of wood, with high gables for the winter snows. Out here there are forests of firs, dark and thick, their branches heavy with winter snow, and stands of elegant birch trees with mottled, silvery bark.

The driver and I don't talk much on the journey although I make a few remarks about the scenery, and he says, 'Yes, I grew up here. I know this place like the back of my hand,' but he asks no more questions.

*

He waits in the taxi but I see he's looking at me, checking I'm not about to step onto the ice. Here, it's far colder than in Sundsholm. A freezing wind is barrelling down from the north, blowing white flurries off the tree branches and the sky is pearly-grey, a paler imitation of the pebbles on the shoreline. The stones are frozen together and, where the ice meets the water's edge, it has formed frills like the lacy edge of an old-fashioned petticoat. Stalks of frozen grass and rushes poke through in places. Further out, the icy surface is snow-covered, and the relentless wind has blown the snow into a series of serried ridges, almost blue in colour. There is beauty here, but it's a bleak and desolate beauty.

I turn my head again. The driver is reading a paperback.

As I walk along the shoreline, I start to shiver. Even in my warm clothes the cold is seeping into my body. It wouldn't take long to die in a place like this. I think of the dreams I once had; Tam and I living by Grandma's lake, children of our own. Those were girlish fantasies. Yet not even in my worst nightmare could I have imagined how our country and our family's life would play out. I have a good life here; I shouldn't keep looking over my shoulder. But Kaz has brought the weight of the past with him, and it is such a heavy burden.

I head towards a stand of birch trees. In midwinter the sun barely skims the horizon; already the temperature is plummeting fast. I stamp my feet and place my gloved hands deep in my jacket pockets. I'm perhaps half a mile from the taxi now. It looks lonely up there on the ridge and I wonder what the driver thinks of me, this crazy woman wanting to walk around a frozen lake.

The clouds suddenly part. A ray of sunlight falls onto the lake's frozen surface and it shimmers like a thousand spider's webs caught in early morning grass. Too soon the light is gone. Time for me to go too.

Close to the taxi, a reindeer bounds out from the fir forest. It freezes when it spots me. I, too, stop moving, not wishing to frighten it. It's a magnificent beast, half-coloured white like the snow, with patches of slate and dun like the bark of the trees. There's a yellow tag on its ear. I remember the deer I saw in the forest when we were fleeing our country and I think, *I'm still fleeing, still running.* But perhaps we always are, in one sense, fleeing from ourselves and our secrets, from the things we do not wish to face.

We gaze at each other, the deer and I. Then it bounds off and I soon lose sight of it.

'You were lucky to see that,' the driver says, as I get into the taxi.

'It was lucky,' I say.

We move off, down the road. 'Are you warm enough? You're shivering.'

'It's cold out there today.'

He turns up the heating. 'Coldest day so far this season, I reckon.'

'I think so, yes.'

'A boy drowned in the lake last year. Did you read about it?'

'No, I didn't. How awful.'

'He went out on the ice too early, and fell through. He wasn't a kid: he was nineteen.'

Nineteen – the same age Tam had been when he was killed by the sniper. I start to cry; not small, silent tears but wrenching sobs that wrack my body. I can scarcely breathe. I gulp air like a drowning fish.

The cab is slowing, stopping. I pull a tissue from my coat pocket and wipe my eyes and snotty nose. The driver turns to me. 'The lake is sad in winter. It remembers the boy who drowned.'

'Why have we stopped?' The light is fading fast and there's no traffic: we haven't passed even a farm truck and now I feel afraid.

'My heart is breaking for you,' he says.

I look at him. His eyes are not blue – the left is – but the other is green like Tam's.

'What makes you cry like this?'

'My father is dying in hospital.' Another tear rolls down my cheek.

'And this is why you wanted to visit the lake?'

'We used to come here, as a family.'

'It's good to come to a place like this when you are sad. I too come here when I am sad. But now I must get you home.' He starts up the engine and we drive back onto the road. My phone beeps. It's Tomas. 'I come tonight,' his message says. 'If this okay with you.'

'Someone missing you?'

I tell the driver about my work and explain Tomas' situation. It's a relief to think of something else.

'I can help,' he says. 'I live alone and have a spare room. I could take this Tomas in until you can find him somewhere.' He sighs. A small sigh. 'I suppose you have to vet people.'

'Surely cab drivers are vetted, aren't they?'

'Yes,' he says. 'Of course.'

I shouldn't trust a man I hardly know. Yet somehow I do. 'Normally we'd need to carry out additional checks but perhaps I can bend the rules, just this once. I'd put Tomas up at my place again but I have my brother over from Australia and with my father ill ...'

'My name is Isaak, by the way.' He pronounces it *ee-sack*.

'I'm Mira.'

He doesn't ask where I'm from but, like the nurse in the hospital, he must guess. I still have the accent, the olive skin and dark hair.

'Mira. What a beautiful name.'

We ride in silence for the remainder of the journey. It's a comfortable silence. The taxi is warm. I relax. My eyes close. I'm surprised when the taxi slows and stops. We are already at my apartment building.

I hand Isaak my taxi card but he waves it away. 'Please, allow the journey on me, Mira. It's been such a pleasure.'

I hesitate. What is it he wants?

'Get Tomas to call me.' Isaak leans over, hands me his business card and our fingers touch briefly. I look into his eyes and I feel a powerful emotion I've not felt in almost thirty years. But I try not to let it mean anything. I've made too many mistakes with men.

'I appreciate your kindness and generosity,' I say.

'One condition.'

There's always a condition. I should have known.

My face must register displeasure because he bursts out laughing – not a contemptuous laugh but something fresh, like a spring breeze. 'I don't think my request is too terrible. I'd like to take you for dinner one evening but if you feel dinner is too much, I'll settle for coffee.'

I feel my face flush. I've slept with men – too many men – but I haven't been out to dinner with a man in a long time.

He holds up his hands. 'Sorry. I'm being an ass. Just say no. Then it's over and done with. No hard feelings.'

'It's not that.' I move across the seat. Before I open the door, our eyes lock again. I turn away and fumble in my bag. 'Here,' I say, scribbling my number on a scrap of paper. 'Call me.'

As I run up the steps to the apartment, I feel light as a snowflake.

I call Tomas and explain about Isaak. He seems more than happy with the arrangement. Then I run a bath and soak in it for ages. I'm still there and half-asleep when the phone rings.

'Where are you? You're supposed to be here by now.' It's Pearl.

'Sorry. I got delayed.'

She makes a sound like Ma used to do when she was irritated with us. A kind of hissing. 'When will you be here? We were expecting you an hour ago.'

'I'm coming. I'm just getting dressed.'

'You could have called to say you were running late.'

'I'm sorry,' I say again. She thinks I'm like Kaz. Unreliable. Crazy.

I get out of the bath and call for a cab. There's no chance of it being Isaak this time. It will be a city driverless one. Somehow I'm strangely disappointed. I slip on my clothes, walk down the stairs and go out into the snowy square.

21

The past: Isara Camp, Sufra.

In the field of armed conflict an extraordinary shift has
that has compounded the problem of missing persons.
Battlefields have spread into villages, towns and cities,
and the physical abuse of civilian populations has
become both an objective and an instrument of war.
This has produced a huge rise in the number of civilians
missing in conflict.

www.ConflictandWarStudies/missingpersons

My shirt was sticking to my back, dust in my nose, dust
everywhere and that damned dog barking in my ears and
driving me crazy and he was echoed by another dog and fuck,
how many people were there? How would I ever find my sister
among all these people: the boys kicking a football in the rising
dust, the huddles of men smoking and talking, the girls giggling
and washing clothes, the women by the stalls examining the
cheap goods, cheap dishes, cheap fabrics, cheap shoes, cheap
everything. And all the while the sun beating down on my neck.

'Pearl, Pearl!'

Trucks belching fumes at the main entrance. Men unloading crates. More shouting. Throngs of people. Entering. Leaving. Waiting. Hoping. The mad man shouting for God and people sitting in the dust and the kid selling cheap cigarettes and lighters and the boy with one leg, hopping, hopping as if he were a bird and the sweat trickling down my back and my throat so dry it was like sucking on a stone.

Pearl wasn't with the girls skipping or the girls playing hopscotch. She wasn't by the water pipe, or in the concrete wash house, or in the school tent in which a group of women sat, heads together, as if discussing a secret. On and on I walked, to the edges of the camp where torn plastic bags clung to discarded rolls of barbed wire like nameless flags. On and further. Along the paths between the tents, the dust causing me to sneeze, the smells of cooking making my stomach grumble, with my shirt still stuck to my back and my hair turning to wet straw.

'Pearl, Pearl!' Over and over I called her name until my voice was shredded and hoarse.

Once, I thought I saw Nadia and I ran, and almost grabbed a girl by her arm. I stopped just in time. She wasn't Nadia; she was just a girl in torn, thin clothes, snot running down her face, her dark hair tied with a dusty pink ribbon.

I turned south, to the camp's other dusty edge. Soon that space would be filled with tents and broken families like ours, families wondering what had sent their lives out of orbit, families bewildered, homesick, uprooted like trees after a storm. I stood at the wire fence, looking north, towards Lyrian, my bleeding, dying country. Somewhere, up there, were Kaz and Pa. Somewhere up there was our house, or what remained of it. I turned back to face the mountains. Maybe Pearl and Nadia had run in that direction. But the truth was, they could have gone anywhere.

*

The man at the office by the gate wore a military uniform. He was sitting on a half-broken chair smoking a cigarette.

'My sister has gone missing,' I said.

'Name? Age. Description.' He had a thin moustache and spoke with a strange accent. He wrote down Pearl's name, her age and what she was wearing. Then he looked at his watch and said he would do what he could.

'She's with a friend. Nadia.'

He wrote Nadia's name under the piece of paper with Pearl's name on it and looked at his watch again. I left.

Ma was spooning rice into Moe's mouth. She stopped when she saw me, the spoon still in her hand.

'I can't find her anywhere. I reported her missing.'

Ma dropped the spoon. Moe closed his mouth and opened it again.

*

It was dusk when Ma and I went out together, Ma carrying Moe in her arms. This was the time in the camp I normally liked the best: the heat of the day gone, the distant mountains catching the last dying embers of the sun, the smoke of the fires rising. But that evening I felt emptied out. Nothing mattered any more but finding Pearl.

Nadia's grandmother was sitting on a threadbare rug, sipping from a chipped china cup. When we walked in, she looked up and I saw that her eyes were moist as if she'd been weeping. Nadia's trembling brother stared at us and shook from head to toe. The other kids, scattered about the tent, were silent.

Moe had fallen asleep on Ma's shoulder, but he woke and started to whimper.

211

'Have you no idea where your granddaughter might have gone?' Ma asked. The grandmother put the cup down, wiped her eyes with her thin, old hands and shook her head. 'Do you have other relatives here?'

A tear tracked down the grandmother's face. 'We have no one.'

Moe whimpered again and Ma stroked his hair. 'Sh, shh,' she said, before turning back to the grandmother. 'Do you have a mobile?'

'Here,' one of the girls said, the one I'd seen stirring the pot earlier in the day.

'Take my number, will you?'

The girl stood up and walked over to Ma. The mobile she held was old-fashioned and worn. I wondered if it even worked.

'If they turn up you must let us know immediately. Is that understood? We'll come back first thing in the morning.'

The girl took Ma's number and mine, and typed them into the phone. 'We don't know where she is, lady. We want her to come back too. We'd tell you if we knew. We would.'

The grandmother nodded in agreement though she said nothing.

'Of course you would,' Ma said.

The sky was almost dark, the first stars now visible, but we kept our eyes fixed on the camp and the people passing and called Pearl's name. But Pearl did not call back.

*

I said I'd go out again. Moe had fallen asleep and Ma and I had run out of things to say. Ma didn't want me to go but I went anyhow.

The moon had risen, thin and silver in the sky. It looked kind of lonely up there. Myriad stars glittered too but I didn't care for them, or the moon. It was almost ten, but the air was still hot and oppressive and a sickly smell of burning plastic hung over the camp.

I walked to the main gate. If Pearl and Nadia had gone outside the camp, this would be the best place to spot them when, or if, they returned. I stood in the glare of the security lights so that I could be seen. A skeletal dog nosed at something in the dirt. People came in. Some went out. Then a man sauntered up to me, a large man with polished shoes that gleamed in the light, a gold watch glinting on his hairy wrist. He appeared to be around Pa's age. He smiled and said, 'Isn't it rather late for a pretty girl to be out?'

I said nothing and walked closer to the gate but I heard his footsteps in the dirt, following me. I spun round. 'Leave me alone.'

'Steady, girl. I mean no harm.' I meant to sidestep him but I wasn't fast enough. He caught me by the arm. I could smell alcohol on his breath. 'I'd marry a girl like you.'

'Let me go,' I hissed.

His grip tightened. 'What a high-spirited girl, you are. Just like a young filly.'

'I'm not a fucking horse,' I said.

'There's no need to use language like that. I'm an honourable man and I'd like to ask your father for your hand. I can give you a good life. I have money.' He reminded me of a man who'd once come to our house in Zazour trying to sell us bogus insurance: his voice, like this man's, had been oily and disgusting. Ma soon saw him off. But Ma was not here.

'I'm not marrying anyone.' Now that the camp had swelled in numbers a trade had begun in temporary unions. Many of these were little more than prostitution. Again, I tried to pull away from him but he wouldn't let go. 'I'm not old enough to marry,' I said.

His eyes went to my breasts. 'When your father learns what I have to offer, he won't turn me down. Why don't you take me to him now?'

'My father is dead.'

'May he rest in peace.' The man smiled again, the smug smile of a man used to getting his own way. 'Then you must be in need of funds. If you'd take me to your mother. Unless it's too late, of course. In which case ...'

'Let me go. Or I'll scream.'

The man relaxed his grip. I stepped back. 'Perhaps later on, you'll see the sense in it,' he said. 'I'm offering you a way out from this stink hole but if you don't wish to take it you are free to go.'

Now I could see people staring at us, the people waiting at the gate to register; mostly women and children, and a couple of wizened men with faces like old walnuts. No one spoke but a woman began to mutter.

'Low-lying scum!' I shouted. And I spat in his self-righteous face.

As I ran back to our tent, I thought about the man and others like him who preyed on the vulnerable. I just had to hope and pray that Pearl was safe. I would say nothing to Ma about what had happened to me. She had enough to worry about.

She was lying on the mattress, Moe asleep at her side, the lamp still burning. The crying I'd suppressed for months spilled out in a flood. I thought about the girl who'd drawn bullet holes on her doll. The boy playing dead. The toy guns. The man with lust in his eyes. Nadia's trembling little brother. But most of all I thought of Tam, Kaz and Pa – and now Pearl. All gone.

*

Though I was exhausted beyond measure, sleep would not come. How I wanted to hear Pearl's soft breathing, to feel her presence close by, to reach over and stroke her hair. It was my fault she'd disappeared. I was jealous and I'd pushed her away and now there was nothing left but her empty bed.

I hardly slept that night. I lay awake, listening to Ma's breathing, her odd mumbled mutterings. To the dog that barked on and on and the man shouting about God and Satan. To faint cries of a baby. Then a woman began to sing. It was a mournful song, yet there was something hopeful in her sweet, clear voice. Later, all fell silent. Silent except for my heart. Boom, boom, boom. As if shells were falling in my chest.

22

Present day: Sundsholm, Neeland.

Anxiety is a psychological, physiological, and behavioural
state. Both humans and animals can experience anxiety.
It is caused by either a real or a potential threat to the
subject and is characterised by increased arousal,
changes in the endocrine system, and specific behaviour
patterns.

Neeland Journal of Psychiatric Studies/Jonssondottir, P/
Vol61/22

'What happened to make you so late?' Pearl is standing in
the hall in a printed apron, a halo of light behind her
head.

I was expecting Stefan to open the door, not Pearl in that
apron, a dark look in her eyes. 'One of my clients disappeared.
There wasn't anyone else who could deal with the problem.'

Five pairs of boots are lined up on the wooden rack. Kaz's
are easy to spot – they are larger than the others and the leather
is worn. They're boots for dust, sand and deserts, whereas the

family's boots are fur-lined, sturdy, almost new. I can't quite understand how Pearl has managed this life, its normality and ordinariness, how she has turned her back on the past.

A murmur of voices from the living room – two deep voices and the high chatter of Oscar. I can detect nothing from Lucas.

'How's it going?' I take off my coat.

'Good. The boys like him.' Pearl attempts to smile but the smile leaves her face almost as soon as it's arrived.

'That's something, I suppose.'

'Yes, it is something.'

As I take off my own boots, an aroma of spices and cooked chicken reaches my nose. 'Smells great,' I say.

'Never let it be said that I don't make an effort.'

'I know you do. I appreciate it. I'm sure Kaz does too.'

Pearl smiles, a genuine smile this time. That's progress too. 'Any news of your cat?' she asks. 'Kaz said you've been worried about her.'

'No. I'm worried she's gone for good.'

Pearl puts her arm on mine. 'I came back, didn't I?'

Kaz is sat on the sofa next to Oscar and Stefan is in his usual chair, close to the solar fire. Lucas is sprawled out on the other sofa. Everyone looks relaxed, except for Lucas. His mouth is set in a thin line and he's jiggling his legs, like Kaz does.

'It's so cool,' Oscar says. 'Uncle Kaz has seen a real shark.' He turns to Pearl. 'Can we go to Australia and see a shark, please Mum, please.'

Everything in the room gleams like a Christmas bauble. Tea lights burn on the shelves and the solar fire casts a warm glow. It ought to look welcoming but the red cushions scattered on the white furniture remind me of patches of blood.

'Sharks are rare now,' Kaz says. 'The great whites are almost extinct.'

'That's tragic,' Oscar says, and he makes a sad face.

'It's all due to ocean warming,' Lucas says. Even when he's not speaking his jaw is moving.

'Hunting. Killing. That decimated their numbers too,' Kaz says. 'But we've had a shark-breeding programme in place for some years and the oceans are much cleaner than they were a few decades back. There are strict controls. Dumping plastic can get you a prison sentence.'

'Please sit,' Stefan says to me, gesturing from his chair. 'You're making me nervous, the two of you standing there.' He glances at Pearl. I sense anxiety in his expression and perhaps a little protectiveness. I don't quite know what to make of Stefan, though I've known him for many years. Sometimes I get irritated by his sense of entitlement, and the way that opportunities appear to have fallen so easily into his lap, but I know he loves Pearl and the boys and that, in his way, he loves and cares for me too.

'I need to get back into the kitchen,' Pearl says.

'Would you like help?' Stefan asks, although he makes no move to get up.

'It's okay,' I say, and I follow Pearl to the kitchen.

'If you could get the dishes out of the top oven where they're warming.' Pearl frowns. 'Are you okay? You look pale.'

'Like I said, it was a difficult day at work.' I wonder if Kaz has mentioned Tomas.

'You'll feel better after some food.' She hands me an oven cloth. 'I do so want everything to be okay with Kaz but ...' Her voice wobbles.

'He's not drinking, is he?'

'No, no.'

'What is it then?'

'I don't know ... just a feeling I have.'

'Do you think he's hiding something?'

What made me say that? Now Pearl will be suspicious again. I pick up the warmed dinner plates but a strange sound fills my ears. Like static. And I lose track, until I hear Pearl calling my name.

'Mira! Mira ... you're standing in the middle of the kitchen with the plates in your hand. They must be heavy.' Pearl shakes her head. 'Where were you?'

'Sorry. Miles away. In a dream, I suppose.'

'Well, pull on your seven-league boots and come back to my kitchen.' She laughs. I like it when she laughs.

I carry the plates into the dining room and Stefan shows us to our places at the table. Pearl only uses the dining room for special occasions, or for entertaining Stefan's clients. She's covered the table in a white linen cloth. Six fluted glasses sparkle in the glow of red candles. Ma used to love coming to dinner at Pearl's house. She was so proud of Pearl and her house, but perhaps a little envious too. Oh, how I miss Ma. We all miss Ma but we don't talk about her much. It's too painful, especially now that Pa is fading.

'White or red wine?' Stefan asks.

I wonder if we should be drinking in front of Kaz, but I take a glass to help settle my nerves. 'White, please.'

Stefan pours for the three of us. There's a bottle of mineral water by Kaz's place, and apple juice for the boys. 'Here,' Stefan says, lifting his glass. 'To family.'

We clink our glasses and I think of Pa lying in his hospital bed, hardly able to drink at all. I feel a pang of guilt. Of sadness too.

'To Uncle Kaz,' Oscar says but Lucas says nothing and he doesn't pick up his glass with the rest of us.

Pearl serves the food. Tonight she's made chicken casserole. It smells delicious and spicy, like the chicken Ma used to cook back home. There's rice too, and fried aubergines, courgettes, yoghurt sauce and flat breads. Quite a feast.

'There are kangaroos where Kaz lives,' Oscar says. 'Can I have more rice, Mum? I'm starving.'

'They're called marsupials.' Lucas has food on his plate but he's just turning it over and over with his fork. I haven't seen him take a mouthful.

'What's a marsupial?', Oscar asks, biting into a chicken leg.

'Please don't eat and speak at the same time,' Stefan says, rather sharply.

I look at Kaz but his eyes are fixed on his plate.

'Marsupials are mammals who keep their babies in pouches, like kangaroos and opossums.' Lucas stabs the fork into a piece of chicken.

'I want to see one,' Oscar says. 'Can we?'

'Maybe we'll visit Uncle Kaz after ...' Pearl hesitates. Her cheeks are flushed from the kitchen and the wine. 'After Grandpa gets better.'

'Don't be stupid,' Lucas says. 'Grandpa isn't going to get better. That's the only reason Kaz is here. He never came before. He didn't bother.' There's an awful silence, broken only by the clink of cutlery. 'Isn't that true?' Lucas adds, with a sneer.

Lucas has always been so kind and polite. His outburst is quite a shock.

Colour has flooded Stefan's cheeks and his mouth is set thin and taut like a tightrope. 'Enough, Lucas. Kaz is a guest here. If I hear another word out of you like that, you'll go to your room, no questions asked.'

'I'm going anyway.' Lucas jumps up from the table and runs out. We hear his footsteps on the stairs, the slam of his bedroom door.

'Well,' Pearl says, 'of all the—'

'It's okay,' Kaz says, quietly. 'He's only speaking the truth.'

We eat on in silence. Even Oscar is quiet. The chicken is delicious, perfectly cooked, and the sauce is sublime; but I no longer feel hungry. Each mouthful is an effort and I can't help thinking of the meal we ate together after Tam died and how desperately Ma wanted everything to appear normal and how the harder she tried, the worse it became. Pearl, too, is struggling with her food, but she's gulping the wine.

I'm grateful when Stefan breaks the uncomfortable silence. 'The food is wonderful, darling.' We murmur assent. 'Tell us, Kaz, about life down there. We'd like to hear.' He leans over and ruffles Oscar's hair. 'Especially Oscar.'

Kaz talks. He talks a lot. He talks of indigenous rights, and the big mining corporations. He talks of forest fires, cyclones and desert tracks. I'm surprised at how knowledgeable he is. I didn't know that at one time he worked as a ranger. I suppose that was before the drink got him. He talks of how the Australian government is researching new ways to rebuild the bleached, dead reefs and if it will ever be possible. I try to concentrate, to stop my thoughts from wandering in blind and difficult directions, but the reefs remind me of the dead and bleached-out cities from our war, and the people left wandering those empty spaces like the fish in the dying seas; I imagine the fish gasping for air in the algae-ridden, poisoned water and how we too had to gasp for air, how we're still gasping for air.

It's stifling in here. Airless.

'Guess what's for dessert? It's Ma's special semolina-and-pistachio pudding,' Pearl says. 'Let's hope it's up to Ma's standards.' Pearl's voice is over-bright and there's silence from Kaz. She starts to clear the plates. I get up too, and carry the almost empty casserole to the kitchen, relieved to be gone from the table and the heat of the room.

'Do you want me to check on Lucas?' I ask.

Pearl's skin flushes, even though it's cooler here. 'What came over him? That was so wrong. I mean, I understand the emotions but he's old enough to know better.'

I know that Lucas has done wrong but I want her to understand, just as I want her to understand about Kaz. About me, too. Yet those things unspoken from our past lie between us like a vast desert. But I can speak up for Lucas. 'Oscar said Lucas is having some trouble at school.'

'What trouble?'

'Bullying.'

Pearl raises her eyebrows. 'He hasn't said anything to me.'

'Perhaps you should try and talk to him about it.'

'I will, but now isn't the time and you going up there, that's just pandering to his bad behaviour.' She walks to the fridge. Opens it. Takes out a dish.

'Please, Pearl. I'm worried about him.'

She sets the dish down on the marble worktop. 'I made a lemon mousse, too. I know it's one of your favourites.'

'Thank you,' I say, and I kiss her on the cheek.

She taps her fingers on the kitchen counter, then lifts her hands and smooths her hair. Her cheeks are still pink and her mascara is a little smudged. Now she sighs, a long, almost plaintive sigh. 'All right. You go and see Lucas but please, Mira, don't be long. Stefan won't be happy if he knows.'

*

Lucas's door is closed. I knock softly. 'It's me, Mira.'

I wait but there's no answer. I click the handle. Lucas has a lock but at least he hasn't used it. If I had a kid, not that I ever will, I wouldn't allow a lock on the door.

Lucas is lying on his stomach, his head buried deep in his pillow. I don't think he's crying.

'It's me, Mira,' I say again.

He kicks his legs, crumpling the duvet. The cover matches the blue and turquoise seascape on the wall opposite. I was with Pearl when she bought it for Lucas's thirteenth birthday. I wonder how many thirteen-year-old boys are bought expensive paintings. But that's not what matters right now. I'm not here to make judgements. 'Lucas,' I say. 'Lukes.'

'What is it?' He sits up and draws his knees to his chest.

'Is it okay if I sit down?' I gesture to the beanbag on the floor. He nods, and I ease myself into its soft folds.

'I know it's not easy having Kaz here, but it doesn't help to talk like that. It just upsets everyone, you included.'

'I don't care. It's the truth. Why are we all pretending?'

His room is so tidy. Nothing is out of place. Oscar's room is always messy, toys and books strewn everywhere, clothes in piles. Here the books are neatly lined up on the shelves and the desk is bare except for Lucas's electronic notebook. 'Can we open the window?' I ask.

Lucas gives me a quizzical little frown. 'Are you hot?'

'A little.'

He presses a small black box at his side. The window makes a slight purring noise and opens. 'Is that enough?'

'I think so. If it gets cold we can always close it again.'

'Have you got one?' He points to the box. 'It operates the heating too, but Mum gets mad if I change the settings.'

I laugh. 'My apartment isn't that sophisticated.' I realise he hasn't visited for a while. Not since before I was in hospital. 'You should come and see me again sometime.'

'I will,' he says. 'I promise.'

I breathe in the welcome cold air. 'Kaz was in the war. Has Mum ever talked to you about the war?'

'No,' Lucas says but he lets go of his knees. 'Well, not much.'

'Kaz left the camp. You know about the camp. Remember, I talked to you about it once?'

He nods.

'He left to go and fight. He saw some very bad things and sometimes when people see bad things it can affect their minds.'

'Is that what happened to you? Did you see bad things?'

We've never discussed my illness, but Lucas was old enough to understand and I suppose Pearl must have said something, 'I did, yes, but Kaz saw worse and to try and block it out, he started drinking too much and then he got really sick.'

'Mum says she'll never forgive Uncle Kaz for not coming to Granny's funeral.'

'She will forgive him. Give her time. It's important that we forgive people ...'

'Even people who try to hurt you?'

'To a degree, yes. Though there must be justice too, proper justice.' I stop. I want to tell him about Tam but perhaps now is not the time. When he's older. Yes, then. I promise myself that. But whenever I think of justice, I think of the soldier too. 'Has someone hurt you?'

Lucas's bottom lip quivers. 'A boy at school keeps taking my packed lunch but he doesn't eat it, he throws it in the gutter and he says I don't deserve to eat because I'm only half a person and halves don't deserve to be fed.'

'Half a person?'

Lucas gives me a 'Come-on-are-you-stupid?' look. 'Because I'm half from somewhere else. My skin is dark; not black like some of the people you work with, but it's not white like most of the people here.'

'Oh,' I say. 'Now I understand. I'm slow off the mark sometimes. I expect it's old age creeping up.'

He smiles.

'Have you talked to anyone else about this?'

'Only Oscar. I told him not to tell Mum or I'd ... please don't tell her. She'll only go and make things worse. She'll march up to the school and ... you know what she's like.'

'I won't tell her. But you should. How can she help and support you if she doesn't know?' I feel like a hypocrite. It's all too easy to dole out advice. I do it every day at work, but when it comes to my own life, I'm blind.

'Maybe,' he says, though he doesn't sound certain.

'He's weak, this boy. That's why he picks on people like you. Make out you don't care. If you don't react, he'll soon grow bored. If you show weakness to bullies, they always see it. Why don't you ask your mum to make you a bigger lunch one day? Offer it to him. That'll take the wind out of his sails.'

'What if he throws it away?'

'Tell him that your mother has won cookery prizes.' I have no clue if this will work.

'It sounds like an idea,' he says. 'And I'll be nicer to Kaz.'

'We all make mistakes, but some of us make bigger mistakes than others.'

We sit in silence for a moment. Then Lucas jumps off the bed and gives me a hug. 'I'd better go,' I say, pulling away. 'Or I'll be in trouble too.'

*

Stefan and Kaz are drinking coffee in the living room. I expect Pearl is having green tea or some other drink she considers has health-giving properties. Oscar is on the floor, playing with a toy robot. Pearl frowns at me but she doesn't say anything. I haven't been gone long, though perhaps long enough to arouse suspicion, but if Stefan has noticed my absence, he's not showing it. The talk now is of cricket. I'd no idea Kaz and Stefan were interested in the game but they're discussing it in an animated manner.

'It's time for bed, Oscar,' Pearl says, yawning. I can see that she is bored with cricket. 'Come on, I'll go up with you and check on Lucas.' She catches my eye but I keep my expression neutral.

'He needs to apologise to Kaz, to us all,' Stefan says.

'In the morning,' Pearl says. 'Let's get him to do it then, eh?'

'All right,' Stefan says, grudgingly. He stretches and gets to his feet, looks at Pearl. 'I thought I'd wander over and have a nightcap with Lars.'

'What? At this time?' Pearl's voice rises. 'It's late and we have company here.'

Stefan puts his hand on her shoulder. 'Lars's house is only two blocks away. I thought I'd give the three of you some time together.' He glances at me and then at Kaz. 'If that's okay.'

I nod. Even though it's not okay with me. But what choice do I have?

'I see.' Pearl rolls her eyes. 'Just don't stay out late, Stefan, eh?'

*

Pearl goes upstairs with Oscar. When she comes down again, it's just the three of us together.

An owl hoots in the tree outside. I don't think I've ever heard an owl in Pearl's garden before. I pick up my wine glass but it's empty.

'We have to talk,' Kaz says.

'Isn't that what we've been doing all evening?' Pearl says.

The owl hoots again and then all is silent and still. Nothing moves but the candlelight flickering on our faces, like the candlelight in the cellar all those years ago, before the explosion. I hope this explosion won't be too big. At least I know this one is coming. Whether that is any consolation or not, I have no idea.

23

Present day: Sundsholm, Neeland.

'Everyone sees what you appear to be, few experience
what you really are.'

The Prince, by Niccolò Machiavelli

I can't recall when I first read Machiavelli, but now I think on
his words. We are siblings and yet we hardly know each other;
we have been afraid of knowing. Now the three of us sit in Pearl's
living room, none of us looking at each other; the silence like an
impending avalanche.

'Pearl,' Kaz says, softly. 'There's something you need to know.'
His lip is trembling, and he's leaning forward in the chair, one
hand on the knee of his dark trousers – the only pair he brought
with him that are even half-decent.

'Pearl,' he says again.

Maybe I can stop him, I think. Or, like Mimi, I can walk
out of the house and into the dark, snowy night, and never
return.

Pearl is biting her nail. Now she wiggles her stockinged toes and looks Kaz up and down as if she is about to interview him for a job. 'What is it?'

There's still time to put an end to this. But I say nothing.

'Are you both going to sit there like stuffed dummies? If you have something to say, come out with it.' Pearl's face flushes and the candlelight catches the diamonds in her earrings.

'Do you remember the day we left the house in Zazour?' Kaz says.

'Of course I do.' Pearl's voice is as snappy as a dog's bark. 'How could I forget something like that?'

'And you remember Tam?' Kaz continues, tugging at his white hair. A few strands fall out and float down onto the sofa.

'Of course I remember him. He was your best friend, Kaz. A tragedy.'

'I wouldn't call it a tragedy,' Kaz says. His dark eyes seek Pearl. 'He was murdered by government soldiers.'

Pearl crosses her legs neatly and sits back in the chair. 'If I remember correctly, it was Mira who told me that. At first you all kept saying he'd had an accident. Are you saying something different now?'

My throat is dry. I reach for my wine glass but it's empty.

'No, I'm not,' Kaz says.

Pearl takes another bite out of her thumbnail. 'What are you getting at? Spit it out, for God's sake.'

'Kaz,' I say. I hear the desperation in my voice. But he ignores me. I should get up and leave right now. I must. But I don't move. I just sit in the chair, my hands in my lap.

Kaz clasps his hands together and leans further forward, as if he is praying. He swallows. Sits upright. I hear him take a deep breath. Here it comes. 'A week after Tam got shot, Mira and I went out looking for bread.'

Kaz, please. You promised.

'We got bread, and oranges, but that isn't the story. You see, we went to the cemetery and ...' He looks at me. I turn away. I imagine this is what it's like to sit in the dock in court, waiting for the verdict. My heart is all over the place and I feel vaguely nauseous. 'Mira and I ... we killed a soldier.'

I dare to glance at Pearl. Her face is drained of all colour. 'What? Did he attack you?'

'I agreed to meet him,' I say, my voice quiet now. I can't let Kaz take all the blame. Not now.

'You planned it?' Pearl jumps to her feet. 'You planned that?' One of the candles splutters. She blows it out.

'It was my idea,' I say. 'The soldier said he'd get me bread in exchange for sex.'

'Oh my God,' Pearl says, clutching the edge of the wooden sideboard. 'Oh my God.'

*

It's cold and I can't stop shivering. I lean against the rear of the shed, sheltered a little from the biting wind. The wind sounds like a baby crying. In the distance the marker stones of the dead look like rows of soldiers standing to attention.

I wait. Five minutes. Ten. I keep checking my watch. He's late. Perhaps he won't come. I think to go home. To abandon my idea. But suddenly he's here, his hands in his pockets, flakes of snow on his green army jacket. 'I thought you might stand me up,' he says. 'But then I saw the footsteps.' His cheeks are red from the cold.

'Where's the bread?'

'In the rucksack.' He places his heavy pack on the snowy ground and opens it. 'Here. See?'

At the top are two loaves, wrapped in thin paper. My mouth waters at the sight of them. We haven't had bread in weeks. I reach out but he grabs my arm. 'Not so fast. We agreed. The payment. No payment. No bread.' He shoves me against the wooden wall and pulls at the zip of my parka. I try to push him away but with only one working hand, my attempts are futile.

'You want the bread or not?' He's breathing heavily. Today his breath smells of mint.

'You said oranges too.'

'I have oranges.'

He slides a cold hand under my clothes and cups my right breast. I feel his thing grow hard against my leg.

Where are you, Kaz?

'Do you like that?' the soldier says. I say nothing. My heart thuds in my chest. I am sick and afraid.

He pins me against the shed. And he's strong. Stronger than I imagined. Now he tugs at the zip of my jeans. I struggle. He knees me in the belly. He doesn't try to kiss me. He shoves his fingers hard up inside me and I cry out. 'You're hurting me.'

Where are you, Kaz? Where?

He laughs. 'You're a virgin, that's why it hurts. It always hurts the first time.'

'Please stop,' I say.

He pulls me down. I smell pine resin and something else, sharp and animal. The ground is cold and wet under my bare skin. I push my knees together but he forces my legs open. His penis stabs at my thigh. I struggle and spit. He slaps my face. Bruising, thrusting, fingers, mouth, flesh, horror.

Everything turns white. Just like before. A world without shadows. There is nothing now but silence.

The soldier's body jerks and flounders. His grip loosens on my thigh. He makes a strange noise like a staircase creaking in the dark.

A dark shape against the white of the snow and the sky: Kaz. His arm is raised. He holds a knife in his hand. This is what we agreed. His arm comes down. Again. Again. Again. Blood pools into the white snow. I think of a film I saw. Hunters clubbing baby seals to death.

The soldier is quite still now. He's staring up at the white sky.

'Get up. Mira! Get up!'

There's blood on my thighs. I can't move.

'Clean yourself up.' Kaz hands me a wad of tissue. There's blood on his face; his hands. He wipes his own jacket clean in the snow. A waterproof. It doesn't stain. 'We have to go,' he says. 'Now.'

'Is he dead?'

'Yes.'

'We can't leave him here like this.'

'What else can we do, Mira? Bury him?'

We run along the edge of the cemetery through the trees and the snow blows in our faces and bile rises in my throat and I vomit and Kaz grabs my arm and we're running – running forever through the whiteness and I think perhaps we're flying.

*

There's a candle flickering somewhere, a smell of wax, an owl hooting. Are there owls here? I haven't heard an owl in camp before. I pull on my clothes: I've lost weight and have to pull the belt in another notch. It's too dark to see my face properly in the small mirror on the crate that serves as our dresser, but even in the dim light I can see I look tired.

Ma and Moe are asleep, curled up together. Neither of them stir as I leave the tent.

A sliver of moon hangs above the mountains. The sky is already paling, a golden glow in the east; another day dawning in camp, another day like the one before and the one before that. But today isn't like other days because Pearl is missing.

People are getting up, fetching water, calling their children. A black cat slips under the canvas of a tent. A baby cries. I walk to the toilet block, the ones we always use, but Pearl isn't there and she's not at the water pipe and how stupidly I've been clinging on to that small hope.

I sit on a wooden crate and call Pa. *Please answer, Pa, please answer.*

'You're early,' he says.

'Pearl is missing.' My voice is breaking, my heart breaking, everything breaking into smaller and smaller pieces.

'Missing?' he repeats. 'How long has she been gone?'

'Two days and we don't know where she is.'

'Two days? Why haven't you called me before? Why didn't your mother call?'

'You're so far away. What can you do?' I start crying. 'Oh, Pa, why has she gone? It's not like we had a big argument but ... you know how she's not talking ... and ...'

'It's not your fault, sweetheart. You can't blame yourself.'

'Please come back, Pa. We need you. Please come.'

'I'll get back as soon as I can, Mira. But I don't know how long it's going to take me. This is a war zone. I can't just get on a bus.'

I shout at him then. 'Why did you have to go back there, why?'

'Please, sweetheart. Be strong. Call me the second you have news.'

Now I shuffle along to the main gate like an old woman. There are people lined up outside the fence, always people lined up here. Some of the children's faces are pressed up against the mesh but I try not to catch their eyes. I can't face seeing their desperation today, or the small glimmers of hope that will soon turn to resignation and despair.

Next to the gate is the Portakabin where the guards sit. I came here only yesterday but it might have been a lifetime ago.

One of the guards is outside, remonstrating with a woman and her husband. I consider going in to ask if they've had any news of Pearl and Nadia. I don't. I know it will be a waste of time. And I wonder how many kids go missing, and if anyone in authority here even bothers.

I wait at the gate for around half an hour. Then I walk back into the camp, following the rows of tents. A small boy peers at me through a hole in the canvas of one tent. He doesn't smile. Between the rows, washing is already hanging up to dry. As I pass through I see a pink sweatshirt hanging on a line. Just like the one Pearl wears. It isn't hers.

*

'Mira!'

Who's that calling?

'Mira!'

It's Pearl. What a relief. I must phone Pa and let him know. I must run and find Ma.

'Call Pa,' I say. My voice sounds thick and hoarse. 'Tell him.'

'Tell him what?'

'You're found, Pearl. You're found. Tell him that. It is you, isn't it? Where's my mobile. Give me my mobile. I have to call Pa.'

'You don't need your mobile, Mira.'

Someone presses a cold towel on my forehead, and someone else says, 'Is she all right?' A man's voice. Kaz, isn't it? What's he doing here? Isn't he fighting in Lyri? He must have come back.

'She's gone like this before.' It's Pearl's voice and yet it isn't quite her voice. Where is that girlish squeakiness? And I'm surprised she's talking at all. She doesn't like talking. 'You do know she was in hospital last year?'

'Yes, she told me.'

You know I was in hospital. My hand got burned.
'She's opening her eyes. Does she need a doctor?'
'She'll be all right in a minute. It's the shock.'

*

I'm in the bathroom. Pearl is here. There's vomit on my clothes. She's washing me, washing my face, my hands. The soap smells of roses. She's pulling off my top now, wrapping me in a thick towel. I'm shivering. My teeth are chattering. The bathroom is white, everything bright and clean, not like that awful stinking toilet block. It's warm too. But I can't stop shivering. I'm so cold.

'I thought you were gone,' I say.

'I'm not lost,' Pearl says. 'We're both at my house in Sundsholm.'

I should be looking after her, my little sister. She needs protection. She might run away again. Or a bomb will fall on the house and bury her alive. Isn't that what happened to her friend? The house fell on top of her, on top of the whole family and there was dust and the snow fell and I saw a doll on the ground and its head had come off.

My head is on Pearl's lap. I'm crying and she's running her hand through my hair and holding me tight.

*

Pearl and I are still sitting in her bathroom, our backs against the tiled wall, our knees drawn up. Kaz is downstairs talking to Stefan. It must be late but I've no idea how late.

'I'm sorry,' I say. 'About everything.'

'It's okay. I said it was okay.'

'I didn't want Kaz to tell you. I never wanted you to know. What must you think of us? It was murder, Pearl, cold-blooded murder.'

'We were at war then. Different rules applied. Let's not talk of it now. Do you still feel sick? Perhaps you should go to bed?'

A blue towel is lying across my lap, a frieze of fish on its edge. 'Kaz went missing at the same time. Did you know that?'

Pearl shakes her head. 'No, I didn't. I mean I knew later but I never really understood.'

'Two days you were gone,' I say.

She nods. 'I remember.'

*

Two days, hot, long and merciless.

Pa called me again later. He was weeping down the phone. 'No one knows where Kaz is,' he said. 'How can two of my children go missing in one day?'

'Kaz is missing?' I never thought a heart could ache like mine did when I heard those words.

'Someone from his brigade contacted me. They were searching a house and he suddenly vanished.'

'What are you going to do?'

'There's nothing I *can* do.' Pa sounded despairing. 'I need to come back to you and your mother, and Moe. I need to find Pearl.'

I didn't tell Ma about Kaz, not at first. I was afraid the news would finish her. Ma and I continued our search. A kind man gave us a lift into Isara. It was noisy and busy in town. Dust flew into our hair, and the fumes of scooters and cars filled our noses. We walked up and down the narrow streets endlessly, but we didn't see Pearl. When we came back to camp we walked again, taking it in turns to carry Moe. We hardly ate. We were exhausted. Only Moe kept us anchored. His small needs. His fists tugging at our hair. His smiles. His greed for Ma's breast at nightfall.

*

Mid-way through the following morning a shadow fell across the entrance to our tent, and a reedy voice called my name. I got up and there was Nadia's grandmother, with her bent back and her paisley scarf. Next to her, stood Pearl.

'I said they'd be back.' The grandmother was a small woman but there was something fierce about her. No sign of Nadia. We heard later that the grandmother had threatened to set a knife to Nadia's throat if she so much as moved an inch from their tent.

'Pearl,' I said, almost falling to my knees. 'Thank God.'

Pearl stood, unsure. Then Ma leapt up and slapped Pearl across the face. She'd never laid a finger on Pearl before. 'What were you thinking?' Ma's cheeks were burning and her eyes were burning and for a moment I thought she'd hit Pearl again.

Pearl opened her mouth wide but she didn't cry.

'I'll let you be,' Nadia's grandmother said.

'Wait,' Ma said. 'Where did you find them?'

'They came back of their own accord.' She turned to Pearl. 'Mind you tell the truth. Your mother's slap is nothing compared to the fiery pits of hell.'

Pearl hung her head. Her hair was ratty and dusty. There was an oily stain in the middle of her dress. She continued to stand close to the entrance of our tent, her arms at her sides, her head bowed. Part of me wanted to go to her but another part of me wanted her punished. Ma turned to the stove and picked up a pan and banged it down hard. But Moe, dear sweet Moe, wobbled his way over to Pearl and scrabbled at her feet. 'Pel, Pel,' he said.

Ma marched over and scooped up Moe. 'Sit down,' she said to Pearl.

Tears were now running down Pearl's dirty cheeks. She sat down on the mattress, hugging her knees and her whole body convulsed with sobs. Ma and I looked at each other, then Ma handed Moe to me and held Pearl in her arms.

After Ma let her go, I went to Pearl and she quietened and I remember how she smelled of dust and kerosene.

'What happened, Pearl?' Ma said.

'Nadia said we could go to Isara and get ice creams and chocolate. She had money and she said maybe we could even buy a new dress, or ribbons or ...'

'Didn't you ever think how Nadia might have got that money?'

'No,' Pearl said, in a tiny voice.

'It doesn't take three days to get to Isara and back.' Ma was trying to be patient but I could hear the anger in her voice.

Pearl knotted her fingers so hard the joints clicked. 'A family Nadia knows gave us a lift into Isara. We went to the market and bought some fruit but later we got lost and it got dark and we didn't know how to get back. We found an empty building. It was horrible and cold and dirty and I was really scared.'

My mobile rang: Pa. 'Thanks be to God,' he said, when I told him our happy news. 'Let me speak to her.'

After, I said to Pearl, 'You were gone two nights. Why didn't you return the next day?'

'Nadia was too scared. She said she'd be in terrible trouble. I didn't want to stay but I couldn't leave Nadia on her own. But then I said we had to go. I said you'd be sad and I said I'd leave her on her own.'

'How did you get back?' I asked.

Pearl hung her head again. 'We found a taxi. I think Nadia stole the money. I'm so sorry.'

I wasn't convinced by Pearl's story and I don't think Ma was either. But we dropped the matter. Pearl was safe, that was the important thing. Moe wouldn't leave Pearl alone. He kept pulling at her clothes. He was too young to understand but he knew she'd been gone and it bothered him.

*

I'm lying on the bed in Pearl's small second guest room. It's cosy in here. I don't like big rooms. They make me nervous. 'Pearl,' I say. 'What happened that time when you and Nadia went missing?'

She's sitting on the bed next to me, cradling her knees. 'We've talked about this before … haven't we?' Her face is in shadow. I can't see her expression.

'We never talk about the past. You don't like talking about the past, remember?'

'I guess we all have secrets, stuff we are ashamed of.' Pearl rocks a little. Back and forth. As if we were back on the boat. But it's quiet in the room. Quiet and safe. 'It's so long ago, I'm not sure how much I remember. I know we met this man. He said he'd buy us new clothes and stuff. Then we got in his car; that's how stupid we were. He drove us to an abandoned house out on the edge of the town … what was it called?'

'Isara.'

'Yes, Isara. The man promised to take us shopping for new clothes if we kissed him. We said no, and he started shouting. I was so scared. I thought he'd drag us into the house, kill us and cut us up into little pieces but Nadia was devious. She said he could do anything with us if he took us to get the clothes first. Lucky for us, the man wasn't that bright. He took us back into the centre of town and we managed to escape. We wanted to go back to the camp that night but we thought he might come looking so we hid behind some large dustbins. When it got dark we heard rats running about. The next day I said we had to go, but we were terribly afraid.'

'Why didn't you tell us at the time?'

'I was ashamed. And I thought Ma would go crazy if I told her.'

'I'm sorry,' I say.

'There's no need to be sorry. We weren't harmed. We escaped.'

'Why keep the truth from me all this time?'

She laughs and shakes her head in disbelief. 'You ask me that, today of all days?'

'Can you forgive us … for what we did?'

'It's a shock.'

An owl hoots, then another. I turn to look out of the window but the blind is pulled down. 'It was a terrible thing.'

'Yes,' she says, 'it was. But the soldier would have raped you if Kaz hadn't stopped him.'

'You still don't understand.' I move to the edge of the bed, and reach for her hand. 'I lured the soldier to the cemetery. Kaz and I had it all planned. In revenge for Tam's death.'

'Mira, he was going to rape you.'

'Is that enough of an excuse to kill a man?'

'Stop tormenting yourself for something you did almost thirty years ago. Seriously.'

'I should be punished. It was murder, Pearl.'

'Haven't you and Kaz been punished enough? What would that do to me, to the boys, to Moe, if you decided to confess? Think about that. Are you certain it wouldn't be to assuage your own conscience?'

'What about justice?' I say.

'Justice? You think there was justice in our war? In any wars?' She gets up off the bed and kisses me on the forehead. 'It's late. Go to sleep. We'll talk about this another time.'

When she's gone I slip under the duvet and turn off the sidelight. I hear the front door open and Pearl calling Stefan's name. I hear the three of them murmuring together and then coming up the stairs, the bedroom doors opening and closing, Kaz using the bathroom. The house quietens. From time to time there's a crack as the floorboards contract, but I don't hear the owls again.

Did we think we were being heroes, Kaz and I, or that our actions would change the course of anything? I don't know. I don't even know how such an idea could have entered my head, let alone that my brother and I could have taken a life. But then the senseless taking of life became part of it all, something none of us could get away from, and in that way we were all culpable. Although I can't speak for Pearl or Moe because they really were too young.

Here in Neeland, a murder is considered so abhorrent that each one, no matter how it was committed or for what reason, reaches the news channels. No murder is considered too banal, too ordinary, to remain uncounted. In Lyrian we lost count of murder because there were simply too many murders to count. Behind Tam's death lay many more deaths. Thousands upon thousands of deaths. In prisons. In police cells. In cities and villages. In fields and backyards. In orchards. At the edges of rivers. Anywhere and everywhere.

Yet we, too, committed murder, Kaz and I. We took a life in revenge for Tam's death and in doing so we left another family grieving, just as we grieved, just as Tam's parents grieved. Three families left weeping over the senseless loss of young life, left mourning the lives that might have been and, as a consequence, holding revenge in their hearts, so that the cycle might begin again, no end to its repetitions, until we all grew tired of it and, for our part, we could no longer remember the one pure thought we'd had at the beginning: to free ourselves, to spread our wings and soar.

I think these thoughts as I settle into sleep, and in my sleeping I dream I am a bird flying over Zazour and once again it is a green and lovely place.

24

Present day: Sundsholm, Neeland.

A moral conflict is created when a person violates what
society and the individual himself considers 'right'. An
inability to reconcile wartime actions with a personal
moral code will have lasting and negative psychological
consequences.

www.Neeland_Veterans_Foundation/PTSD

At first when I wake I'm not quite certain where I am and I
feel as if I've just resurfaced after diving somewhere deep. I
blink and focus. Of course, I'm at Pearl's house. I've slept in this
room many times before. Here is the crisp white cotton duvet
cover and a pale light filtering in through the venetian blind.
Here's the painting on the wall opposite, a sprig of flowers set in
an abstract landscape, a lovely thing.

Kaz and Pearl are sitting at the breakfast bar. They look
comfortable together. I suppose after last night I shouldn't be
surprised about anything, but I am, all the same.

'Did you sleep well?' Pearl asks.

'I did, thanks.'

'Coffee?' Pearl pours me a cup, offers breakfast. The boys are running about, getting ready for school. Stefan must already have left for work. I turn on my phone. There's a message from Isaak. In the drama of the night before, I'd forgotten about Tomas. 'All good here. Tomas and I are getting along just fine. XX.' I notice the two kisses, but perhaps they don't mean anything.

'Who's that?' Pearl asks.

'Work again.'

'I thought you didn't have work today.' Kaz's eyes are puffy but he's not jiggling his legs or pulling at his hair.

'I don't,' I say. 'But I need to get home. I've got stuff to do.'

'Has your cat come back?' Pearl asks.

I shake my head and Pearl reaches for my hand. She says nothing about last night.

*

After the boys have left for school, I kiss Pearl and Kaz goodbye, and leave the house. The streets are busy but the air is clear and cold, and the walk settles my mind. At the end of Pearl's street I cross snowy Valmaparken, and then I head up Kathina, with its boutique shops and oddly lopped trees. As I pass the police station at the top of Kathina, I consider stepping inside. I don't. Instead I stop at the mini-market to pick up a few things.

'I have good news, Mira,' Mr Engman says, beaming. 'Someone has spotted your cat. I told you she would come back.'

'Where?' I ask.

'In the park here.' He gestures to the door. 'A boy came in earlier. He said he'd seen a cat matching Mimi's description early this morning. He told me he'd call you. Has he?'

'No. No one has called.' I dump my shopping on the counter. 'Keep these for me, will you? I'll be back to collect and pay for them later.'

There's no sign of Mimi in the park. I call her name. I check the bandstand and walk around the frozen pond. I check the bushes. Nothing. Not even a mouse. I go back to Mr Engman, with tears in my eyes.

Back at the apartment I tidy up, put on a wash, and check my e-mail – the first time in over twenty-four hours. I'm already upset about Mimi and shaken up by last night and now there's a message from Eka. He wants to speak to me. They have discovered the remains of six men buried in one of the orchards close to Zazour. A bitter taste comes into my mouth. I pace up and down the apartment and stare out of the window. I pummel the cushions. I kick the bathroom door and stub my toe. 'Don't get your hopes up,' Eka said.

I call him but there's no answer. I leave a message and check the blog. The guy who calls himself Adam is there, the one who lost his father, but I too am losing my father and this morning I feel like I'm losing my mind again. I try to hold on to the calm I felt sitting in the bedroom with Pearl, but it has fled like Mimi. I log off, make myself a strong coffee and stare out of the window. A small black cat is padding across the snow. He looks lonely. Then I think maybe Mimi doesn't want to come back to my apartment after her taste of freedom. Perhaps she yearns for a wilder life.

The door entry rings. It's Kaz. I wasn't expecting him.

'I thought you were staying at Pearl's today?'

'She's rushed off to the hospital. She asked me to go with her but I said I'd come later.'

He sounds out of breath. He must have run up the stairs instead of taking the lift.

'Oh, God. Is Pa okay?' Everything is breaking apart again. Just like before.

'The hospital called after you left. It can't be anything too serious or Pearl would have said.'

'Do you think I should call her now?'

Kaz shakes his head. 'She'll call us.' He takes off his boots and coat. 'I'm not used to this cold. It's freezing out there.'

'It can get a lot colder than this, believe me. I'll make you a coffee to warm you up.'

We sit opposite each other at my small kitchen table. I wonder whether to tell him about the message from Eka, but I decide to wait. My mobile pings but it's not Pearl or Eka, or the boy who thought he'd seen Mimi; it's Tomas. 'Thanx. Isaak is great man.' One good piece of news in all this mess.

'Who was that?' Kaz taps the table. He looks tense.

'Tomas. I managed to find him some temporary accommodation through a friend.'

'I meant to ask about Tomas but with all that went down ... I plain forgot.'

I turn my head to the window. The early morning dawned calm but now the wind is up, blowing snow, and people are hurrying across the square, heads down. There's no sign of Mimi.

'About last night,' Kaz says. 'You must be so mad at me.'

I stare into my coffee cup. Am I mad at him? I should be. He broke his promise. And yet what I feel is relief, a heavy boulder lifted from my shoulders.

'Pearl didn't say a word this morning,' he says. 'I'm surprised she wasn't more shocked. I expected condemnation. Hysteria, even.'

'I was the hysterical one,' I say. 'I was scared. I thought Pearl might throw us out of the house or call the police.'

'Even though we're family?'

I nod. 'Yes. Even though we're family.'

Kaz sighs softly. 'I don't know her like you do.' He taps his fingers on the table again and drinks his coffee. I'm sure he's here for a reason but I decide not to push it. Whatever he wants to say, it can wait. The wind whistles round the building and Kaz continues his tip-tapping. As if he were typing on one of those ancient typewriters, the ones that fetch a fortune these days.

'Pearl hated it when we first came to Neeland. She blamed me,' I say.

'She likes it here now. Says she wouldn't want to live anywhere else.'

'Now it's me who wants to go back.' I give a little snort. 'Ironic, isn't it?'

'You want to go back to Lyrian?' Kaz opens his eyes wide. 'To Zazour?'

'Maybe. Though not for good. It's too late for that. I'm settled here. I have my job and …'

'Are you sure you're not mad at me?' Kaz looks at me. No, not just looks. His gaze is piercing. As if he is trying to see inside.

'Do I look like I'm mad?'

'Maybe you keep your anger inside. Depression is often internalised anger. My therapist told me that.'

'You went to therapy? I thought you said you didn't.'

'I only had two sessions. Then I quit.' He laughs, a nervous kind of laugh. 'Do you think it would have made a difference to our lives if we'd come clean?'

I snort again. 'But you did tell. You told Pa.'

'I didn't tell him everything.' Kaz puts one elbow on the table and cups his head in one hand. He closes his eyes, opens them again. The wind catches the edge of the building and groans.

'What didn't you say?'

'Does it matter?'

'You have to get it out now.'

'Like shitting, you mean?' His voice is sharp. Like a knife. He was the one who used the knife. He killed the soldier.

'Forget it. Let's just talk about the weather.' I sweep up the two coffee cups and rinse them in the sink. From the corner of my eye I can see Kaz staring out of the window; my window.

'You won't want to hear what I have to say.' Kaz gets up and starts pacing about the tiny kitchen. 'You might regret it.'

He's right. I might regret it. But we can't turn back, not now we've come so far. 'I'll regret it, will I? That sounds like a threat. Well, if it's confession time, why don't I start? We might as well put everything on the table.' I pull out my chair and sit down.

'No need to be so sarcastic.'

'Two can play, Kaz. You want to hear me or not?' Kaz doesn't answer. I continue anyway. 'Before I got taken into the psych ward last year I'd been picking up young men in bars – guys who reminded me of Tam. I brought them back here for sex. I fucked around twelve guys, although I lost count in the end. Maybe there were more.'

'Mira …'

'You want more? I'll give you more. I was drinking vodka. Having sex in doorways. Taking sleeping pills. One morning I saw blood dripping down the bathroom walls and his face staring down at me – the soldier's face. Do you remember his face? Because I do.'

Kaz sits down in the chair. 'There's no need, Mira.'

'I used to get so drunk I couldn't remember. But of course you think you have the monopoly on pain and guilt. It's fucking nonsense, Kaz. We all feel it.'

Kaz holds up his hands. 'Okay, okay. We went to this house in the south of Lyri. Posh area. Used to be, before it got smashed up.' He grabs at a chunk of his hair.

'Who went?'

'My brigade. The six of us. They were like brothers to me.' He rocks back and forth in the chair, his eyes half closed, as the wind outside gusts and moans.

'And?'

'He was downstairs, the father. We'd had a tip-off. He was some kind of general so they claimed, a big fish anyhow. Well, he got what was coming to him. Bang, bang and he's lying dead on the floor. It was pretty clean.'

'Was it you who shot him?'

'No. Would it have mattered if it had been me? I've shot people. You must know that. It was war. In war you kill and maim, and your moral compass gets fucked up. It's shoot or be shot at, there's no time to think, no time to wonder, no time for anything but killing and shitting and if you're lucky you eat and sleep a little.' Kaz is tapping his leg on the floor, as if trying to dance. Or waiting for a chance to run. Yes, that.

'I know,' I say.

'No, you don't. Know.'

'You were saying … about the house.'

'Yes, the house. We thought it was just the father at home but we had to check. The daughter was upstairs, hiding under the bed. She was so beautiful. I've never seen a girl like that before or since. Perfect. A rose. Deep blue eyes. Freckles on her nose. Must have been about fifteen. Same age you were back then. That's what killed me about it.'

'Oh my God, Kaz …'

'I never touched her and that's God's honest truth. Never touched a hair on her head. But I never saved her either. They all took turns. Jakka went first. Jakka was my friend. I'd have trusted him with my life, but after …' He leans forward on the chair and his voice drops almost to a whisper. 'I didn't say a word. Not a single word. I stood there and watched. I left after Jakka was done. Went back downstairs. Couldn't take any more. She was screaming at the beginning but they shut her up.'

'You waited downstairs while they raped her?'

'They treated her worse than an animal. She was dead when I went up again. Rope round her neck. Where did they get that rope from? And we were supposed to be the good guys.'

'Oh God, I'm so sorry.'

'There's no need to be sorry.' He cuts the air with his hands. 'It's done. Gone. Like the soldier.'

'Did you tell the therapist? Cindy?'

Kaz looks down at his hands, those hands that used to be so familiar to me; hands that have killed. There are age spots on the skin, like small islands. 'No. I told no one.' He lets out a long sigh and we're silent, looking at each other, trying to measure the weight of it. When he speaks again, his voice is softer. 'That's what broke us, me and Cindy. There were times when I couldn't make love to her, many times. I'd want to but then I'd start thinking about the girl.' He points to his crotch. 'And as soon as I thought about her I'd shrivel up.'

'What could you have done? You mustn't blame yourself.'

'I had a gun. I could have shot Jakka when he started. I could have shot them all.'

'They might have got you first. You must have thought of that.'

'I did. Maybe that would have been better than this hell.' He points to his head. 'This hell in here.'

'It's not a crime to want to live.'

'I'm not so sure, Mira.' He pulls at his hair again, pulls and pulls. I reach over and gently move his hands.

'What about us, what we did?' I say.

He sighs, such a small sigh. 'How can you quantify something like that? We took someone's life, didn't we?'

'It was quick, though. He didn't suffer. Not like the girl.'

'Didn't he? I don't know. Why would I know? We left. We didn't exactly check.'

'Oh ... I never thought ...' I never have considered that. If the soldier suffered. If he slowly bled to death. I never wanted to think of it.

'Best not to. I still dream about her – the girl. I never think about the soldier; but her face ... I won't forget it. She had a tiny mole on her left cheek. Funny what you remember, isn't it?'

I get up and go to the window. The sky is white. I'm waiting for snow to fall. I'm waiting for Pa to die. I'm waiting for Tam. Waiting for Mimi. All this waiting. I turn back to Kaz. His bottom lip is quivering but his eyes aren't so dark and blank any more. Yes, that's one thing I'm sure of.

'There's something else,' I say. 'It's Tam. They might have found him.'

When I say that, big, fat tears run down Kaz's cheeks. We leave the kitchen and sit together on my sofa, our arms linked, and it feels like I've found my brother at last; really found him. But there are always losses, even in gains. Because that's how life is. One thing comes back, another vanishes. My mobile buzzes. It's Pearl calling. 'You need to come to the hospital now. Pa is very sick.'

'We're coming,' I say.

'What is it?' Kaz asks.

'It's Pa. He's going, Kaz, he's going.' I snatch up Isaak's card, and we pull on our boots and coats and race down the stairs.

25

Present day: Sundsholm, Neeland.

Justice cannot be achieved just by the cessation of injustice. It requires punishment and/or reparation for injuries and damages inflicted.

www.issues_talk.com/justice

I'm glad Isaak is driving us. He makes me feel safe.

I wonder if it's another scare. If when we arrive we'll find Pa sitting up in bed, a smile on his face, but then I remember the panic in Pearl's voice and I get a bad feeling in my gut. None of us talk. As Isaak negotiates the city streets Kaz sits, hunched forward, staring out of the taxi window.

I retreat into myself. Into my memories of Pa. We were happy to see him, but it was a shock to all of us when he returned to camp. His hands shook, he had bouts of coughing that left him breathless, and he looked as thin and tired as our blankets. His skin was grey too, everything about him was grey, the colour leached out of him. Yet he'd only been gone a few weeks.

Pa tried to lift Pearl into his arms but he couldn't manage her weight any more. 'You've grown big and strong,' he said, but Ma and I could see that wasn't the real reason. His own strength was gone. He wasn't the same man, and he never would be again.

Pa embraced Ma. He held Moe and kissed him on his head, and then he hugged me and I felt how thin he was. 'How was it back there?' I asked, once he had sat down. He waved his hand dismissively. 'You don't need to know, Mira. No one needs to know that.'

'Shouldn't Kaz be here with you?' Pearl spoke with confidence now. She was almost back to her old self. 'Is my doll safe?'

'Kaz has gone to Lyri. Your doll will be safe.' Pa's hands were shaking so hard, the tea slopped out of the cup Ma had given him.

'Why has he gone there? Did you go?' Pearl kept staring at Pa.

'He was sent. And no, I didn't go.'

'Why doesn't he call us? He used to call. Grandma doesn't call either.' Ma and I hadn't quite got used to Pearl's chatter after her long and painful silence.

'It's not so easy for him to call from where he is,' Pa said. He turned to Ma. 'You still haven't heard from your mother?'

Ma shook her head. She seemed to fold into herself. We had spoken of Grandma often but we had resigned ourselves to the fact that we might never see her again. I could see how that pained Ma, and how she sometimes cried in her sleep, but what could we do?

'Might she have gone somewhere else?'

'I don't know.' Ma was cradling the tea mug in her hand and biting her lip, but she didn't say anything and we didn't discuss the war again. We talked instead of school and the number of new arrivals in camp, the weather and the dust and the price of everything, but then we ran out of things to say because the war had lodged itself inside us like a virus and our words felt heavy and false.

Ma and Pa sat together in the corner of the tent drinking tea. Sometimes they spoke quietly to one another, sometimes they did not. Pearl and I allowed them some privacy. We kept Moe amused and we took him outside to see if we could find the cat that lurked in our area, but we did not see it. Later, we had lunch together and then Pa excused himself and went off to smoke with the other men.

'He shouldn't be smoking with that cough,' Ma said, after Pa had gone.

Pearl picked up her pencil. She had stopped drawing shuttered and blasted houses. Now her theme was gardens. Gardens scattered with rose bushes and fruit trees. Gardens where cats roamed along twisting paths. Gardens lush with ponds, fountains, birds and butterflies. But that afternoon she drew a single, large and bulbous tree, like a baobab. She placed our family in the tree: Ma in her printed apron next to Pa; Moe on the same branch crawling towards a leaf; and the three of us – Kaz, Pearl and me – on another branch. The black kitten she put at the top.

'I like that,' I said. 'It's one of your best.'

Pearl smiled. 'Do you really think it's good?'

'I do, yes. I think it's splendid.'

'Do, do, do,' Moe said.

We laughed to hear Moe saying his first word and I gave Pearl a hug and she hugged me back and we hugged Moe too and I thought, *There is hope, even if it's as faint as the tiniest star in the night sky.*

But that night, after Ma had put out the lamp, I heard Pa whispering. 'Even on the border the situation is bad. I can't tell you how bad.'

'Why didn't you tell me Kaz had gone to Lyri?' Ma whispered back.

'You know why.'

'We haven't heard a word from him in over two weeks. Mira understands, but Pearl …'

I lay motionless under my blanket.

'He's joined a brigade in the opposition area. That's all I know. The war is spreading, Sara. It's spreading everywhere. I don't see it stopping any time soon.' Pa coughed, and blew his nose.

'Kaz will be all right, won't he?' Ma said, once Pa had got his breath back.

'I hope so. Now let's sleep. It's late and I'm bone tired.'

I lay awake listening to Ma breathing and Pa coughing, to Moe snuffling and Pearl murmuring in her sleep, to all the noises of the night, and I made up my mind. We would leave that place, whatever the cost. If Kaz wasn't back we'd go without him. He could always follow us later.

*

Isaak is leaning on the horn.

'What is it?' Kaz's hands are clenched, the knuckles white with tension.

'A van blocking our path.' Isaak sighs and taps his fingers on the dashboard. 'I thought it would be quicker this way.'

'Maybe we should get out and walk,' I say.

'It's still too far.' Isaak hoots again. 'Don't worry. Someone is coming.' He turns his head to look at me. Our eyes meet, and something passes between us like a wave coming up to shore but then it is gone.

The taxi rumbles down the narrow, cobbled street, and then we turn left into Karlkvagen, the long, wide, tree-lined boulevard that leads to the hospital. We pass the History Museum and the snowbound park with its bandstand and elegant lamps. Though the traffic is light, the journey seems slow but at last the glass and concrete hospital building rises up before us.

Kaz and I hurry in through the large glass doors, and make our way to the emergency desk. 'I'm sorry,' the receptionist says. 'You can't go in just now.'

'My sister is with him,' I say.

'Your sister arrived earlier. They're doing all they can. If you could just wait.' She gestures to the waiting area.

'Please.'

The nurse picks up her computer pen and taps the screen. She's no longer looking at me. Kaz slips his arm through mine. 'Come on, Mira. Let's do as she says.'

We sit down in the waiting room, on blue fabric chairs. We're not alone. A family of four is huddled in one corner. I wonder who they're here for. A grandparent, perhaps. The youngest child, a boy with white-blonde hair, is playing with coloured wooden bricks but his sister is sitting on her mother's lap. The girl's face is turned away from me but I can see the mother's face, the anguish in it; the light gone.

I close my eyes.

*

Fixer was standing outside his tent. He looked thinner, his cheekbones showing; a hole in the knee of his jeans. But his smart shades were gone. Maybe he'd sold them.

'Ma says we can go.'

'You have the money?'

'Half. We'll have the rest for you next week.' After arguments and counter-arguments our departure had been agreed. Ma would sell her jewellery and Pa would withdraw the last few funds he'd deposited.

'How many are you?'

I counted on my fingers. 'Five. My brother's only small. He's not even one year old yet.'

'Your brother doesn't have to pay.'

'That's good because he's not earning and he has no savings.'

Fixer laughed. I liked it when he laughed. It made him seem friendly. But he soon turned serious again and named his price and it was higher than before. When I asked him why, he just shrugged. 'Take it or leave it. I fix the details, I don't set the price. There's a group leaving a week Wednesday. The bus takes twelve hours. It leaves from the main gate at seven in the evening and arrives at the docks the next morning. Keep your luggage to a minimum.'

'Do we get a ticket?'

'A ticket?' He grinned. 'You'll be lucky.'

'And then?'

'We wait.'

'We?' He'd talked of going but somehow I hadn't believed him.

'Yes, I'm leaving too. I'm sick of this place. No proper work. No education. Only trouble. Just trouble ... sorry. I don't remember your name.'

'Mira.'

'Mira. Of course. Mira.' He said it nice. Like it mattered.

'What's your name – your real name?'

'Best you don't know. No hard feelings. It's for my own security. You understand?'

I nodded but I was disappointed. I thought he might trust me but he did not. 'When are you off?'

'Same as you, if it works out. Next week.' He waved his arms. 'Every day more and more people are arriving. The war's not going stop anytime soon. It's only going to get worse. What do you think it'll be like here in camp next winter? Best to take our chance, even if ...' He stopped again and put one hand in the pocket of his jeans. 'Fuck. Where are those cigarettes?'

'Even if what?'

He looked into my eyes and I saw a sadness there and I wondered if he had any family in the camp. 'It's no ferry service. You do realise that, don't you?'

Behind Fixer, the mountains shimmered as if they were made of water. 'I'm a good swimmer,' I said.

He went to pull down his shades. Not finding them, he sought the loops on his jeans instead. 'It's not enough to be able to swim. Make sure you're one of the first on the boat. There's never enough life jackets, that's what I've heard. Maybe you can buy some at the port but they have to be proper ones, not toys. We're heading across in summer but a storm can blow up fast and it's a long way across. Not everyone makes it.'

'We'll take our chance,' I said.

'You have until next Wednesday – the week before we leave – to get the rest of the money to me. Otherwise your place goes to someone else. Okay?'

'Okay.'

I handed him what Pa had given me. Fixer counted the notes and I left.

*

We're packed in like sardines. There's a smell of engine oil, sweat and vomit. A baby is crying but we're mostly silent, holding on to our bags, holding on to each other, trying not to think of the glassy depths below and the churning waves, trying not to think of the seaweed floating like long dark hair, trying not to think of what might await us down there. I look up. At Pearl. Her face is wet. The small boy next to her is holding an orange brick in his hand.

I reach for Pearl's hand. 'Where's Pa? He doesn't know how to swim and he hasn't got a life jacket.'

'What are you saying, Mira? We're in the hospital. Pa is gone. He's gone.'

The small boy pulls at my trouser leg. 'Do you want my brick?' he says. Doesn't he have a jacket? All the children should have life jackets. It's wrong to travel without them.

'Leave the woman alone,' I hear a woman say. 'She's upset.'

'We're in the hospital, Mira,' Pearl says. 'In Sundsholm.'

'Why are you upset?' the boy asks, still tugging at my trousers. 'Did someone die?'

'My father died,' Pearl says.

'How did he die?' The boy's hair is the colour of pale sunlight.

'Peter, that's enough.' The woman's voice again.

'He was old,' I hear a man saying. His voice reminds me of my brother Kaz, but Kaz is not on the boat. He didn't come with us. He refused. 'It's very sad,' the man continues. 'But it's what happens when people get old.'

'Pa is dead?' I say.

'I'm sorry,' Pearl says. 'They couldn't save him this time.' She's crying; that's why her face is wet. We're not on the boat; we are on solid ground.

*

Pa's face is pale and waxy and his eyes are closed, but he looks serene and there's a trace of a smile on his lips. He's with Ma now, where he wants to be. I lean over and kiss him on the forehead; the skin is still warm. We sit together, Kaz, Pearl and I, at the bedside, in silence. After a while we're led into a carpeted room. Green curtains at the windows. Soft chairs. The three of us stand in a huddle, our arms around each other. A woman in a charcoal-coloured suit brings us tea and biscuits. We sit again. We don't touch the biscuits.

Pearl picks up her mobile and calls Moe. I hear Moe's tinny voice but not the words.

'He wants to speak to you,' Pearl says.

I take the phone. Moe is crying. He sounds like the baby he once was, soft in my arms. 'I should have come earlier,' he says.

'We thought we had more time,' I say. 'Pa took a sudden turn for the worse.'

Moe knows Kaz is here but he doesn't ask to speak to him. I understand. There will be time for this later. Time for talking. Time for speaking the truth. And it will be okay, I'm sure of it. For now I'm just sad that Moe will be coming to a funeral instead of visiting Pa, but I guess that's how it goes. Life is always a matter of chance, of being in the right place or the wrong one and in that respect we were lucky. We escaped to freedom and our family stayed intact, in its fashion. So many others did not.

The woman who brought us tea returns. She asks if one of us will sign the necessary papers. 'I'll do it,' Pearl says. 'Is that okay?'

I nod, say yes. What do I care for papers?

'I'll go with Pearl,' Kaz says, 'Unless …'

'You go. I need some air.'

*

The church is empty. It smells of wood, incense and polish, and the curved wooden roof beams remind me of a boat. I sit in one of the high-backed pews and think of all the boats that didn't make it; the people who drowned trying to get to a place of safety, the people who continue to drown seeking refuge and a better life. Then I think of Pa and his life. He and Ma never quite settled here. They were always tied to Lyrian, to the memories of what had been lost, what might have been. Yet it wasn't a bad life. Pa didn't work again but he had his vegetable patch and his friends, and he had Ma. After Ma died, something died in him too.

The door to the church opens and closes. I turn but I can't see anyone. I was half expecting Kaz to walk in but he went off with Pearl. He doesn't know I'm here. I am alone with my memories.

Kaz walked into the camp a few days after Pa. He didn't call in advance. Like Pa, he'd lost a great deal of his body weight. When he took off the filthy, ragged shirt he was wearing I saw how his ribs poked through his chest. There was a scar on his back too, but when he caught us watching he quickly covered himself again. Yet what bothered me most wasn't his physical condition but the look in his eyes. They reminded me of a bombed-out building – dark and vacant.

Ma wasted no time in informing Kaz of our plans to leave. He shrugged and said tonelessly, 'I agree. Time you got out of this place.'

'You're coming with us,' Ma said, picking up a cloth. 'Aren't you?'

'No, I'm not.'

'What do you mean you're not?' Ma flicked at the dust aimlessly.

'Give the man a chance,' Pa said. 'He's only just arrived and you're talking of leaving.'

'You can't go back to that madness.' Ma twisted the cloth round and round in her fingers. 'I'm begging you, Kaz.'

'I have no intention of going back.' Kaz's eyes flickered momentarily with life.

Ma startled and the cloth dropped on the faded rug. 'Where are you going?'

Kaz got to his feet. 'I'm going outside for a cigarette.'

There was a short silence. No one moved, not even Moe. Then Ma picked up the cloth she had dropped and folded it carefully. 'Of course he's coming with us.'

Pa put his hands together, as if he were praying. 'Let me talk to him, Sara. I'm sure he'll come round.'

'You think?' Ma wiped away a few beads of sweat away from her face. 'He sounds very determined and you know what he's like. Once he has an idea in his head ...'

I left Ma and Pa to their argument. I found Kaz slouched at the side of our neighbour's tent. 'Why didn't you call us? Ma was frantic. You know Pearl went missing for a while?'

'I lost my mobile.' He took a drag on his cigarette. 'God, these are foul. Cheap bloody rubbish.'

'Couldn't you have borrowed a mobile?' I studied his face, but his expression betrayed nothing.

He shrugged and sucked on the cigarette.

I attempted a more conciliatory tone. 'Are you serious – that you're not coming with us?'

He gave me a cursory nod. No answer at all.

'Is it because of the soldier?'

'Why would you think that?'

'What is it then? If you come with us you can start a new life. Finish your education. Get a job as an architect. Surely you want to do that. It's what Tam would have wanted.'

'How do you know what Tam would have wanted?' Kaz's weathered, browned skin took on a deeper tone. 'For fuck's sake, Mira.'

I took a step back.

'Okay, that was low of me, speaking of Tam like that. But I need to make my own way. You of all people should understand that.'

'You're going back to fight, aren't you?'

'No, I'm not. If I go back I'll end up a corpse, or some kind of psycho. You have no idea, Mira, no fucking idea.' He drew on the cigarette, until it was burned down to the stub. I waited. My heart was a stone. The sun beat down on my head. Sweat trickled down my back. I waited. A ball thudded against a post, over and over. A cockerel crowed in the distance. The mountains faded into the early afternoon heat.

Kaz dropped the cigarette stub into the dust and ground it with his foot. 'Do you know what the real truth is? I'm a coward. I can't take war; the killing and the blood. Tam would have done better. Yes, even peace-loving Tam.' He put his hand on his chest. 'My heart is gone. All that's left is a hole where it once was.'

'You're not a coward, Kaz.'

'It's hell in Lyri. Worse than anything you could possibly imagine.' He met my eyes and I thought he was on the verge of saying something, but he turned away and the moment was lost.

Kaz left the following morning. He refused to say where he was headed in spite of Ma's entreaties. Three weeks later we, too, were gone. There was a delay in our leaving though we weren't told why: our questions were met with shrugs and evasions. There were so many questions which could – or would – not be answered. Like why Kaz wouldn't come with us. All we had was heartache.

But now I know. Now I understand.

*

I call Pearl from the church. She suggests I head home. If I'm okay with that. There are more papers to sign, items of Pa's to collect. But I can wait, if I like. I say no. I'll catch up later.

Isaak is standing outside the church door, in corduroy jeans and a thick down jacket. I was too caught up with Pa to notice his clothes earlier.

'Your father? How is he?'

I open my mouth. The words won't form. Tears spill down my face. And there, in the cold winter light, Isaak holds me tight and he smells of moss and earth.

We go home, to my apartment. In his taxi. We go home and sit at the kitchen table, opposite each other, like Kaz and I did not so long ago. Already the light is fading from the sky, the short winter day turning to night.

'There's something I should have said to Pa and now it's too late.' My tears splash onto the kitchen table. 'Pa knew but he never said a thing. Why didn't he? Why didn't I?' My voice breaks.

'Things are always left unsaid. This is the nature of relationships.' Isaak reaches for me across the table. He has large hands. Like my brother's hands.

Now he falls silent. Somewhere a radio is playing. Notes of music like small splinters in the air.

'Too late for Pa but not too late for you.'

Isaak smiles, a gentle smile, but he does not speak and it is this patience in him, the space he allows, that gives wings to my words. 'If anything is to happen between us you must know this.' I take a deep breath. My tears have stopped but I'm shaking. 'My brother and I killed a soldier. Pa knew, but he never said.'

Isaak continues to regard me, his expression unaltered.

'Did you hear what I just said? My brother and I murdered a young soldier. It was my idea. You hear me?' I bang on the table. 'Kaz told our sister and now Pa is dead.'

Isaak leans forward. 'I hear you, Mira.'

'Do whatever you like. I don't care. Go to the police. Turn me in. It's what I deserve. The soldiers shot Kaz's best friend, Tam. He was my friend too ...' Now I put both my hands on the table. I'm not wearing gloves. Isaak's eyes flicker as he registers the scars on my right hand, the way my fingers curl. 'The soldiers did this too. They shot at a tree close to where my sister and I were standing. The tree exploded and a piece of burning bark hit my hand. I was going to be an architect, you know.' My voice rises. 'They took that away from me.'

Isaak cups his hand around my scarred one.

'The soldier we killed wasn't the soldier who killed Tam. He was only a young recruit. Now, do you see? My brother and I did the most terrible wrong. We can never put it right.'

Isaak gets up and walks over to my side of the table, and wraps his arms around me.

My tears fall again, hot and salty. Isaak brushes my tears with his fingers. Then he kisses me on the lips and I kiss him back. While we kiss I think about the one kiss Tam gave me, and the kiss I gave the soldier and how it was twisted and wrong, and of all the other kisses I've traded since and how they've meant almost nothing. I'm sad Pa has died but I'm happy for this kiss, whatever it means.

26

Present day: Sundsholm, Neeland.

Reconciliation is a place of trust and mercy, of justice and peace.

www.issues_talk.com/reconciliation

It's dark when I wake. At first all I can think of is how Pa is dead and how much I miss him. The pain of this is physical. My heart aches and I draw my knees to my chest and then I'm aware of someone else in my bed: Isaak.

I lie in the warmth and the dark and listen to Isaak's soft, steady breathing. When I reach out and wake him, he holds me. I need this embrace. It's not like the times before. It's like coming home.

*

Dawn is breaking when we leave the apartment, the sky threaded with pink and gold and I think of the dawns in camp, Pearl struggling with the water container, our breath steaming out in the winter air and how we tried to pretend everything was okay when it wasn't.

Isaak puts the taxi into gear and we move off down the empty street. As we pass through the city and the suburbs, we stay quiet, lost in our own thoughts. At the edge of the vast forest that blankets this country, I break the silence. 'When we first came here I thought the fir trees were soldiers.' I shiver, even though it's warm in the cab.

'Why would you think that?' he asks.

'They're so tall and forbidding. We drove through a forest like this when we left our home for the refugee camp.'

'How long were you in the camp?'

'Six months. I was the one who organised getting us out. I thought if we didn't leave, we'd be trapped there for ever.'

'You came by boat?'

'Yes. First we had to take a bus. It wasn't one journey, it was many journeys.'

'Life is always many journeys,' he says.

I will tell him one day, but for now I say nothing. I will never forget that journey. We travelled as others had travelled before us: with few possessions, our passports clutched tightly in our hands, all packed into an ancient bus and surrounded by the smells of sweat and body odour, assailed by the cries of babies, until we arrived at the port. The port town was a pretty place, the harbour awash with blue fishing boats, the sky filled with wheeling gulls, but the place was crowded with refugees and we weren't welcome. We had to wait for our boat; days of waiting in dirty rooms, praying for the wind to die down, with nothing to do but walk along the sand and watch the breakers. The final pieces of Ma's jewellery were sold, as were the final pieces of everything else, until all we owned were the clothes on our backs.

One morning, the wind calmed and word went round that the boat was ready. We gathered up our things and rushed down to the quay. I hadn't expected much but when I saw that the boat was nothing more than a rusted fishing trawler, I was afraid. As we pushed forward, almost fighting each other to get on, I spotted Fixer on the deck. I waved to him but he didn't see me, lost in the crowd. We met later, on the boat, but after we landed I lost sight of him.

'Tell me ... how was the sea voyage?' Isaak asks.

'We were crammed in like cattle being herded for slaughter.'

'I heard about those boats,' Isaak says. His voice is sad. 'So many did not make it.'

'We were lucky. Only one person died – a young woman. I don't know why.'

Isaak falls silent again. I have silenced him with my words. It's all too easy to silence people with such stories. They don't want to hear of death, of a country smashed almost to dust, its people ground down like meat in a mincer. They want stories of hope. Of heroes and heroines. Those stories exist but there was so much brutality and madness; stuff that can never be told.

I fix my eyes on the unravelling road, but something unravels inside me too. I hear voices calling my name, a sea of voices. Who are they? Do they mean me to join them? I cry out in fear.

'What is it?' A man's voice. Is it Pa?

'Who are you?' I ask.

'It's Isaak. I'm stopping the cab. Look at me, Mira.'

I do as he says. I look. There's a young man in a white shirt but he isn't Tam; he doesn't have Tam's hair and he's not so tall. A group of soldiers is walking the young man over a broken wall into a field of maize. I thought it was wintertime – how can maize grow in winter? I continue to watch. I don't look away. I watch as the soldiers shoot the young man in the back. Like Tam, he is not carrying a weapon, but still they shoot him.

He falls into the maize. He is gone.

The boat lurches and the engine cuts out. There's no maize field, not out here. I'm mistaken, confused. We're at sea. The boat lurches again. The engines die. We're going to drown. Now I'm in a world that casts no shadow, white as a wordless page. I call for Pearl but she doesn't respond. She's not speaking. She has not spoken in days. Only the man speaks. 'Mira, Mira. Open your eyes.' He has a quiet and steady voice.

'Tam is shot,' I say. 'He's fallen to the ground. But where is Kaz? Kaz should be here.'

A gentle hand on my arm. 'Mira, look at me.'

There is no boat. No choppy sea. No field of maize. No soldiers. No sniper on the street, his rifle pointed at Tam's back. I'm in Isaak's taxi and we're stopped at the side of the road close to a clearing surrounded by fir trees. In the centre of the clearing is a red barn.

'I got lost,' I say. 'My sister was lost once: my brother too.'

'You're not lost. You're here with me.' Isaak takes both my hands in his. 'We're going to the lake, remember? It's going to be beautiful, I promise.

*

I'm back at the apartment. The lake was beautiful, just as Isaak said it would be. He has gone now. He said he would stay but I wanted time alone. I told him to go and look after Tomas. We'll see each other tomorrow, and maybe the next day and the next.

I call Moe. He'll be arriving in the morning. Isaak and I will pick him up at the airport.

When the call is ended I stare out of the window. Even though it's dark I've not pulled the blind. Snow is falling softly, the white flakes dazzling in the pools of light.

Tam was one of the first to die in that long war. In that sense he was lucky. He did not live to witness what came later. The slaughter. Blood flowing in the streets. People suffocating. Hospitals and medical centres collapsing under the weight of bombs. Churches burning. Mosques burning. Schools burning. Whole towns dying. He did not witness the sieges and hunger, the great tragedy that was our country. Thousands followed Tam; so many thousands that none of us could keep up with their names. But their mothers, fathers, sons and daughters will know. They will remember, and their cousins, nephews, nieces, friends and lovers. Please, let us not forget the lovers.

And what of us, the exiles, who had to leave everything behind and adapt to a new way of living; who had to face poverty, prejudice, guilt, trauma, and even madness? Only we know the difficulty of this.

I turn away from the window, check my messages. There's one from Eka. The results of the DNA tests are inconclusive. It's disappointing. This time I'd really hoped. I write back to say thanks. Eka will go on with his work and I'll continue with mine. Whatever happens between Isaak and me, I won't stop searching for Tam. I won't stop until I, too, lie in my grave.

Maybe tomorrow or the next day or the next, there will be news.

I think of the friends I lost, like Rey who has vanished into the mists. I miss her laughter, the crazy way she used to dance. I miss the black kitten and the family of sparrows who used to chatter outside our window. I miss Pa's jokes and the five of us – then six with Moe's arrival – eating at the breakfast table, Ma brewing coffee, the smell of it mixed with fresh bread. And in summer, the scent of jasmine and roses, wafting in from the garden.

All that is gone forever. This is what I have now. My family who still remain. My work. This apartment. This view. And perhaps it's enough because now I'm ready to forgive myself and

Kaz, and it's the biggest thing. We lived through that war but we're not going to stay broken forever.

I stare into the darkness. In a few weeks the light will return. Soon, in Zazour, the orchards will bloom like spring snow and under our fruit trees everything will smell of earth and promise.

I can almost taste it.

Oh! But now what do I see? There's a shadow crouched under the streetlight in the square. I catch my breath. It's Mimi, I know it's her.

I fly down the steps, light as the snowflakes that now fall from the city sky. This is now. This is home.